WANTED BY THE BIKERS

AN MC REVERSE HAREM ROMANCE

STEPHANIE BROTHER

Copyright © 2023 by Stephanie Brother

All Rights Reserved. This book or any portion thereof may not be reproduced or used in any manner whatsoever without the express permission of the publisher except for the use of brief quotations in a book review.

This book is a work of fiction. Any resemblance to persons, living or dead, or places, events or locations is purely coincidental. The characters are all productions of the author's imagination.

Please note that this work is intended only for adults over the age of 18 and all characters represented as 18 or over.

WANTED BY THE BIKERS

AN MC REVERSE HAREM ROMANCE

1

KAYLEE

Deep breaths, deep breaths.

A retro neon sign glows bright over the door of Haunted Ink Tattoo. This is definitely the right place, but the neighborhood's rougher than I expected, even for South Side. The front has huge display windows, but they're completely blacked out, with nothing visible from out here but tattoo designs to advertise the business and beat-up posters for local shows and concerts taped to the glass.

I reeeaally wish I could see inside, because this is my first real interview since getting my cosmetology license. Working at Mom's salon has given me a lot of experience, but I didn't exactly have to work hard for the position. I glance at my watch and take one more deep breath, hoping my car will still be by the curb when I'm done. A little bell dings as I push open the door.

The shop is well lit and nicer than I expected from the outside. Black walls are covered in framed tattoo art, and the floor is tiled in red and white checkerboard. A blue velvet couch and a slouchy leather chair surround a wrought iron coffee table with tattoo magazines strewn across the top. On the wall, a framed leather vest catches my eye, with a big logo on the back that reads, "Screaming Eagles." A reception desk sits off to the side, empty.

Can I really see myself sitting there?

"Hello? Um, I'm here for the interview?" I call out towards a doorway leading into the back. This is the right day, right? Or did I manage to screw things up before I even started?

A rough voice yells through a doorway. "In the back! I'm finishing up a client, but he doesn't give a fuck."

Alrighty then.

I straighten my pink blazer and give my curls a shake. At Mom's place, my subtle auburn balayage highlights are the most shocking thing I can get away with, but here I bet I could dye my hair neon green and nobody would bat an eye.

Not that I want to. I don't think anyway, but maybe some peekaboo streaks?

"Yo! You still there?"

"Coming!"

I rush through the doorway and immediately spot the hottest man I've ever seen. He's got long dark hair with a deep red streak, and a thick black beard. The guy looks like he does a sit up, a push up and a pull up between each line he inks, because all the impressive designs covering his bare chest highlight nothing but tanned muscle and rugged perfection. Dark eyes draw me in like a wolf sizing up a particularly tasty deer.

I'm sooo out of my league here.

"Fuck," he curses under his breath, and I'm not sure if I should take it as a compliment or if he's wondering what a girly girl like me is doing applying for a job in a place like this.

It would be a very valid concern. "I—I'm Kaylee. I'm here for the receptionist job?"

"That a question or a statement, sweetheart?"

"What? No. I mean I'm here to interview for the receptionist position."

"You hear that? She's interested in your position, Wraith," the guy he's working on jokes.

"Ignore this fucker and have a seat. I'm nearly done."

I try to imagine calling the clients in Mom's fancy salon 'this fucker'. Mrs. Wilber's eyes would pop out of her overly botoxed face.

My nervous laugh is cut off when I sit down and get a better view of what my potential new boss is doing. And who.

Wraith, the owner I'm supposed to be interviewing with, is wearing tight rubber gloves and wielding a tattoo needle quickly and confidently, the buzz a constant sound as he works on a drawing that is right about…

Oh.

Oh my.

His client is a giant bear of a man, stretched out in the tattoo chair with his shirt pulled up and his pants opened to expose his powerful hip and an expanse of skin that definitely falls into the delicate manscaping zone. I wet my lips nervously and try really hard not to look too closely. Otherwise I might already see a lot more than I bargained for. My cheeks are so hot I bet I'm practically glowing.

If he pulled those jeans down just a little more…

"Like what you see?" the big guy rumbles.

I snap my eyes up immediately. I bet everything I was just thinking is written all over my face, and he has no problem reading it. "I—"

"Jesus fuck, Tank. Sit still or I swear to God I'm gonna stab this right into your dick. Come take a look, Kaylee. What do you think?"

Tank huffs a laugh and crosses his arms behind his head, showing off his anaconda size muscles. "Just making sure the lady has a good view."

I get up and step closer, wondering if anything else is anaconda sized on him. No matter what happens with the job, I'll be saving this memory for the rest of my life.

"Who's Little Miss Muffet here?" a new voice asks from the doorway. This guy's wearing a T-shirt at least, though he might as well not be considering how it should be paid overtime for how much work it's doing to keep him contained. I can make out every single plane and angle of his ripped torso.

Green eyes. I've always been a sucker for pretty eyes, and he's got the deepest green I've ever seen. I could tumble over and over into those mossy pools until I drown. I'm so lost in them I hardly notice how he's looking me up and down, pausing at my chest before dragging his gaze back up to my face. His lips twist in a wicked smile and he rubs a hand over his five o'clock shadow. His short blond hair is a sexy mess, like he just rolled out of bed after... well, you know.

"Nitro," both Wraith and Tank say at the same time in greeting.

"Don't any of you have real names?" I blurt out before I can stop myself, though I do manage to not ask if they're really Gary, Bob and Arthur. Three flat stares are the only answer I get. I guess they're too cool for that.

Does Nitro work here, too? They all seem like they know each other well, teasing each other like siblings. I feel out of place in my stylish pink interview suit. Wraith shakes his head and goes back to the tattoo. It looks like the handle of a gun that would be pointing right at Tank's, um, gun. At first it's interesting to watch as Wraith strengthens the outline of the grip, wiping away excess ink and blood, but a wave of nausea washes over me and I have to grab the edge of Tank's chair.

"You okay?" Wraith asks, picking up on it immediately.

"Absolutely!" I say, my voice way too bright and strained.

"She's cute," Nitro says, strolling over to a fridge and grabbing a beer like he knows the place well. "Why are you here, princess? Is this a sorority thing? Because if you need to bang a bad boy to pledge or something, my dick is available."

"She's here for the fucking job, asshole," Wraith mutters.

Nitro winks. "My offer stands. Just like my—"

Wraith cuts him off. "What kind of experience do you have? Your resume said you work at a salon?" The tattoo gun buzzes one last time before Wraith wipes off the tattoo, applies some sort of cream and then pastes a transparent patch over the work.

I swallow hard as he starts cleaning up the equipment. I've never liked needles, but I didn't think I'd have a problem with tattoos. "Y—yeah. I'm sort of the everything girl. I work at the front desk with appointments and payments, help with shampoos, waxing, eyebrow shaping. Sometimes I do touch-ups, and if they're busy I help with makeup for events. It's good experience but their clientele is older and it's super rare that anyone wants anything interesting. I feel like—"

Wraith holds his hand up for me to stop. "Sweetheart, don't take this personally, but this is a fucking tattoo parlor, not Budget Trim."

"Oh, yeah, totally. And I know I'd just be in reception at least to start, but I saw on your website that you used to offer piercings, and I have my certification so I thought maybe if it worked out, I could offer other stuff too. I just really want to work somewhere where the most creative choice in my day isn't brown or black mascara."

"Kaylee. Kaylee. Take a breath. You're not on fucking trial here."

"That's good, because all the lawyer would have to do is look at her and she'd tell them her life story," Tank says with a laugh.

I feel myself flush. He's not wrong, but still. Rude.

"Don't take this the wrong way, sweetheart, but I'm not sure this is a good fit. This is a rough neighborhood for a girl like you, and I saw the way you turned a little green when you watched me ink Tank."

"It's fine! I'm fine. I really want this opportunity."

"And you don't have a problem with the way these guys were talking? Because we're fucking boy scouts compared to some of the people who come in here. I wouldn't let anyone fuck with you, but I can't be mopping up your tears if someone says something rude. And the way you look? Words are gonna be said, Kaylee."

Should I be scared or flattered? No one's given me this kind of attention, like ever. And especially not guys like this. I'm never thin or perfect enough for the types of guys my friends hook up with, and guys like these don't even notice I exist. They're always with cool, badass chicks.

"I can do this. I know I can."

Tank pulls his massive frame out of the chair and walks up to me, taking his time with refastening his jeans. I have to crane my neck to look up at him when he hooks his finger under my chin, his skin rough against mine. "You think so? Because a sweet little thing like you? The guys won't be able to stop themselves. Shit, I dunno if I can, and I'm a fucking gentleman."

Nitro snorts.

"Go home to your Mama's salon," Wraith says, shaking his head. "I need someone who can deal with the monsters who come through here and I can't be worried about babysitting your fine ass."

"Some of the old ladies can be real monsters, too," I blurt out.

"We're not fucking joking, princess." Nitro's voice is deadly serious as he raises the edge of his shirt and reveals the hilt of a gun, and not a tattoo one like Tank's.

My eyes go wide and I see on their faces that they know the point was made. "Um, maybe I should…" I trail off.

"Appreciate your application, though. Good luck on the job hunt," says Wraith, with a note of dismissal in his tone.

"Right. Thanks." I feel about three inches tall as I turn around and show myself out with my tail between my legs. For a little while I let myself think that maybe my life could be more than it is.

It was stupid to think I could fit in at a place like Haunted Ink, with men like that. I could barely make eye contact with them or watch Wraith work, never mind actually hold down a job. Maybe I should aim for something a little less exciting and work my way up.

With a defeated sigh, I start my car and pull away from the curb. I'm going to need a treat to deal with Mom's 'I told you so'.

2

KAYLEE

I take a deep drag on my blue raspberry slushie, almost welcoming the brain freeze when it hits. Sometimes, even in mid-February, it takes the completely synthetic flavor of a fruit that doesn't even exist to hit the spot.

"Rough day?" The guy behind the counter asks. He's probably around my age, wiry with a friendly face and a name tag that says Gabriel.

"You could say that. Be honest, was I stupid for wearing this to an interview at a tattoo parlor?" I gesture at myself, loving everything about the pretty pink outfit, but knowing in my gut what his answer will be.

Yep, his expression says it all. "Was it like, a fancy one?"

"No."

"Then yeah, kind of. You look really nice, though."

There isn't enough blue raspberry in the world for this situation. "Thanks."

"Anything other than the slushy and the gas?" His question is nearly drowned out by the roar of motorcycles pulling into the station.

"No, I think that's—"

A loud crack splits the air, immediately followed by one of the front windows shattering inwards, sending glass flying our way.

"Fuck! Get down!" Gabriel shouts, dropping below the edge of the counter, "Come back here. It's reinforced."

It isn't until he says that, that I realize what the sound was. Holy crap! That was an actual gunshot. I drop to the floor, desperately trying to remember my school shooter training. Crawling like a turtle with its butt on fire, I scamper behind the register and huddle in place next to Gabriel.

"Just stay down and it'll pass," he says, voice strained but not nearly as shocked as it should be given the situation.

"I thought South Side was safe these days," I hiss at him.

"It is! Mostly. Shit like this hardly ever happens anymore. The Eagles will make sure whoever is messing around here pays."

The Screaming Eagles vest at Haunted Ink Tattoo should've been my first sign that this area isn't just the fun kind of exciting. Everyone knows they are the most notorious biker gang in the city, probably even this whole coast, and their compound is right here in South Side. But I thought they kept it safe here, not… whatever's going on outside.

I can't help it. Gripping the counter, I raise myself just enough to peek over the edge.

"Lady, stay down!" Gabriel whispers harshly.

Stacks of wiper fluid and shelves full of snacks block my view, but it looks calm. "Maybe they're g—" A flurry of gunshots and yelling sends me right back on my butt.

"You have a death wish or something? Keep your head down!"

An eardrum-shattering explosion takes what's left of the front windows with it. I scream even though I can't hear my own voice, pressing my hands over my ears as glass and burning debris come flying over us.

The stillness that follows is an eerie blessing, and I'm not sure if I've just lost my hearing until Gabriel starts swearing. Then something crashes to the floor, and there's the sound of fire.

I never thought I'd experience what it felt like to be in a warzone, especially not right here in the city.

"That was one of the tanks. Those fuckers are destroying the place!" He grabs a fire extinguisher.

"You said stay down!"

"Yeah, when stray bullets were our biggest problem. This counter isn't going to do shit if the place explodes. There's a door out the back, follow me." Head down, he sprays down any flames in his path as he leads the way.

I move to follow, but glance out the front where things seem to have gone quiet for the moment. "My car!"

"Move it!" he screams, just before something booms inside the station, shaking the floor so I nearly lose my balance. Another explosion? Candy bars and bags of chips on fire spill from the shelves, and a fridge full of energy drinks topples over, right between me and Gabriel.

It's okay, I can climb over—

With a creak and a crash that has me jump back a step, the one next to it falls too. There was a crate of some kinds of car accessories stored on top of it, and suddenly there's a big pile of rubble blocking the door with just a tiny gap for Gabriel and me to see each other through. There's no way I'm squeezing through that.

We stare at each other helplessly, two bystanders caught in someone else's war. I'm quickly learning that I should stop wishing for more excitement in my life because I'm not cut out for it, but I know I could never live with myself if something happened to someone else because I froze. "Go! Don't be stupid. I'll chance the front."

He hesitates, but nods. "I'll call for help," he yells, already on the move.

I make it as far as what's left of the front door before the gunfire starts back up and I throw myself to the ground. This is insane. I have no idea what to do. Outside is deadly, but inside is on fire.

There's a black SUV in front that probably looked a lot better before it was filled with bullet holes and scorched by the explosion. A man in a suit is using the front for cover as he shoots at a group of guys in jeans and leather jackets on the other side of the pumps. The pump that blew up is a fiery wreck, and I'm not sure what's scarier, the guns or what will happen when the flames keep spreading. There are a bunch more pumps that can go up. My car is still more or less untouched, and I make the—probably stupid—plan to try to get to it and get the heck out of Dodge.

I keep as low as I can, inching towards my car and hoping no one sees me. At least until I trip over the arm of a man in a white dress shirt lying face down in a pool of his own blood. The only thing that keeps me from screaming and bringing everyone's attention my way is that my scream won't come out. I'm literally too terrified to make a sound. Time passes like in a dream as I dash to my car without a thought in my head but putting one foot in front of the other until I get there. Somehow, I do.

The guy hiding behind the SUV cries out in pain and the gunshots stop. I hold my breath as the bikers walk right past the other side of the pumps on their way to the SUV. One last gunshot pierces the air and I know in my gut the man in the suit is just as dead as the guy by the door.

"It's done. Let's get the fuck outta here," says one of them in a gruff command.

Tears stream down my face and I make myself as small and still as possible as the murderers run to their bikes.

Don't see me. Don't see me, I chant in my head. There's no way they'll let a witness get away.

I'm almost convinced that I've gotten away with it when one of the monsters stops. I can just see him through the car windows. His face is deeply scarred, the disfiguration continuing from his chin and well down his neck. Then I realize that if I can see him, he can see me, and I huddle down.

"Come on," snaps one of the others. "Cops are gonna be here soon."

"I thought I heard…"

He takes a step in my direction.

3

WRAITH

"Get your asses to West and Fifty-second," Eagle Eye barks into the phone. "Shots fired at the gas station. Something big's going down and you're closest."

"On our way." Tank and Nitro watch me closely, waiting for the order as I jam my phone in my pocket. "You heard that?"

"I think they fucking heard him across the street," says Tank, but other than that, any trace of the laid back jokers they usually are has vanished. Shit's about to go down, and there's no one I'd rather have at my back than Tank and Nitro. The Screaming Eagles are my family, and these two assholes are my brothers, not by the blood in our veins, but by the blood we've spilled pulling each other's asses out of the fire over the years.

We adjust our pieces for easy access as we run to our bikes. When things turn bad, every second matters. A moment later, we're screaming out of the alley and towards who the fuck knows what trouble.

Sirens are just starting to be audible in the distance, so we don't have a lot of time before this turns into a total shit show, but if someone's moving on our territory, we need to find out before this city's joke of a police department is on the scene.

The first thing I notice is smoke spiraling up from the pumps. Fuck.

And when I spot the expensive looking black SUV with tinted windows, I get a really fucking bad feeling about what we're about to find. Not every car that looks like that belongs to the mob, but with everything else, the odds are really fucking good. A half dozen bikers are scrambling over the place like rats fleeing a sinking ship. From a distance, I don't recognize their bikes or their patches.

Who the fuck are they?

I raise my hand to direct Tank and Nitro to follow them, but then I spot the bodies, and a flash of the same bubblegum pink that walked into my studio less than an hour ago.

Motherfucker.

We brake fast, screeching into the gas station with a good distance between us and the burning.

Nitro takes one look at the situation and shakes his head. "It's too late. This whole place could blow any second."

I point to where the familiar pink figure is slumped down next to a car by the pumps and he swears. "You two check the others. I'll go look."

Tank nods, but he looks like he wants to tear someone's head off and I'm right there with him. That beautiful, innocent girl was only in this neighborhood because of the interview. If she's dead, it might not be directly my fault, but her blood would be on my fucking hands.

Moving fast, I go over expecting the worst, but her shoulders move. There's blood on her clothes and she's huddled on the ground, but she's not dead.

"Kaylee!" I kneel and brush back her hair. "You hurt?"

At my touch, she seems to break out of the shock she's in. Sobs rack her body, but she shakes her head and throws herself at me like a drowning woman, desperate to stay afloat.

"Three dead," Nitro shouts, running our way. "Two on the pavement and one behind the wheel. Multiple shots but each has a hole right in their fucking foreheads. This wasn't random."

"Pray they're not Giordanos, 'cause if they are, this is going to be real fucking bad," Tank growls. "Did you catch who was flying out of here?"

"Guys? Talk later, run now." Nitro's already on the move as something pops and the sirens get closer.

"We're going to get you out of here, Kaylee. Can you hold on?"

"To what? I don't—Oh, God." Her eyes are squeezed closed like she's trying to block all this shit out. I don't fucking blame her.

"We're about to find out." I scoop her into my arms and follow Nitro and Tank to our bikes. She squeaks in protest, but buries her face in my shirt. I throw my leg over my bike and flip her so she's straddling me. "Hold on, sweetheart."

"But—"

Whatever she was going to say is drowned out by the roar of our bikes as we peel out onto the street, three abreast with Kaylee safely tucked against me. She feels good there, and not just because her tits are pressed into my chest and her skirt is way up her thighs. I only get a moment to appreciate the feeling before a wave of heat licks at our heels as the gas station blows sky high.

4

KAYLEE

If Wraith, Tank and Nitro hadn't come when they did... I'd be gone. A shiver so strong it nearly makes me lose my grip tears straight through me. This morning all I wanted was the chance at a new, more exciting life. I got exactly what I wished for and almost died because of a stupid blue raspberry slushie.

I don't know how or why they found me, but I owe them my life. Not only was I a complete wreck back there, I'm pretty sure the sound of their bikes was what drove off the other bikers before I ended up like the rest of their victims.

I cling to Wraith, breathing in the clean, masculine scent of him underneath the stink of gas and fire.

The weather is mild today, but it's still February. After the blast of heat from the explosion fades, I start to really notice the chill as the wind whips against my back. My front is nice and warm, pressed tight against Wraith.

He curls an arm around me, holding me even closer, making sure I don't fall off. Sitting the wrong way on a motorcycle going full speed down a city street after everything that just happened, I shouldn't feel safe. But I do.

Maybe it's the adrenaline, but the vibration of the bike and the feel of the big, strong body that's protecting me is actually kinda nice. They might have been a little rude at the interview, but they weren't mean or anything. Maybe they're not so bad, after all.

My car!

It was a pile of junk, but it ran and it was mine. I don't have the money to buy a new one, and even if my insurance covers gas station explosions, I'll probably get pennies for it.

But I'm alive to worry about stupid things like cars.

I rest my head against Wraith's chest as thoughts whirr through my scattered brain like popcorn. My sleeve has a big red stain. It's blood from the man I tripped over. A man who'll never worry about his car insurance again. His blank expression is burned into my memory.

The bike slows and I dare to look around. We're deep in South Side and I don't know the streets or where they're taking me. How the heck am I going to get home?

They pull up to a bar called The Eagle's Roost, where there is already a long line of motorcycles parked outside. Wraith passes me off to Tank who lifts me right off the bike like I weigh absolutely nothing. When he puts me down, he doesn't take his hand off my shoulder. Is it for support, or so I don't run away?

"What are we doing here? Shouldn't we call the cops or something?" I ask as they guide me to the door.

A scary looking biker is watching it, his long hair tied back, revealing a vicious scar on his face. He nods in greeting. "Prez is down front waiting for you. Everything good?"

"Does she look like everything's good?" Nitro fires back.

The guy shrugs. "She's breathing and none of that blood looks like it's yours. Coulda been a fun time for all I know."

"Read the fucking room, Animal," Tank growls. Animal laughs as the guys take me past and in through the door.

It's the middle of the afternoon, and the bar is quiet, with classic rock and mostly male voices filling the space. A few people turn to look our way, but nobody seems overly shocked at the sight of the three of them surrounding a blood covered woman. It's their lack of reaction that freaks me out more than anything. What kind of world did I stumble into where this is normal?

At the bar, Wraith nods to Tank. "We'll go report, get her a drink and keep her out of trouble."

"Sure thing."

Wraith and Nitro head down into a lower section of the bar where there's a stage with a topless woman in booty shorts dancing with another woman whose breasts are all but falling out of a tiny bikini top. A grizzled old biker sits with several other scary looking men. He looks up as Wraith and Nitro approach, and then his gaze slides over the space between us and lands right on me.

I freeze, unable to look away from the piercing stare of the man with one white eye. That has to be the man the guy at the door said was waiting. Prez is short for president, right? When he looks away, it's like being dismissed.

"You want a beer or something?" Tank asks, gesturing to a couple free bar stools.

"Um, I'm not really a drinker."

His eyebrows go up, but he shrugs. "Suit yourself. I'm sure they've got something back there for you. Hey, Badass! Get me a Bud, and my friend here wants…"

The bartender, a guy big enough to make Tank seem normal looks at me expectantly. Everything about this is so surreal. I left the house for an interview, nearly died in a shootout, almost got blown up, and now I'm sitting here in my wrecked clothes ordering a drink.

"Just… just a Coke, I guess."

"Sure you don't want anything stronger? Nothing personal, but you look like you could use it."

I shake my head and then pause. "Um, could you put a couple maraschino cherries in there?"

"Coming right up." He grins and turns away to get our drinks.

I spin on the stool, looking around. On the surface, this looks like a pretty normal bar, but these aren't frat boys. They're men, muscled and tattooed, filling the place with the tang of leather and musk that competes with the usual scent of beer and cigarettes. There's a couple in a shadowy corner, and she's straddling his lap facing away from me, but from what I can see, he has her shirt open and they're getting real friendly.

Who does that in public? Not that anyone but me seems to notice. When her hands move towards his belt and start to do something, I spin back around before I can see anything more. This place is nuts!

Tank slides my Coke in front of me. "See something interesting?"

"Nope."

"You sure? Nobody here would mind if you wanted to take the edge off after a rough morning."

My jaw drops and I spin his way. "Are you insane?"

Tank leans closer, his striking blue eyes only inches from mine. "Don't play innocent. I saw how you were looking at me earlier back at the shop. I promise I can give as good as I get. You aren't even a little bit curious?"

A low, throaty groan from the corner punctuates his question. I must be beet red, but I shake my head with conviction. "Not even a little," I lie. "I don't know why you guys brought me here instead of straight to the police, but I'm not like you. I don't see this kind of stuff every day and I'm hanging on by a thread, okay? If I get down on my knees, it's going to be to pray that this was all a bad dream and not to suck your dick. Got it?"

I wasn't aware of how loud my voice had gotten by the end of that until I realize everything's gone quiet around me. Even the music seems to pause to maximize my complete embarrassment. I slap a hand down on the bar and take a long gulp of soda, pulling in one of the cherries and biting down to get the satisfying gush of sugar syrup mixed with Coke.

Tank throws his head back and laughs. "I like you. You're pretty and mouthy."

"We miss something besides Kaylee not wanting to blow you?" Nitro asks from behind me.

He and Wraith join us at the bar along with the burly old biker they were talking with. His short cropped hair is pure silver with only a sprinkling of dark, and his mustache is thick and bristly. He walks with the easy confidence of a man who knows he's in charge and doesn't have anything to prove. His tanned, leathery skin is furrowed, and close up, his pale white eye isn't any less unnerving. It doesn't make him look less focused—if anything it makes the shrewd calculation in his good eye more obvious. Even if I didn't have any other clues to tell me he's the boss around here, you couldn't mistake him for anything else.

"So you're Kaylee," he says, watching me closely.

I nod.

"My boys tell me you've had a rough day, honey, so I'm going to keep this short. What happened at the gas station is unfortunate, but this is our territory and we'll handle it. You should go home and do your best to forget about all this. Do you understand me?"

His tone is friendly, but there's an implied threat in there that is impossible to miss. "I've had a chat with Gabriel, and he tells me that you were inside with him when everything went down. It's a miracle you both made it out through the back safely."

"Oh, no. The way got blocked and I had to go out the front, so—oh, right." I'm naive, not stupid. I know what that look means.

"Are we going to have any problems?"

Wraith puts a hand on my shoulder and squeezes. Support? Or a warning?

I shake my head, scared silent for the second time today. "No, sir."

"Drink's on the house. Finish up, go home and get the fuck on with your life. If anyone asks, you tell them what I just told you. Got it?"

I nod and he watches me for a long moment before nodding back and walking away. My shoulders slump and it takes another cherry before I manage to speak. "He's terrifying."

"Who? Eagle-eye?" Tank asks. "He's a teddy bear as long as you don't get on his bad side."

"What happens if I do?"

They all share a look. "How about you don't," Nitro says softly.

"Those men. The ones who were shot. Someone will pay for that, right? I need you to tell me that all that won't just get swept under the rug. I'm not a little kid. I know this city is messed up and you guys are… who you are. But it's wrong if people die and nobody cares. Right?" I look up into Wraith's eyes.

He nods slowly. "You have my number. Promise me that if you start feeling funny about this or you need to talk, you call me and nobody else."

I trust him. I don't know why or if it's stupid, but I do. "Okay."

The world they live in scares the crap out of me, but my gut tells me that while the three of them might think it's funny to shock me, they would never hurt me, not on purpose.

This time, I get to ride behind Nitro as they escort me home. It's a lot less awkward than straddling the front of him, and there's something nice about having my arms wrapped around his waist and hiding from the wind behind his broad torso. It's actually kind of fun, especially with Wraith and Tank flanking us like an honor guard.

It's dark by the time we stop in front of my parents' house. The air is cold and the wind sends fallen leaves swirling over the sidewalk. Wraith helps me off the bike, and before I can stop myself, I stretch up on my tip toes and press my mouth against his. I only meant for it to take a second, but his arm goes around me and he nips my lip, making me open for him.

His tongue slides into my mouth and what was meant to be a tiny thank you turns into a deep, hungry kiss. He tastes like danger and possibilities. Possibilities I'll never see, and that's probably for the best, but when I watch them drive away, I know for a fact the heat of the flames won't be the only thing I remember from today.

5

TANK

Arturo Giordano pauses his measured pacing of the meeting room above the Roost and turns to the table. "This looks very, very bad, Eagle-eye. You must understand that."

From what I've heard, Papa Giordano is still the Don of the Giordano Mafia family, but Arturo has taken on most of his father's work at this point. Sharp-eyed, with a hawkish expression and a crisp designer suit, he looks every inch the capable second in command. When he steps into control, I don't see him being any easier to work with than his father.

Good for their business, but kind of shit for us since right now easy to work with would be really fucking useful. At least that's the way it seems to me. Not that anyone asks.

I cross my arms over my chest, flexing a little for emphasis. Our VP King and Viking, one of the officers, sit at the table with Eagle-Eye. Wraith and Nitro sit off to the side, but I'm standing in back. It's what I'm good at. The muscle, the threat. All this political shit? I totally understand why the Giordanos are pissed, but I'm glad I'm not the one having to figure out what the fuck to do about it. I'd probably just get everyone killed.

"My men were passing through your territory after a meeting in Abbeville. It had nothing to do with biker business, and yet I'm sure you've seen the latest news? The images the police put out in search of more information? The images that show men with your patches attacking completely unprovoked?"

"Of course I have," growls Eagle-eye, the words coming out like gravel from a rock crusher. "But they aren't mine. I haven't seen a single one of those fuckers before and none of my men are unaccounted for."

Arturo throws his hands up. "*Cazzo!* I don't know what to believe. The only reason we're here asking questions instead of shooting up the place is because of the years of truce that have benefited the both of us. And Alessa, of course. The Fabbris weren't the only part of the Family that weren't happy about our cooperation, and this only fuels the rumors."

Old history and more fucking politics. Alessa's the Giordano Mafia princess who ended up the old lady of four Eagles. Yeah, I'm glad I'm not the one in charge of this.

"What rumors?" King asks with a hint of danger in his tone. He never likes being questioned, and as VP, he's in a similar position to Arturo. They both need to make sure that not only are their people safe and under control, but that their authority as second isn't in question.

Too much fucking stress if you ask me.

"That Alessa is nothing but a hostage you're holding over Luca and she should be considered an acceptable loss." Arturo nods his head at Luca Giordano, Alessa's father. "There are those who think the safety of the truce will make us soft and that you're testing the water to see if our internal conflict has weakened the Family."

Luca, like most of these mob guys, usually shows about as much emotion as a rock, but at Arturo's words, he snarls. "My daughter and grandchildren are not pawns."

Viking grunts in agreement. He's one of Alessa's men in addition to being one of Eagle-eye's officers. "We had nothing to do with this mess, but if you've got people looking for a fight, let them come here and say that to our faces."

Whoever set us up knew exactly what buttons to push. Alessa shacking up with bikers nearly started a war between the Screaming Eagles and the Giordanos when it went down, but if there's one thing both organizations have in common, it's family and fucking loyalty. Throwing that into question is a quick way to piss everyone off.

"Enough! The Fabbris have been pains in both our asses," Eagle-eye snaps. "Are they trying to cause trouble again? Neither of us would profit from a break in the truce. Or has that changed?"

Arturo and Luca share a look before he shakes his head. "No. It's not impossible, but we're watching every move they make and we haven't heard even a whisper." Arturo sighs. "I need more than your word that the men on the video weren't yours."

I've had enough of these bullshit accusations. "We told you what we saw! Are you calling us liars?"

Eagle-eye raises a hand. "Tank. Stand down."

"I just think it's really fucking shitty that after all these years, an obvious fucking set up like this is all it takes to make them question us."

"They lost three men. If it had been the three of you, don't you think we'd be riding in and demanding some fucking answers?" Eagle-eye says, fixing his clear eye on me. His expression is dark.

I fall back, still not happy.

"They weren't just lost. They were executed," says Arturo icily, glaring daggers at me. "On your territory, with evidence that your people were behind it. By your own admission, you were there! Even someone like you can understand how that looks."

"What the fuck does that mean?" I growl. "You think you're better than me? Than us?" Of course he fucking does. Wraith and Nitro get up and stand with me, an obvious show of support. "I'm good," I bite out between clenched teeth.

"The man asked a fucking question," Eagle-eye says, his tone smooth and deadly—a warning for Arturo to not wear out his welcome.

"I don't believe you did it," says Arturo finally. "We wouldn't be here if I did, but the good of the Family comes first, just as I'm sure your club does with you. I'm not here to make accusations, but in the end the future of the Giordano family is more important than my personal feelings."

"Then stop dancing around the point and tell me what the Giordanos want. I don't want a fucking war. You don't want a fucking war. So where do we go from here? I'm being as fucking understanding as I can because three of your men are dead, but mine are being framed for shit we didn't do. Neither of us can afford to let this go and if we spend our energy fighting each other we are playing right into their hands." Eagle-eye crosses his arms over his chest and leans back.

"A week. You can have a week. After that, we must take action or it will be seen as weakness. This isn't a threat, it's simply all I can give you. I bury my nephew on Sunday and I need to look his mother in the eye and tell him that we will make those responsible pay."

"A fucking week?" King cracks his knuckles. He's been mostly silent so far, but nothing has slipped past him. I wouldn't fuck with him any more than I would Eagle-eye. "That's not much time, not if we have to pursue multiple leads."

Arturo picks up his phone from the meeting table and slips it into his pocket. "No, it isn't, but all we ask is that you find the guilty party. The revenge we are more than happy to arrange ourselves."

Eagle-eye rises slowly, leaning his weight on the table and looking Arturo dead in the eyes. "You realize that we're not going to bring the war to you, but if you start one, we'll burn your fucking empire to the ground."

"You may try. I'd expect nothing less."

They stare at each other, and I get the feeling that while they might look nothing alike, they both have a feral streak that would mourn the casualties but absolutely glory in finding out who would win.

Luca clears his throat. "Alessa is expecting me to visit with her and the children after our meeting. Is that going to be a problem?"

"Not today." Eagle-eye gestures towards the compound. "But go with Viking so everyone knows to keep it fucking friendly."

When they're gone and it's just Eagles left, he lets out a long breath and leans back in his chair. "What a fucking mess. That girl you pulled outta there. Where's she now? I think it would be good for us to have a longer chat. Were there any other witnesses?"

King leans forward. "Gabriel was working that day, one of the neighborhood guys. I've known him since he was a kid. We can bring him in, but he was the one that called to tip us off and I'm pretty sure if he saw anything useful we'd know by now."

"Do it," Eagle-eye orders.

"I've got Kaylee's contact info from her application. The only reason she was even anywhere fucking near us was because she had an interview at the studio. We'll get her," Wraith says.

"Fuck. I won't mind seeing her cute ass again," Nitro says with a grin. "But it's fucked up that she almost fucking died because you were trying to keep her safe from our shit."

He's not wrong. She was fucking adorable. When Wraith told her she wasn't cut out for the job, I wanted to punch him. It would've been entertaining as hell to watch her shocked little face adjust from some frou-frou lady salon to a fucking biker tattoo joint. I'd give her a week before she worked up the courage to follow through on some of the long looks she was giving us at her interview.

King growls. "This is serious shit. There's a war coming if we don't get some real information. Keep your dicks in your pants, for fuck's sake."

"You mean like you did when you kidnapped your old lady from her bedroom just to fuck with her father?" Nitro says with a snort.

I'm pretty sure the only thing keeping King from kicking his ass is how loud Eagle-eye and Viking laugh.

Eagle-eye stands. "King, talk to Snark and have him watch the cops. They've got the fucking tapes, so if they so much as pass around a dirty joke I want to fucking hear about it. Viking, keep Alessa safe. If anything happens to her, we're fucked. Wraith? You and your boys need to scrape your fucking brains to see if you remember anything, and bring that girl back in. It won't take a genius to realize that if her car was there, so the fuck was she."

6

KAYLEE

THE DOORBELL RINGS AS I SIT AT THE COMPUTER redesigning my resume for the hundredth time and nibbling a cookie.

I'm not expecting a delivery, and not particularly in the mood to talk to anyone after the week I've had, so I ignore it.

My parents are both at work. When Mom found out I was nearly caught in the big gas station explosion two days ago, she gave me the rest of the week off. They don't know the whole story, of course, but I came home looking like an extra in an action movie. They took one look at me and I had to say something. Especially since what's left of my car is probably still smoking outside the station.

The whole day keeps running through my head, and it's all tangled up together. My interview with three hot guys, nearly getting shot in what must have been a gang fight, and then nearly getting blown up. It was a little glimpse into a world I've never seen before. One where every day could be your last.

I know I wanted some more excitement in my life, but that was a bit too much, thanks. Too bad, because Wraith, Tank and Nitro? Even one of them would almost make it worth the risk.

News about the explosion and fire is all over TV, but they are saying it was a technical fault. Nobody's mentioned anything about a shooting or bodies being found.

The bell rings again, and this time whoever it is really leans on it.

What the heck is so important? I glance over to the door, still thinking about those three hot bikers. It wouldn't be them, right? But it could be.

Curious and more than a little hopeful, I close up my laptop and shuffle over to the front to peek out the window. Two police officers are standing on our porch, looking annoyed and impatient. One is right at the door, the other standing farther back with his arms crossed over his chest.

Oh crap. What should I do? Pretend not to be here? They have to be looking for me, because nothing ever happens in our neighborhood to bring out the cops aside from when Cal's teens ride their ATVs through peoples' lawns.

Are we going to have any problems? Eagle-eye's question runs through my head. I bet he would definitely classify this as a problem.

The cop standing in the back catches sight of me behind the curtains. I jump out of the way, but the damage is done. They start pounding on the door. "Ma'am? Answer the door. We need to have a word."

Double crap.

I ease open the door just enough to peek through. "Can I help you?"

The guy in front looks like a caricature of a cop. He has a jaw a superhero would be envious of, not a hair out of place, and a suit so stiff it looks like it could stand on its own. Right away it feels off. He's trying too hard and just ends up looking very, very into his job. His partner seems slightly more relaxed, with a ruddy complexion, unruly red hair and a lopsided grin.

The redhead speaks first. "Kaylee Thompson?"

I look nervously between them, not wanting to give an inch if I don't have to. "Yeah, that's me."

"I'm Officer Anderson and this is Detective Harris. May we come inside?"

Anything other than yes would be suspicious, so I let them in. "Sorry, I wasn't exactly expecting company." I gesture down at my sweats. "What's this about?"

I hate lying, probably because I'm not any good at it. Even when I was little I never got away with anything. I gave my word that I wouldn't say anything about what I saw, but lying to the police? This could be bad. Really bad.

"I'll be brief, Ms. Thompson. A car registered to you has been found at the Red Kite service station. We're still analyzing the security footage, but this would go faster if you could confirm that you were there at the time of the explosion. I'm sure the shock is why you haven't been in touch yet," Anderson gives me a patronizing smile.

Security footage. I should've expected that. Even if they haven't seen it yet, they'll eventually see me and maybe even the guys. "Um, I was there, but it all happened so fast, you know? I don't know if I can help you with anything."

"Right... right. That's understandable, but all the same, we'd like to bring you to the station, ask some questions and get an official statement."

"Can't we just talk here?"

Detective Harris shakes his head. "I'm afraid not. As a person of interest, the interrogation has to happen in an official space so we can ensure everything's by the book."

"Person of interest?" I squeak. "You don't think I had anything to do with it, do you? I mean, I totally get that you guys have all sorts of rules and stuff..." I back up a few steps. "How about I come in later this week and—"

"We're going to need you to come with us now. I'd prefer not to have to force the issue, but we will if we have to."

"I'm sure you understand how important it is to cooperate with the investigation," says Anderson, sounding totally reasonable and a little threatening at the same time.

It's not a request, I realize that. Him being polite is just a pretty little bow on top of a brick they intend to throw if they have to.

"C—can I get changed first?"

"Of course, and how about you throw together a bag with some things. You know, just in case this takes longer than anticipated."

"Um, thanks. I'll be right back." I make a break for my room, trying not to look suspicious. I need to call Wraith. The last thing I want is to end up in deep shit with both the cops *and* the Screaming Eagles.

Footsteps follow me up the stairs.

I spin around. "Excuse me?"

"Standard procedure." Anderson holds out his hands apologetically. "Since we had to track you down, you're considered a flight risk."

"Flight risk? Are you serious? I'm a twenty-one year old salon assistant who still lives with her parents and currently doesn't even have a car. Do you think I'm moonlighting as an explosive expert or something? I had a bad morning, went in for a slushie and ended up in the middle of something I had nothing to do with. That's it!"

Detective Harris gives me a flat stare, taking over with a dark, gruff tone. "There's no need for theatrics. We're only doing our jobs. This case has serious implications for the safety of this city and we can't afford to take any risks because it makes you uncomfortable." He gestures to Anderson. "I told you we should have done this my way. She's resisting. Cuff her."

"What? What are you doing? Stop that! I was just surprised. I'm not resisting anything!" No matter how much I beg, it doesn't stop Officer Anderson from pressing me up against the wall, pulling my arms behind me and snapping cuffs on my wrists. "I haven't done anything wrong!"

"Then you have nothing to worry about, do you? Let's go down to the station and get all this worked out."

These are supposed to be the good guys? Yesterday I met a bunch of men that these guys would call criminals, but even when they were being scary like Eagle-eye, they treated me nicer than this.

They confiscate my phone and I'm marched out of the house and into the back of their cruiser. Harris slams the door shut, while Anderson goes around to take the wheel. When we get to the main station downtown, I expect to get signed in, my fingerprints taken, something, but instead I'm locked in a completely bare interrogation room and left alone. There's nothing but an uncomfortable chair, a metal table and a door with a frosted, reinforced window. On the wall is a gigantic mirror that based on the crime shows I've watched is probably one-way glass.

This really doesn't feel right.

Don't I get a phone call? They could keep me in here and nobody will know what happened to me. One day I just vanish. Poof. Gone.

I stand up and pace around the room in the rainbow fleece lined crocs I wear around the house as slippers. The clank of the door opening sends me running right back to my seat. I clasp my hands in my lap and focus on looking cooperative. The truth is on my side. I haven't done anything, and the video will show that Wraith and the others weren't responsible either.

It's Harris and Anderson again.

"Sorry about the wait. Something came up," Anderson says in a soft voice. He's carrying a glass of water that he takes a sip from and puts down in front of himself, not me. Right up until I saw it, I didn't realize how thirsty I was. "Now how about you start at the beginning and tell us exactly what happened yesterday afternoon."

I've been running it over and over in my head since they put me here, but I still don't know what to say. "I told you back at my house. I had a bad morning."

"What happened?"

Nervous, I pick at the corner of my thumbnail. If they check my email, they'll know, right? Can they do that if I'm not arrested? What about GPS? Best to stick to the truth. "I… I had a job interview but it didn't go that well so when I stopped to fill gas on my way home, I figured I would go in and grab a slushie to make myself feel better. I was chatting with the guy behind the register when something exploded outside."

"What did you talk about?"

"I don't know. My job hunt I guess? Anyway, we ducked behind the counter when stuff started blowing up, and then we—"

Detective Harris reaches into his jacket and pulls out several grainy photographs which are stills from a surveillance camera. In one you can see me coming out the front where a body is clearly visible, in another I'm hiding by my car, and in the third, Wraith is leading me away.

Shit.

"Like I was saying. We started running for the back door because of whatever was going on out front, but he was faster and the door got blocked so I had to go out the front. I really didn't see much, I swear." Between thinking about yesterday and the stress of being interviewed, it's all too easy to let the tears come. Hopefully they'll get me some sympathy. "It was so scary. I saw the body and just... I ran to my car hoping I could get away, but was too scared. I hid and hoped they wouldn't see me."

"Who wouldn't see you, Ms. Thompson?"

"I don't know who they were. I told you, it happened fast."

"Could you pick out any of the shooters if I showed you some pictures?"

"M—maybe. I'm not sure." Lie. I've been trying to forget, but I can still picture the scarred face of the guy who nearly found me and I'm pretty sure if I saw them again, I'd recognize at least one of the others.

"Good, excellent. Now I'd like you to tell us who the men were that you left with." He frowns and taps the picture where Wraith is visible. "They looked very similar to the shooters didn't they?"

My heart's racing a mile a minute. I'm walking on very thin ice. "You think? I guess they both were riding motorcycles, but that's pretty common. They were just Good Samaritans."

He snorts in disbelief. "Do you really expect me to believe that someone was driving by, saw a shooting in progress and the gas station burning, and they just scooped you up and left?"

"Why is that so hard to believe?"

"Nobody in that area does anything unless they have something to gain from it. Let me be perfectly clear. We've run a background check on you and there's nothing that indicates even a hint of connection to anything that happened aside from you happening to be in the wrong place at the wrong time."

"Then why am I here?"

Detective Harris stands. "Because we have reason to believe that the Screaming Eagles are behind those cold blooded murders. You're either keeping your mouth shut to protect them or you're afraid of them. I don't know which it is, but either way, you could be the key to making sure they pay. I'd start thinking long and hard about what you saw."

"I didn't... I really didn't... When can I go home?"

Anderson leans back, and his grin turns crafty. "Oh, Ms. Thompson, I'm afraid that would be a very bad idea. We'll be keeping you safe for your own good."

"What? You can't just—"

"We can and we will. Someone will be in to get you soon." Anderson finishes the water and crushes the paper cup on the table right in front of me before they walk out, leaving me locked in the room alone again.

This really can't be legal. Can the police really just pick me up and hold me without any kind of consent?

I close my eyes and remember Tank and Nitro joking around at the tattoo parlor, and the taste of

Wraith when he kissed me goodbye. I know for a fact the three of them weren't the shooters, and from what I heard and saw after, I'd bet money that it wasn't the Screaming Eagles behind it.

The police department in this city has been a joke since I was a kid. Everyone knows it. Maybe Harris and Anderson are seeing the chance to finally pin something on the bikers and being a little overeager. I'm sure once someone more understanding talks to me this will all work out.

7

NITRO

"Anything?"

Wraith shoves his phone into his jacket with a shake of his head. "No. Her number's going straight to voicemail. Has been since last night. I don't like this."

"Kaylee's ghosting you? She didn't strike me as a kiss and run kinda girl." Tank puts his fingers to his lips and lets out a shrill whistle. "Newbies! Over there! When you're riding with us, you represent the club. I don't want to see you fucking around."

Beast and Shrapnel, both ex-military, yell "Yes, sir!" while Mad Dog gives a curt nod.

"Where are Deuce and Reaper?"

"Here!" Deuce shouts as he and his buddy jog out of the workshop and towards their bikes.

Shit, it feels like a lifetime ago, but I remember being in their shoes. At their age, I was fresh out of service without a fucking clue what to do with my life. After being a Sapper in the Army, a buddy got me a job doing demo for a construction company. I lasted three months before I realized I'd be doing the same fucking thing day after day for the rest of my fucking life and walked off the site. Joining the Screaming Eagles was the best fucking decision I've ever made.

"Let's cruise by her house after the run," I suggest. "Chances are she's just playing it smart and not wanting to get involved in any of our shit, but we're on the clock here with the Giordanos. Like it or not, we have to bring her in."

Wraith nods. "I feel like a fucking asshole for dragging an innocent girl like her back into this mess, but I gotta say, I'm not mad about seeing her again."

"Of course you're not. Last time you saw her you were tasting her fucking tonsils," Tank says with a snort.

"Jealous?"

"Not unless you aren't planning on sharing."

"Fuuuuck," I groan out. "Why'd you have to say that right before the ride? Now I'm picturing her with that little pink interview skirt flipped up and those big eyes looking up at me while she—"

"Roll out!" Eagle-eye booms.

A courtyard full of bikes roar to life as one. Looming war or not, club business has to go on. South Side is only safe if we're here to keep it that way. The people who live here need to know we're paying attention, and we can't give the fuckers trying to mess with us the satisfaction of thinking we're running scared.

About two dozen of us roll out of the compound and hit the streets, ready to make it clear that we aren't going any-fucking-where. Fuck, I love these rides. With the wind in my face and my brothers at my side, it's easy to forget about all the bad shit because the good is so fucking good.

"Stay the fuck in position!" Wraith yells at the prospects who aren't used to riding so tight together.

Keeping an eye on these grown fucking men is like running a fucking daycare sometimes. Was I ever that fresh? With a potential war brewing, we're gonna need all the new blood we can get, but it ain't worth shit if we can't depend on them.

Eagle-eye cruises at the head of the pack, flanked by King and Alpha. They ride like they own this fucking place, because they do. When I was serving I learned real damn fast that being a leader isn't about a title or a rank, it's something you're either born with or you aren't. Sometimes it takes going through real shit to bring it out, but it was always fucking there.

They have it. It's why so many other clubs burn out while the Screaming fucking Eagles only burn brighter and brighter.

The run goes smooth, right up until it doesn't.

Just as we hit the edge of our territory and start looping back around I can tell something's off. Eagle-eye exchanges a look with King. Cars usually pull over and let us through, but this is too quiet and we find out in a second why that is.

Riot trucks barrel out of the streets on both sides right before we hit an intersection. They block the entire road and cover the sidewalks, and in an obviously planned move, officers in full tactical gear pour out, lining up with their shields at the ready. What the fuck is this? The cops haven't been brave enough to challenge us on our own turf in a long fucking time.

The head of the line, including Eagle-eye and Alpha, barely manages to slide to a stop before crashing right into the whole mess. The rest of us form up tightly behind them, only to get blocked in from behind by two regular cop cars with the lights going.

"Prez?" asks King, his hand close to his waist, ready to draw if he has to.

Eagle-eye motions to wait, his expression deadly. I haven't seen him look this furious since the day we rode to get his daughter back from the Pit Vipers. "No iron, not unless we have to. It's their fucking move."

All of us, even the prospects, go still. Whatever the fuck happens, we meet it together.

"If this turns ugly, we're sure as hell gonna be the ones who walk away in the end," Tank growls under his breath.

"What the fuck is this about?" Eagle-eye shouts. "This is a public road you're blocking. We're just out for a little ride."

A man in a crisp black suit steps forwards, still safely behind the riot shields. He's broad-shouldered with a cartoonishly square jaw. "I'm Detective Harris, and I'd hold off on filing a complaint until you hear me out if I were you."

"If you were me, you'd know you just signed your own fucking death warrant," King snaps. Several of the guys around me nod in agreement.

One of his own tries to hold him back, but Harris walks to the front of the line like he thinks his shit don't stink and flicks out some papers, handing them over to Eagle-eye. "I have an order from the governor to bring you all in for questioning and identification in relation to the murders that took place at the Red Kite service station."

"We don't know shit about that. None of us were there and you fucking know it," says Eagle-eye.

Harris shrugs. "That's for the courts and our eyewitness to determine. We'll need the rest of your little club to come in as well eventually, but this is a good start, don't you think?"

"Ask Hawthorne how smart taking us on is," King taunts, standing shoulder to shoulder with Eagle-eye. Harris's eye twitches, but his expression remains stony. "If he couldn't do it, your little army surplus parade here sure as fuck won't either."

The Hawthorne clusterfuck was before I joined the club, but everyone old enough remembers how Hawthorne was put in his place by the Screaming Eagles those years ago.

Wraith motions to me and Tank. We lean in. "Think. The only two people we know for sure were there when it happened were Gabriel and Kaylee. King visited Gabe last night, so if they really got someone I don't think it's him."

"You think they got Kaylee?"

If Wraith's jaw was any tighter his teeth would fucking crack. "It would explain why she's not answering."

"I'm not saying you're wrong, but no fucking way she's flipped so fast," Tank whispers. "I might not be a genius, but I know people and I trust her."

"Trust doesn't mean shit if they play dirty," Wraith says. "I don't want to think she'd run straight to the cops either, but we've known her what? A couple hours?"

Alpha, a big ass motherfucker who's shacked up with Eagle-eye's daughter Faith, drifts closer without taking his eyes off the cops. When he speaks, his lips hardly move. "On my signal, you and your boys charge the front and make as big a fucking distraction as you can. The rear is vulnerable. We'll blast a hole and get hell out of Dodge. Be ready to follow. Clear?"

I nod. "Crystal."

Harris gives us a dark look. "Whatever you're whispering about—"

"Is none of your fucking business. Go home, Detective Harryass," I yell, leaving my bike and walking his way. Wraith, Tank and several others do the same. "There's fuckall for you here and if you think you have the manpower to bring us in, you're a fucking idiot. South Side belongs to the Screaming Eagles."

"Not for long," he spits. "I know exactly who you are, Corporal. I believe our witness added you to the short list of people we need to have a good long talk with. Don't make us do this the hard way."

I grin, letting all my crazy show as I taunt him. "I left my rank behind long ago. Not my fault if keeping it hard is a problem for you."

He looks like he just sucked on a lemon, but his expression changes really fucking fast when my gun is right up in his face and he realizes how far away from his own men he's moved. We're so close I can see his pupils widen as he stares down my barrel.

The scene explodes around us. Half our crew charge the riot police like fucking wild barbarians, while the other half take the opportunity to blast through the back where only a half dozen cops are standing around their cars.

"Go! Go!" King orders, directing the charge towards the back.

Fuck, this is nearly as good as sex. Adrenaline courses through my veins as I bounce on my toes, keeping my gun on a furious Harris until my intuition tells me it's now or never. I swing my arm up fast and fire. Harris hits the ground in panic, scrambling like a cockroach back to safety.

The whole street is in fucking chaos. Harris might have brought a lot of men, but they are all green as hell. We're on our bikes before they can react, with the prospects just ahead of us. This is a hell of a trial by fire. There are many reasons to join the

Screaming Eagles, but living a safe, quiet life isn't one of them.

We blow past the rear police guard and Deuce weaves. I correct for it, but then his front wheel bounces like he just hit one hell of a pothole. Fuck! Is he gonna—

He manages to get his bike back under control, but not before veering in front of Shrapnel and Mad Dog, nearly sideswiping Tank. Tank dodges, but the two prospects don't have a fucking chance. They touch wheels while trying to avoid Deuce and go down, hard. Beast slams into the other two and flips over the front of his bike. He slides across the asphalt.

Everything happens in what feels like slow motion but is over in the blink of an eye. The front riders, including Eagle-eye, Alpha and King, fall back to protect the rear and buy us time. Finally getting their thumbs out of their asses, the cops are closing in fast.

Wraith and Tank lead Deuce and Reaper clear as Shrapnel and Mad Dog get back on their bikes, scraped and bloody but moving. Beast is still on the ground, clutching his shoulder.

"Prez! Go!" I yell, swinging into a stop and abandoning my bike to help Beast.

"Get the fuck on your bike!" Eagle-eye fires right back.

"Screw your hero complex, old man," Alpha snarls. "Get the fuck out of here. Let us take care of it."

The cops are on us, sirens blaring, and this time there's no cocky detective wanting to give us his fucking villain speech first. They hit the streets hot, guns out.

Fuck!

Eagle-eye and Alpha face the cops. "Go! Get that fucking witness! They don't have shit on us and they know it. King's in charge."

I fucking can't…

Fuck!

I throw myself on my bike before they can surround me too. I know it's what I was ordered to do, but I feel like a coward running while the cops round up Beast, Alpha… and fucking Eagle-eye.

8

KAYLEE

"Rise and shine!" Officer Anderson comes into my room without warning and turns on the fluorescent overhead light.

I wince and sit up, still in the sweats I was wearing when they picked me up. "I want to go home. Can I at least talk to someone? Tell them where I am?"

Has it been one day? Two? I'm pretty sure it hasn't been any longer than that, but the apartment they brought me to for 'protection' has the windows blacked out and my internal clock is totally screwed up. With no way to check, it could easily be more or less time than they tell me. The only thing they've fed me are the disgusting, unsalted scrambled eggs

Anderson keeps making. It could be breakfast, lunch or dinner for all I know.

"We told you last night, Ms. Thompson. Don't you remember? Your parents have been informed that you are in protective custody. I'm afraid anything else could jeopardize your safety and you wouldn't want that, would you?"

"You did? I... I don't remember that, and I already told you everything I know. I don't understand why I'm even here! Am I under arrest? Shouldn't I have to sign something to agree to this? I think maybe I should talk to a lawyer. That's what people always do on TV. I mean, I don't know much about police procedure, but this seems—"

"Don't be ridiculous. You can't believe everything you see on TV. It's true that normally you would have more time to prepare, but sometimes it's important for us to move quickly when it's for the public good. The Screaming Eagles are a dangerous criminal organization, and you witnessed them brutally murdering several men. It's a miracle you're still alive. If they were to find out you're working with us and get their hands on you, you'd be dead."

I'm all too aware that everything I say or do is on camera. They're mounted in all the rooms, and I feel like a bug in a jar. Watched, and in the very real danger of never seeing freedom again.

"But I didn't! I don't know..." No matter how many times I tell Harris and Anderson that I didn't see what they say I must have seen, they don't seem to believe me. It's getting hard not to second guess my own memory.

"Well I do. Mayor Hawthorne's tactics might have crossed some lines, but ever since he was arrested, those animals have been free to terrorize this city. But no longer, thanks to you, we may finally be able to start dismantling their organization."

"But, it wasn't—"

"Ms. Thompson, Kaylee, I can see you still have concerns. Are you hungry?"

I nod cautiously, already dreading more of the eggs. When I first got here, nobody remembered to feed me at all but I was too exhausted to care by the time they took off my handcuffs and showed me my bed. I drank water straight from the tap using my hands and slept. It wasn't until later that I noticed there are no doors, only curtains in the doorways, and cameras can follow what I'm doing no matter where I go.

Everywhere.

Anderson grabs my arm and practically drags me through the curtain into the open plan living area of the small apartment. Detective Harris is waiting at the table with another man I don't recognize. Harris looks up when I walk over and immediately I can tell something has changed. He's absolutely radiating fury.

Not that Anderson seems to care, he hums as he cracks eggs into a pan. At first I thought he was the nice one, but there's something really creepy about how he never acknowledges how messed up this is.

"What's going on?" I ask nervously.

"Good morning, Kaylee. I'm Lieutenant Lancer. I work with the organized crime unit." He's tall and thin, with a strange leer that gives me chills.

He flips open the binder, and inside is a whole catalog of men I'd cross the road to avoid at night. Hard, jaded eyes look out at me from the pictures. Some are mug shots, some are grainy like they were pulled from security footage, some are candid, probably taken from a long ways away. Some have names and other information jotted down underneath, but many are blank.

"You want to do the right thing, don't you, Kaylee?"

"Yeah, um, of course."

"Good, good… I want you to look through those pictures and see if any of them jog your memory."

There are hundreds of pictures in the binder, and all of them look like the kinds of guys you could totally believe would be capable violence. I keep my expression flat, not wanting to give anything away when I see first Tank, and then Nitro on another page. Wraith is in there too, along with Eagle-eye and I'm pretty sure the guy who put cherries in my soda.

"What am I looking for?" Is it stupid to feel loyalty towards a bunch of probably dangerous criminals who just happen to be incredibly hot? "None of these are the men I saw shooting people."

Harris jumps on that like a wild dog on a rotisserie chicken. "But you've seen some of them before?"

Reluctantly, I point to Wraith who I already know they have a picture of me with. "I guess him, but he was the man who saved me. He didn't shoot anyone."

I keep flipping through the binder, and a face that's burned into my brain stares back out at me. It's the scarred guy who nearly found me before Wraith and the others showed up. My hand hesitates.

"What? Who do you see?" Lieutenant Lancer asks sharply.

"Nobody. Nothing… I don't know. Everyone here is starting to look the same." Is that guy in the Screaming Eagles? If he isn't, then telling them would be good, right? But if he is, then… But he did shoot people.

I'm so bad at this.

Lancer and Harris exchange a look. Harris finally stands up and grabs the binder, he rips a half dozen pages out and puts them on the table in front of me. Eagle-eye. One I don't know. Nitro. A few more I don't know. He points to each in turn. "These are the men who did the shooting." It isn't a question.

"No! I'm sorry I can't tell you what you want, but I definitely didn't see any of them there. They aren't the shooters."

"Of course they are. You're clearly confused."

Anderson comes over with what looks like a single egg, scrambled and still a little runny. He puts it in front of me, but Harris sweeps it off the table in annoyance and the egg goes everywhere.

"Look closer!" he yells, getting right in my face. "I don't think you fucking understand the situation you're in. I could have you arrested any time I want. You were identified at the scene of a crime, fled with known criminals and attempted to lie about your whereabouts when confronted. I'm giving you the chance to do some fucking good."

"By asking me to lie?" It comes out before I can think better of it.

My head snaps sideways and the sting of his slap is already spreading across my face before I understand what's happened. The only thing that keeps me from falling off the chair is Anderson putting a hand on my shoulder.

Harris looms over me as he rages. "Those are the men responsible for the shooting. No one else, and you are going to fucking sit here and look at them until I ask you again and your only god damn answer is 'Yes, Sir'. They are criminals and a blight on this whole fucking city. Do you understand me?"

I clutch my cheek and feel the wetness of tears running over my fingers. "You can't keep me here! You can't make me lie!"

Harris reaches into his suit and pulls out a pair of handcuffs. Yanking my arms down, he fastens them around my wrist with the table leg between. "Watch me."

Are the others really going to let him do this? I look to Lancer, who is checking his phone, and then to Anderson who looks more annoyed about the egg on the floor than Harris slapping me. I mean, he's probably not wrong about the Screaming Eagles being criminals. They are definitely not boy scouts, but this is wrong.

Anderson sighs. "Should I make more eggs?"

9

WRAITH

King stands at the front of the common room, in Eagle-eye's spot. "Sit your asses down and listen up!"

"I can't fucking believe this. How did you let this happen?" Blade, who usually keeps his cool, at least until he stabs you, is pacing back and forth like a caged panther. He flips a small knife back and forth between his fingers like a fucking fidget toy, and everyone's giving him space just in case he decides to ventilate someone.

I don't blame him. We're all still reeling from what happened during yesterday's run, but for him it's even more personal. Eagle-eye might as well be his father-in-law, and Alpha's part of his family with Faith, their old lady.

"Trust me," growls Tank. "If there was a way to go back and do this without getting us all fucking killed, we would. They put their own fucking skin on the line to get the rest of us out of there."

"Fucking prospects," Blade growls.

"As any of us would," King interrupts loudly, cutting through. "Eagle-eye is the Screaming Eagles. He's loyal to the fucking bone, and when lives are on the line he's not going to leave anyone behind. So stop all this fucking bickering. The old man made his choice and now it's up to us to get them back and not act like a bunch of goddamn idiots."

The door bursts open and Faith, Eagle-eye's daughter and Alpha's old lady stalks into the room like a fucking Valkyrie on the rampage.

"No cunts in Church," yells Snake, an old-timer who moved back into the clubhouse recently after his own old lady kicked his ass to the curb.

Before anyone has the chance to agree or disagree, Snake is on the fucking floor with Blade's knife sticking out of his bicep. It's not deep, but enough to hurt like hell. "What the fuck, man?"

Ripper, Faith's third old man, stalks over and puts his boot on Snake's shoulder before pulling the knife free and wiping it off on Snake's shirt. "Talk to her like that again. I fucking dare you."

Faith's eyes are wide, but she recovers fast. "Anyone else think I don't have a right to be here? My father is in jail, and last night I had to comfort a baby girl who doesn't understand why one of her daddies is missing. So tell me again that I shouldn't be here." She looks around the room, with eyes the same steel gray as Eagle-eye.

Everyone keeps their fucking mouths shut, including Snake who gets back into his chair and tips his head in acknowledgement while clutching his arm.

"That's what I thought." She shifts her glare to King, who takes it without flinching. "So what are we going to do?"

Razor, an old fucker who's known Eagle-eye since his days before the Screaming Eagles, speaks. "We're wasting time if we sit around bitching about who should've done what. That fucker's always going to do what needs doing even he's the one that pays for it. If he was the kind of man that would leave a brother behind to save his own ass, we wouldn't follow him."

"What are they claiming he did?" Faith asks. "He didn't murder anyone." Razor snorts. "Fine. He hasn't murdered anyone recently."

I'd be more shocked at how easily Faith accepts her father's past, but like me, she grew up with this shit. Biker family recognizes biker family. She broke away for a while, but it's in her blood. She might be a sweet little bookshop owner on the surface, but underneath she's tough as fucking nails. I've never given much thought to what I'd look for in an old lady, but they're going to need some steel in their spine to live this life.

King nods. "Something's going on. There's too much fucked up shit happening at once to be a coincidence. The cops are using the shooting to point fingers at us, but they know better than to come after us on our own turf, and if they need another lesson, I'm more than happy to remind them what happened to Hawthorne."

He'd know, since he was at the center of that whole mess when he, Wild Child and Hero kidnapped

Hawthorne's daughter Emily, only to end up shacking up with her before the dust settled. It feels like a whole lot of pasts are coming back to bite us in the ass these days.

"This would be a fuckton easier if we just knew who to shoot," Tank growls.

The room is tense, but everyone nods. There isn't a single person here, even the assholes, that wouldn't put their own skin on the line to protect what's ours.

King laughs. "I know you fuckers want to go in guns blazing, but we've gotta play it cool for the moment. We're calling in some favors to see if any of our connections have info, and our lawyer is working his ass off to get our boys out. In the meantime, we need to keep our eyes and ears open." He points our way. "Wraith, Tank and Nitro. This is your chance to show the club what you've got."

"Anything you need, King," I say with a nod.

"That girl you picked up? I think we got her."

"What? Where?" All three of us snap to attention.

King waves to Snark, smartass and resident tech genius. "Tell them what you found."

Snark moves to the front and starts rattling off some shit about bouncing off servers and idiots who don't know how to change passwords. I don't follow any of the shit he's saying, but I trust that just like I know my art, he knows his.

"And anyway, I was starting to think they were just bullshitting about having someone, but then I picked up an update when they pulled in a new guy and the contact address they put for him pinged as one of the apartments they use for witness protection. I looked a little deeper, and that dipshit Harris is the one who registered him in the system." Snark folds his hands in front of his chest and grins. "You're welcome."

King scowls as he warns us, "It might not be her, and if it is, you all understand that she might be there because she decided to work with the cops."

The guys and I look at each other. None of us are ready to believe that, but he's right. We nod.

"Good, then bring her in, because I think it's time to have another chat. Make it fucking happen."

10

KAYLEE

Anderson slaps the handcuffs back on my bruised wrists as soon as I'm done using the bathroom. They haven't let me sleep since... I don't know when. I think they're doing it to confuse me, to make me so disoriented that I can't make good decisions. To make me doubt myself.

At least Harris left. Anderson is bad enough, always acting like everything is hunky-dory no matter what they're doing. And Lancer is scary, but he doesn't yell and scream at me like Harris. Or beat me when he gets angry.

I don't know how much more of this I can take.

They only give me enough of those disgusting eggs to keep me going, but my stomach's constantly rumbling and I haven't had a real night's sleep in days… I think? I still have no idea how long I've been here, whether it's day or night, anything. My arms are covered in bruises and scrapes, both from wearing handcuffs nearly all the time now, and from Harris's violent outbursts.

Anderson leads me back to the table, where the same pictures are staring right back up at me. I almost feel like I'm bonding a little with Nitro and the other guys, even Eagle-eye. None of us did anything to land ourselves in this situation, but here we are together all the same.

Lancer sits across from me, sipping a coffee as he reads something on a tablet. He glances up as I run a finger over the edge of Nitro's picture. "Are you remembering something?"

"N—no," I whisper, wondering how long it will take before I eventually give in and tell him what he wants to hear.

"But you saw the shooting? You must have if you are so sure that these aren't the right men." He leans his phone up against his mug with the camera facing me.

"I didn't… no? I mean, I saw the men who did the shooting, but I was inside when it happened." Did I really see anything? Nothing makes sense in my head anymore.

"So you saw what? Five men in motorcycle clothes resembling the Screaming Eagles at the site of the murder of three men, but did you actually see anyone shoot? Is it possible that the men you saw actually came after the actual shooters? I'm afraid I can't show you the security footage, but I find it very suspicious that you are resisting the word of three police officers. Harris wants to throw you in jail, did you know that? I'm trying to convince him that you just need more time, but that will only work for so long."

"I don't want to go to jail." My voice comes out weak and a little wobbly.

"Of course you don't, Ms. Thompson."

My stomach growls. I'm starving and I feel like a slime creature, still wearing the same set of grubby sweats I had when they picked me up from my house. I haven't done anything more than spot clean a little in the sink because the idea of stripping in front of their cameras makes me sick. Eventually,

I'm going to do whatever they say for clean underwear.

But I'm not quite there yet.

Lancer lets out a sigh so deep it almost makes me want to do what he says because I'm obviously a huge disappointment. "Go lay down. You're useless like this. We'll start again in an hour."

I could almost cry in relief. When I'm sleeping or napping is the only time I get to feel a little by myself, even if I know it's an illusion. I drop onto my bed and lie back, trying to pretend I'm not trapped. Trying not to think about how worried my parents must be even if the cops did contact them. I didn't doubt them when they told me at first, but after all this, I don't know what to think.

And I keep thinking about Tank, Wraith and Nitro. Do they wonder what happened to me? Or have they even given me a second thought since the day that changed my entire life? Our lives have become intertwined, and they might not even know it.

With the blackened windows, I can't tell if it's noon or midnight, but I can hear the wind blowing, and the distant rumble of thunder. Occasionally it sounds like a branch scrapes against the glass.

I wait to hear rain, or the crack of lightning, but instead the rumble grows louder. Heart racing, I jump out of bed and put my ear against the window. It's not thunder.

It sounds like motorcycles, and they're coming this way.

"It's not them. It's not them," I chant, afraid to let myself even think it for a second.

The Screaming Eagles aren't the only people who ride motorcycles. I know that. We might not even be anywhere near their part of town. In spite of myself, a stupid, irrational hope is building inside.

The roar of engines only gets louder, until I can make out that there are several bikes. And when the sound cuts off, I rush into the living room to see if the cops are reacting. I want to be ready. For what I'm not sure, but something's going to happen. I can feel it.

"Get back in your room," Lancer snaps.

"I'm thirsty."

Heavy footsteps thud outside the apartment door, carrying even through the thick metal. Is that the sound of motorcycle boots? Or am I just so far gone I'm imagining things?

"Back in bed!" Lancer orders again, pointing to the bedroom. "Whatever you think is about to happen, isn't. *We* are your only way out of here." He knocks on the door for emphasis.

There's an answering knock in the same pattern, only louder. I know Harris's knock, and that's definitely not it.

"Shit," Lancer growls.

Immediately, both Lancer and Anderson have their guns drawn. I run, stopping just inside the doorway to the bedroom and crouching down to see what happens.

"Wrong apartment, buddy," Lancer yells through the door.

"Open the fuck up before we tear the whole damn building down!" There's no mistaking Tank's roar, and my heart soars.

"Good luck kicking in reinforced titanium. Our backup will be here long before you wear yourselves out trying to get in."

"One warning, buddy." It's Nitro this time, his voice dripping with disdain. "Kaylee, if you're in there, stay the fuck back!"

What is he—

And then the whole apartment wall explodes inward in a gray-black cloud of dust.

Someone screams. It might be me. I think I hear Anderson swear, but my eyes are full of grit and my ears are ringing. The debris cloud billows towards me, filling the whole room in a microsecond and I literally can't see my hands in front of my face. Even still, I stumble forwards, towards where the explosion came from. If they got in, that's my way out.

A massive shadow emerges from the cloud, hard to make out through my watery eyes. All I know is that it's far too big to be Lancer or Anderson. Massive arms sweep me up, and the person cradles me close to their chest, a hand cupped protectively behind my head.

"Got her!" he shouts.

"Big fucking deal your fancy ass titanium door makes when the wall is fucking drywall, asswipe," Nitro says with a harsh laugh.

A gun goes off, the muzzle flashing from the kitchen.

"Motherfuckers! Move!" Wraith orders, but I can't tell if anyone was hit or not.

All I know is that two guns go off almost simultaneously right next to me and then Anderson screams. I don't know if he's dead or not, but if he never makes another egg, I won't spill any tears over it.

"I can walk," I start to say before coughing up what feels like gravel from my lungs.

"Shut up and don't move," Tank rumbles as they charge out of what used to be a wall and is now a gaping hole. "We need to have some serious fucking words, but not until we're outta here. Until then, keep your head down and let us do the work."

Ooookay. That's not super friendly, but right now I'll take sexy, angry bikers over sadistic, corrupt cops any day of the week.

Lancer stumbles into view. The explosion must have really thrown him around, because there's blood gushing down his front, and I'm not sure his glassy eyes are seeing us. He gurgles and collapses on the floor. I whimper and press my face against Tank's chest. If I had anything to throw up, I probably would.

A fire alarm goes off in the apartment, and then all the connected alarms in the hallway start to wail. I can hear doors opening and people yelling as they carry me out. Tank throws me on his bike just like Wraith did the first night and wraps a strong arm around me, firm as a steel bar. The bike fires to life beneath us and lurches forwards as he turns the throttle, pressing me even closer to his broad chest.

Wraith and Nitro fall in on either side of us, racing off into the darkness. By the time reinforcements have any chance of showing up, we'll be long gone. But I can't help thinking about Tank saying we'll need to have words.

Was I just rescued? Or kidnapped?

11

KAYLEE

Tank's big body is behind me, holding me close, but the chilly winter air still cuts right through my sweats, and there's nothing but thin cotton socks protecting my feet. We race through the city like the Devil himself is on our heels, and the sound of sirens fades away. Wherever we're going, we're in a big hurry, and as far as I'm concerned, the farther away from that hellhole we can get, the better.

I shiver, and his arm tightens, pulling me even closer, so I burrow into his jacket and enjoy the feel of being held and safe. A few tears of relief slip out, quickly dried by the wind.

Are the three of them dangerous criminals? Maybe. Do they have their own reasons for breaking me out? They must, but whatever it is, I can't imagine it being worse than what Harris and the other cops did. I'm nothing special, so I really doubt they all just fell instantly in love with some random girl who showed up at the tattoo parlor one day.

Unless…

God. I bet they think I already sold them out. They told me not to say anything, and then they must have heard I was working with the cops. I'd be an idiot to believe that they would choose me over the club and their friends.

As soon as we cross into South Side, I know exactly where we're heading. It's not really a surprise. Where else would we go? Were they going to take me home and tuck me into bed? Seeing the giant walled-in complex of the Screaming Eagles compound gives me an odd feeling of both safety and fear. If there's anywhere in the city that Harris can't reach, it's here, but also, once I'm inside, I'm completely at their mercy.

It's the middle of the night, but flood lights illuminate the walls and keep the club logo visible, along with a massive metal gate that rolls back slowly to let us in, then shutting firmly behind with a loud clank as it locks in place.

Growing up in the city, I heard rumors about girls going to parties here, but my friends and I were never brave enough. I've never seen the inside, I doubt most people have. The most I've seen is the wall that goes around the whole block, protecting them from the city. Or maybe the city from them? I've seen maps on my GPS and I know they own the whole block, but it's not until I'm inside that it's really obvious how huge the place really is.

Right inside the gate is a central courtyard. A multiple story warehouse takes up most of the space behind it, and it's on that wall the lit up logo is. A huge garage is off to the side, open and lit up with burly guys working on their motorcycles. Down the other way are small but perfectly normal houses, complete with little lawns and even some playground equipment. It looks cozier than I expected. Not a word I ever expected to associate with the Screaming Eagles.

They stop their bikes right at the bottom of the wide stairs leading to the front doors of the warehouse. This time it's Wraith who comes over to help me off Tank's bike instead of the other way around. When he takes hold of my arm, it hits a bruise and I shrink back.

His eyes narrow and his mouth flattens into a grim line. He shifts his grip, putting his hands under my arms and quickly lifting me off and to the ground. "I'm not going to fucking hurt you."

"Sorry," I whisper.

"Come on, cookie. Let's get you inside," Tank says, swatting my butt to get me moving.

I flinch again, and red hot fury spikes through me at the thought that just a few days with Harris and the others has turned me into someone I don't even recognize. Not just because I feel crusty and disgusting from not having showered or changed, but because it broke some subconscious level of trust in other human beings that I didn't even know I had.

Nitro is the one who seems to understand immediately. "Give her a little space."

One tired step after the other, I walk between them up to the warehouse. The ground is freezing and a little damp beneath my feet. I welcome the discomfort because it means I'm not in that apartment anymore, but getting inside sounds good too.

At the top, Wraith holds the door open. "Welcome to the clubhouse, sweetheart."

They lead me into a big common room with ceilings so high they go up into the second floor. It looks a little like how I'd imagine a frat house would be, with pool tables, a long bar and in the back, beat up couches surrounding a flat screen TV that's playing a football game on mute. On the far wall, there's a large golden Screaming Eagles logo flanked by a pair of American Flags. A fair number of members are sitting around, and the mood is subdued, but attention locks on us as soon as we walk in, and they do not look happy.

"This the bitch that talked to the cops?" growls one of them, a tall brute of a man with long hair and a thick beard. He looks and sounds like his day job should be the lead singer of a heavy metal band.

"We don't fucking know that yet. Don't throw shit around before she even gets a fucking chance," Tank snarls.

One of the others snorts. "We're just calling it like we fucking see it. She's got no loyalty to us. I don't owe her a fucking thing."

"Jesus, relax, Sledge." Wraith holds up his hands. "We're taking her to King now. He'll decide what to do."

"Nobody's going to relax while Eagle-eye rots in a fucking cell," the metal guy spits out.

"Eagle-eye's been arrested?" I blurt out. Then why were they trying so hard to get me to point him out?

Sledge crosses the room, his hands balled into fists at his sides. "Like you didn't fucking know that, bitch."

Wraith moves in front of me, and Tank and Nitro shift to slightly behind on either side, walling me in with their tough, muscular bodies. "Sit your ass down. You want me to tell King you don't trust his judgment? Nobody's touching a hair on her goddamned head, got it?"

A big guy with a thick brown beard and a build that rivals Tank's puts a hand on Sledge's shoulder. "Come on, let's get you a beer and rack up another round. Those boys did their job and now it's time to let King do his, you got it? Trust me. I want some fucking answers too, but look at her. Does she fucking look like she's been eating bonbons in a spa for the past couple days?"

I don't know what's worse, their anger, or the slightly pitying looks in the eyes of these angry, badass men who hated me on sight. I tug my sleeves down over my hands, making sure the marks are hidden, and then shift one foot on top of the other to warm up my toes a little. There's nothing I can do about the dark circles I know are under my eyes, or the rat's nest full of drywall dust my hair is right now.

Sledge shakes the guy's hand off his shoulder. "I still don't fucking like this, Bear."

"None of us do," Bear says. His expression is hard to read. He looks like the kind of man who would give great hugs, but also rip someone's head off if they threatened anyone he loved. Honestly, a lot of these guys give off that vibe.

"C'mon, let's get you out of here," Nitro says softly.

I feel like a prisoner as they lead me past the crowd of unfriendly faces and out of the lounge room. We walk down a corridor with doors on both sides like a hotel, but instead of room numbers, there are name plates. Not a single one even resembles a normal name, it's all biker stuff like Thunder and Lightning. From what I can see when we pass a stairwell, there are even more rooms upstairs. How many people live here? It looks like a lot.

"Eagle-eye is your club president, the guy I met at the bar, right?" My voice sounds tinny and unsure.

Tank grunts. "Yeah."

"If that King person decides I got him arrested, what's going to happen to me?"

"Did you?" Wraith asks softly.

"I… I don't think so."

"Look, there's a lot of shit going down right now and your pretty little ass landed right in the middle of it, Kaylee," Nitro says. "Nobody here knows what's going to happen to anyone."

We stop in front of a room labeled Cannon. Tank opens the door and gestures for me to enter. "Come on. There's some people you're going to need to talk to soon, but you can get cleaned up and rest here until we get called in."

"Who's Cannon? Won't he mind?"

Nitro shakes his head. "Nah, he moved in with his old lady and nobody's claimed his spot yet."

The room is small and fairly basic. There's room for a bed, a dresser, and a card table with a couple chairs. There are still small piles of things lying around, like socks in the corner and beer cans on the table. But there's no blinking camera eye on the ceiling, and something inside me relaxes just a little in spite of all the evidence that I'm very much still in danger.

I sit down on the edge of the bed that has no sheets or blankets and draw a shuddering breath. There's blood on my hand and I don't even know where it's from or whose it is.

Wraith crouches down, balancing on his toes and puts his hands on my knees. "You okay?"

"No. If okay was a place, I'd be aaaaaall the way on the other side of the country. I'm just a girl. I'm not cut out for any of this," I answer honestly.

"Listen to me. I'm going to make you a promise. If you trust nothing else, trust the three of us, alright? I can't tell you what the fuck'll happen, but we'll do our fucking best to make sure you see the other side of it. You got that?"

I look between the three of them, from Wraith's dark brown eyes, to Nitro's green, and finally to Tank's clear blue gaze. The only thing I can do is trust my instincts, and right now, they are telling me that these men might be violent and dangerous, but in a world like this one, that's what I'm going to need to keep me safe.

I nod. "Got it."

12

WRAITH

"I'd say it was a pleasure to see you again so soon, but it wouldn't be entirely honest." King sits across the table from Arturo. "I wouldn't have minded doing this in the morning instead of shit o'clock in the middle of the fucking night. Your trust is overwhelming."

It's three AM, but as the club promised, as soon as we had Kaylee, a call was made and the Giordanos demanded a meeting immediately. Everyone is bone fucking tired, but we've dragged our asses back to the Roost to get this over with.

"And give you all night to coach her on exactly what to say? You'd do the exact same," Arturo responds dryly. "Let's get this moving. Where's the girl?"

King nods to Tank, who leaves the room for a moment and brings in an exhausted looking Kaylee alongside Nitro. She sits next to me, with Nitro on the other side, and Tank stands behind us.

She didn't have time to clean up much aside from washing off the worst of the dust, and we managed to find a pair of sneakers that almost fit, but she looks so damn young. When she walked into Haunted Ink, she had a fresh innocence about her that isn't completely gone, but it's a dim fucking shadow of what it used to be. Knowing I'm indirectly to blame for killing that spark kills me.

Bear and Viking sit on either side of King, and next to Bear is Alessa. It's fucking strange to have so many women in a meeting like this, but as a Giordano, Alessa could be the key to keeping this from turning into a bloodbath, and Kaylee's at the center of everything. Luca, Alessa's father, is with Arturo, along with a younger member of the Family I haven't met before, Nicholas.

Three bodyguards stand behind the Giordano side, mirrored by Quickshot, Animal and Badass. Me, Nitro and Tank have been members for a while now, but this is the first major move that we've been in the inner circle for. I've kept my head down and done my job, but I don't think Kaylee's life was the only one that changed when she met us.

"This? This is who's supposed to have a clue about what happened?" Arturo says, disdain dripping from his every word. "She looks like a street rat you found sleeping at the bus station."

Tank actually fucking growls. "If you don't trust us, what the fuck are you doing here?" He gestures to the three of us. "We can vouch for her. She saw what fucking happened. Why do you think the cops had her?"

"Let her talk before you jump to conclusions," Alessa says, leaning in. "We're all tired and we wouldn't be here if we didn't want answers."

"Fine." Arturo crosses his arms on the table and leans forward. "Who are you and what do you know?"

Under the table, I reach out and wrap her small, cold fingers in mine. She takes a deep breath and nods. "My name is Kaylee Thompson. A few days ago I…"

Kaylee surprises me with how steady her voice is as she talks about what happened the day of the shooting. The interview that brought her to the area, her stop at the gas station and then the horror of being caught up in what sounds like a fucking execution.

"Why were your men there?" King cuts in, looking at Arturo.

"We were looking into some rumors. I personally contacted your president to let him know in case there were questions about why we were in your territory and they had every right to—"

"What sort of rumors?"

Arturo's face shuts down and he snaps into perfect, pole up his ass posture. "That is Family business. It's unrelated, I assure you."

"Yeah, because we're all so fucking trusting in this room," Viking mutters.

Luca sighs and leans in. "I give you my word that to the best of my knowledge, their visit had nothing to do with this. It was an internal matter."

"Okay, so say we believe that. You were driving through town and just happened to be stopped at the gas station where a bunch of unknown bikers just happened to be waiting to fucking blow them away. Kaylee, you said you pulled in, filled gas and went into the station. That took what? A few minutes? Max?" King asks.

She nods.

"And then you heard shots and the first explosion and had to go out the front."

"What's your point?" Arturo asks, brows furrowed.

"Your car was at the pumps. The bikes were scattered near the pumps and the SUV was off to the side."

Kaylee frowns and chews on her lower lips as she thinks. "Yeah, that sounds right."

"So if she was the only one there to actually fucking fill her tank, what the hell was everyone else doing there?"

The door to the meeting room slams open and Deuce stands there with his arm over a girl looking confused. Deuce blinks, obviously drunk. "Oh, shit. Wrong room."

"Get the fuck out of here." Badass, closest to the door, shoves him back, hard and slams the door in his face. "Fucking prospects."

Arturo ignores the interruption, his focus completely on King's line of questioning. "Think hard. Did you see or hear anything that made you think they were talking? Was there yelling before the shooting started?"

"I... I don't think so. I don't know. It really did happen fast. They definitely weren't talking when I went outside. One of your friends was already d—dead," her voice hitches for the first time and her fingers spasm in mine. I hold them even tighter.

"Sure as fuck sounds to me like they went there for a reason, and if that wasn't part of why they were supposed to be there, then what the fuck were they doing?"

Arturo scowls. "I don't know, but I promise you we'll find out." He looks really fucking pissed that things are getting turned around on them.

Kaylee continues her description, and when it gets to the part where we show up, King and Arturo ask us some questions about what we saw. Which is unfortunately not much. Then we explain how, not knowing that the Eagles were about to get pulled into the mess, we sent Kaylee home with a warning to not get anyone else involved.

"And yet, she ended up quite cozy with the city's finest," Arturo says sarcastically.

She shrinks back as everyone's eyes are on her. "I didn't have a choice." That doesn't do much to assure anyone. "It's true! They came to my house, handcuffed me and dragged me to the station! I haven't been home or even been allowed to talk to anyone since then. You think I was working with them?"

Tears rolling down her cheeks, she jerks her hand out of mine and stands. With angry, jerky motions, she pulls up her sleeves, revealing red welts around her wrists and deep purple marks about the size of fingers on her arms. "This is what I got for NOT doing what they wanted!"

"What the fuck? Who did that to you?" I'm on my feet, examining her bruises. Someone's going to fucking die, and before it happens, they are going to experience exactly the kind of pain and fear Kaylee has gone through. Looking at Tank and Nitro, it's clear we're all on the same fucking page.

"Sit your asses down," King snaps. "Kaylee, we're going to need you to tell us everything about what happened while you were in their custody."

Tank holds her face in his hands and brushes her tears away. "You've got this."

She nods. "They have the security footage from the gas station and I'm on it. I had to…" She looks at me. "They wouldn't show me the video but they had pictures. You're there too, with me, but I swear I told them you weren't involved. I told them you guys were just driving past when you saw me and came to help. I told them you didn't have anything to do with it."

"Were they asking you to identify Wraith, Tank and Nitro as the shooters?" Viking asks.

"No, not exactly. They just kept telling me that the Screaming Eagles were responsible and they had this binder full of pictures. I don't know if it was all your members, but some of you were definitely there. And your president, too. Eagle-eye. At first they didn't seem to care who I picked so long as it was someone in the binder, but on the second day, the detective pulled out six pictures and told me it was them. He—he locked me to the table and made me just stare and stare at them. I told them they weren't the right men. I told them."

Someone's going to die, and it's not going to be fast.

Arturo, frowning, raises a finger to get her attention. "Miss Thompson, I need you to answer me honestly, and I swear that my people will make sure you're safe even if it angers these men. Did you see any of the men involved in the shooting in those pictures?"

Kaylee looks at me, and I don't like the look on her face. I have a split second to make the decision, because I'm fairly fucking sure that if I tell her not to, she'll keep her mouth shut for us.

"Answer him," King snaps. "If we have people going rogue I need to know about it."

"Um, not the ones he wanted me to identify, but… I think so."

"You think so?" Arturo asks.

Closing her eyes for a second, Kaylee nods. "I saw one that I know was there, and a couple others I wasn't sure about. It isn't anyone I've seen here, I swear."

"Could you describe them?" I ask. "Get me some shit to draw with."

Doing her best, Kaylee describes what she remembers, and in the end, we have six sketches with greater or lesser detail. Four of them are shit. They could be just about anyone, but the others are pretty clear. Especially the guy who almost found her. She gave me a real good description of the scars crisscrossing his face and crawling down his neck. I spread the sketches on the table and all the Screaming Eagles members gather around to examine them.

"Pretty sure I'd remember that guy," Nitro says, pointing to scarface.

King nods. "I don't recognize any of these men. Did you point any of them out to the cops?"

"No, but…"

"But what?"

"But I think Detective Harris noticed when I saw the guy with the scars. That's when he took the book away and just gave me the six photos." Kaylee looks like she's about ready to collapse. She's leaning against Nitro, and Tank has his hands on her shoulders.

"Maybe we should see if anyone recognizes these pictures?" I suggest.

King nods. "Unless you've got more questions. Let's call it for the night."

Arturo leans back in his chair. "This isn't much to bring back to the Family. *Cazzo*. Those who already support our cooperation will continue to do so, those that do not won't find this new information particularly compelling."

"That's nothing new. The same people who called me a biker whore when I met my men and had Izzy will never be happy, but their prejudices don't get to force us into a new war," Alessa says.

Viking growls. "But if they want one, show them my way. We'll put them so deep in the fucking ground that when the archeologists dig them up they'll think they found the fucking missing link."

Luca nods in agreement. Good to see there's at least some cooperation left.

King stands and hands the sketches to Quickshot. "Make a few copies so they have something to take with them." He nods to Arturo. "We'll do our fucking part to keep trying to figure out what happened, you do the same, because if we find out your men weren't just there by random chance, we're going to have some hard fucking questions of our own."

13

KAYLEE

I wake up tangled in blankets and not knowing where I am. Pure panic shoots through me before my brain kicks in enough to understand that I'm not in police custody anymore. I'm in the Screaming Eagles compound and they must have brought me back to that empty room after the meeting.

Yesterday feels like a dream. I feel like I've been asleep for years, but still not quite long enough. Sunlight comes through a high, narrow window on one wall, illuminating what looks like a bullet hole in the ceiling above me. Right, bikers. I'm going to pretend it was from a hook for a hanging plant, but either way it's still a thousand times less scary than a camera staring down at my every move.

Alone for the first time in days, I throw the blankets off and slide out of bed. I haven't eaten in so long I'm not even really hungry anymore, which can't be a good thing. But even worse than that is how insanely grubby I feel.

The room is as bare as I remember it, but on the table, someone left a towel with the logo of a popular hotel chain on it, an extra large t-shirt advertising a motorcycle company, and one of those five in one bottles of shower wash that claim to be good for absolutely everything and smell like mountain fresh carbon power.

The stylist in me cringes, but the girl who hasn't been clean in days wants to marry whoever was thoughtful enough to leave it for me. I head straight for the little box of a bathroom which is about as barebones as it gets. There's a toilet, a sink with a cracked mirror and a showerhead on the wall with a drain in the floor and a track on the ceiling to pull the curtain closed.

Looking at myself in the mirror isn't easy. There are bruises up and down my arms and over my shoulders and collarbone. Harris was good at keeping his abuse out of sight after that first slap, but his anger left its mark. Ugh. I turn away from the ugliness of it all and get into the shower.

The first spray of hot water over my face makes me want to cry in joy. I scrub myself from head to toe twice, not caring that I smell like a male body spray commercial and that my hair is going to be a crunchy, frizzy disaster. I'm going to be clean.

I come out a half an hour later in a shirt that could be a dress, looking like a prune, but feeling like a whole new person. I crawl back under the blanket to keep my bare legs warm and start finger-combing my curls. What's the chance that that Cannon guy left a decent comb or brush lying around?

Expecting to get grossed out but willing to take the chance, I open the dented metal filing cabinet he set up as a bedside table. Tissues and a bottle of something that I poke out of the way with one finger. Ew. But under a fishing magazine, there's what looks like it could be the handle of a brush. Excited, I grab for it, shrieking and nearly dropping it in shock when I realize what I found.

Apparently Cannon forgot to pack his gun.

The door flies open, and Tank is there. Surprised and not thinking about how it looks, I jump out of bed and hold the gun straight out at him like a cat showing their owner something cool they just caught.

"Easy, Kaylee. Let's not do anything crazy," he says in a low, calm voice, holding his hands out so I can see them.

"I'm not—I mean, I know what this looks like but I—"

"What's your plan, baby? You can't shoot your way out of here. There's a lot of people and a lot more guns between you and the gate. I don't know where you got that, but how about you put it down and we talk?" He moves very slowly my way.

Does he really think I'm going to shoot him? "No, I—"

He's on me before I can explain myself, his hands wrapped firmly but gently around my wrists. He spins me so my back is to his chest, and he twists the gun out of my fingers and tosses it on the bed. With the gun out of the way, he loosens his grip and his fingers trace the welts left by the handcuffs.

"I know you've been through some shit, baby, but we're not going to hurt you." Tank's deep voice rumbles against my back. He starts to let me go.

"Wait. Can you just hold me for a little longer?" I whisper. Out of the three of them, Tank feels the biggest and safest, and right now that feels pretty freaking amazing.

After a moment's pause, like he didn't expect that, he moves us to the bed and settles, his arms still tight around me. It takes me a minute to realize that I can feel the steady beating of his heart and another minute to notice that his face is pressed to the back of my head and he's breathing me in. The gentleness is almost too much to take. My throat burns.

Tank shifts me to face him, but doesn't let go. "Where'd you find the gun, baby?"

"It was in the drawer. I wasn't snooping, I swear. I was just looking for a brush. That's the first time in my life I've ever even held a gun."

His sudden laugh bounces me on his broad chest. "He's called Cannon because he's bald as a fucking cannon ball. And I could tell you're not a gun nut, because that's a lighter."

"What?"

Tank reaches over and grabs what still looks like a handgun to me. He pulls the trigger, and instead of a bullet or a clicking sound, an intense red flame shoots out the end. "Yeah, his old lady gave it to him for his birthday a couple years ago. He thinks it's hilarious."

I fall back onto his chest with a groan. "Why did you let me think I was actually holding a gun?"

"Baby, if someone points something at you that looks like a fucking gun, you treat it like one," he answers without even a hint of humor. Tank strokes a comforting hand up and down my side.

I don't notice at first, but each stroke pulls the t-shirt up just a tiny bit, until a big, warm hand rests on my bare thigh. We both freeze.

"Kaylee," he says my name like it's a warning. "We should really get you more fucking clothes."

"That would, um, make sense," I answer, but I don't pull away. It feels too good to be with him like this and every cell of my body is craving affection after being scared for so long.

His hand slides further under the hem of the t-shirt, coming dangerously close to my hip. The way he looks at me, it's almost like the hand's doing it on its own. "This isn't a good idea."

I should pull away. I don't. "I know."

Tank slides his hand right up to my ass and cups it, lifting me higher on his chest. "Fuck, you could get me in so much trouble, little girl."

Thick, strong fingers tease the apex of my bare thighs. He looks at me, his clear blue eyes burning. His touch is so light and teasing, and somehow I get it in my head that it can erase all the things that Harris did. And as soon as I decide that I find I'm desperate for more. I open my legs just a little, willing him to do something.

"Are you doing this because you think it will make us protect you?" he asks, suddenly.

The question is like a bucket of cold water. I pull back and tug the shirt back into place. "I wasn't thinking anything! It was just nice, okay?"

"Easy, I get it. We all get it, trust me. You've been through some shit. I wouldn't fucking judge you if you said yes. People do what they have to to survive. I know I'm not as fucking pretty as Wraith."

"Oh my God! That's not it. I'm not using sex to make you help me. I just…" I can feel a hot blush crawling up my cheeks. "It was nothing. Let's forget it happened."

"You can if you want, but I fucking won't." Tank sits up and gives me a lopsided grin that makes me want to melt into a puddle. "Come on, Trigger. I don't know about you but I'm fucking starving."

My stomach roars at the mention of food. "Trigger? I don't know if I like that nickname."

"Too fucking bad. The best ones are earned, and you should've thought of that before you pointed a lighter at me." He reaches into his pocket and pulls out a granola bar. "Here. I don't share with just anyone, so if you don't want it, just—"

The wrapper is off and the peanut butter and chocolate flavored snack is already half gone before he starts laughing again. "What?" I ask, mouth full.

"Nothing, Trigger. Nothing. Nitro is out with the prospects, so lemme call Wraith and have him pick up lunch. You care what he orders?"

"No eggs. Anything but eggs."

14

TANK

"Yo! Give me a hand with all this shit," Wraith shouts from the other side of the door, giving it a solid kick for good measure.

"Calm your tits, man. I'm coming." I open up and he pushes his way in, white plastic bags full of food hanging from his arms, and his hands full of girl clothes and shit. "What the fuck? You go shopping?"

"Nah. Alessa thought Kaylee could probably use some supplies. She said to let her know if she needs anything else."

Kaylee's face lights up and she jumps out from underneath the blankets, baring her sexy fucking legs as she hurries over to see what Wraith has.

"Clothes!" She grabs it all from Wraith and races off to the bathroom, flashing a good amount of skin as she goes.

"Nice ass," he says under his breath with a low whistle.

"Fuck yeah, it is. And it feels just as good." I meant what I told Kaylee earlier. She might want to forget about how she was fucking rubbing herself all over me, but I won't. In fact, I have every intention of thinking a lot about it later.

"You fuck around with her? That was fast," Wraith asks, sounding surprised.

"Nah, nothing serious. Why? You staking a claim?"

He did make a move first by kissing her the night we took her home, but in my head she feels like ours, not his. The idea of stepping back doesn't feel good to me.

Wrath looks a little thoughtful before shaking his head. "She's a hot little piece. I won't fucking lie, but she's gone through a lot of shit. If she's up for playing, I'm more than happy to be a distraction, but that's her choice."

"And if she wants me to be the distraction?" I ask with a grin.

He growls a little. "Fine."

"What if she doesn't want to choose?"

"I like that better."

Kaylee comes out of the bathroom still wearing the oversized t-shirt with her gorgeous fucking breasts swinging free, but now she has black leggings underneath and her brown hair tamed and up in a ponytail. A bright smile lights up her whole fucking face. "I almost feel human again. What's for lunch? Wait, do I smell fries?"

Wraith brings the bags over to Cannon's table and starts pulling out the food. He bought a fuck ton of it. "I didn't know what you like, but everyone eats burgers, right?" He pauses. "You aren't vegan or keto or any of that shit, are you?"

She shakes her head. "All I am is starving."

"Thank fuck."

Kaylee snorts. "I guess this would be a hard place to be vegan. Your friends don't exactly look the type."

I shrug and grab two burgers and a bag of fries. "Bull's vegan. Nobody gives him shit about it."

"Because he can bench a fucking car. What flavor shake you want, Kaylee? I got vanilla, chocolate, and strawberry."

"I... I'm going to cry," Kaylee says, looking at Wraith like he's her fucking hero. "Strawberry."

We both watch, probably thinking the exact same fucking thing when she grabs the cup, wraps her lips around the straw, closes her eyes and sucks down a big gulp with a low moan. Wraith and I make eye contact and he smirks.

"Didn't they fucking feed you?" I ask.

"Ow. Brain freeze. Kinda." She winces and puts a hand on her forehead before grabbing a burger and taking it to the edge of the bed to unwrap and eat. "They didn't starve me exactly, but they wouldn't tell me what time it was, and Anderson—he was more creepy than mean—only made one thing. Scrambled eggs. That's it. If I asked for food, I got one scrambled egg with no salt or anything. This is the first real meal I've had since breakfast the morning they picked me up."

Wraith looks murderous. "You didn't say shit about that last night."

Kaylee nibbles on her burger. She shrugs and the t-shirt slips, showing a good amount of bare shoulder. "Those men at the meeting knew the guys who got shot, right? And your club has innocent people in jail. The eggs didn't seem very important."

I sit down next to her, close enough that our thighs touch. She jolts a little but leans into me for support and that feels real fucking good. "Everything they did was meant to break you down. You get that, right?"

"I know. It's just... I'm nothing special." She puts down her half eaten burger and stares at her hands, turning them over and looking at the marks and bruises. "I'm not a big tough biker. I'm just a girl who happened to see some stuff I shouldn't have. That's it."

"Bullshit," Wraith growls. He leans against the wall and stares down at us. "Those assholes were fucking professionals who sensed you were loyal to us but vulnerable, and wanted to keep you scared and confused, so you'd do whatever the fuck they told you. I've seen grown men spill their guts because someone fucking looked at them funny. You held out for days and I'm not even fucking sure why. It's not like you know us."

Kaylee looks up, surprise on her face. "You saved me. If the three of you hadn't come when you did, that man with the scars would've found me and I'd be one more body in the morgue."

I flash back to the day of the shooting. The thought of this sweet girl lying dead on the pavement with a bullet in her head makes me see red. "I going to fucking kill the bastards responsible for this. Both the assholes at the gas station, and those dirty fucking cops who touched you." A little shiver goes through her. "Sorry, I—"

"No, it's kinda hot," she whispers with a giggle. "Is it horrible to think that?"

"Fuck no. I like that you're a little savage, and I think you're wrong about yourself, sweetheart," Wraith says with a grin. "When you walked into my studio for your interview, we saw right away you were hot as fuck, but we thought you were too weak to handle us. You aren't. You hide it well, but you've got a tough fucking spine in there, Kaylee."

Kaylee blushes and takes a sip from her milkshake. "You really thought I was hot?"

Wraith comes over and sits on her other side, boxing her in and putting his arm around her. She looks a little nervous, but her eyes are fucking sparkling. Shit. I want to fucking taste those lips, and then do a lot more than that.

She brushes the end of her ponytail off her shoulder. The shirt slips a little more and I catch a glimpse of the hard little peaks of her nipples underneath. Kaylee looks at Wraith, then at me, and fuck me, her breathing speeds up and her pupils dilate. Her tongue darts out to lick her lips. Wraith cups her cheek and turns her face to his. Their kiss is slow and fucking hot, and Kaylee gives a sweet little gasp when it ends.

I turn her my way, needing a taste for myself. Her lips are soft and strawberry flavor, and when I slip her my tongue, she moans and fucking opens for me. Fuck, she's just as sweet as I thought.

"What was that for?" she asks in a rough, bedroom voice.

"Felt like it. Did you mind? Fuck, say no."

"No, I… I liked it, but…" Her cheeks go pink and her eyes flick between us. "Both of you? Isn't it, I don't know, wrong?"

I trace a finger over her bottom lip. "Trigger, around here, it's the kind of wrong that's really fucking right."

15

KAYLEE

"We work well as a team," Wraith says, hooking his index finger under my chin and turning me back to him. I put my hands on his upper arms, not to push him away, but to hold on for dear life as I kiss him back.

As soon as he lets go, Tank is there. He pulls me into his lap until I'm straddling his thighs and facing him with my arms around his powerful neck. Maybe it's the adrenaline, or just my desperation to feel good and be close to someone after everything else in my life has gone from bad to worse, but I put all of myself into the kiss. His big hands go to my waist, holding me in place. It feels naughty to have him between my legs like this, with nothing but a thin pair of leggings in the way, but also very right.

Maybe naughty is what I need, and if there's anywhere in the world that won't judge me for it, it's here with the Screaming Eagles. I remember all too clearly the kind of stuff they were doing at their bar and nobody even batted an eye.

Wraith brushes my hair away from the back of my neck, kissing me there as Tank's tongue slides along my own. His body moves behind me, caging me between them. His hands slide up to cup my breasts on the outside of the t-shirt, and I moan in spite of myself. Clever fingers find my nipples and tease them until they are rock hard and begging for his touch. At the same time, Tank threads his fingers into my hair and cups the whole back of my head, staking a clear claim on my lips.

I catch myself pressing my butt back into Wraith and force myself to stop. There's no question in my mind that they'll let me take this as far as I want. But how far is that? If I give in to the temptation of having sex, I can't just run home and put the memory on a shelf. I'm going to have to keep seeing and talking to them until this is over.

"Relax," Tank says in a low, rumbly voice. "Just let us make you feel good."

Wraith's plays with my breasts as his teeth nip at my neck. He shifts forwards, and I feel the big, hard length of something at the front of his jeans. It's definitely a weapon, but I don't think it's a gun. Especially not when he lets out a pleased sigh when I wiggle against him.

Tank's fingers tighten in my hair and he pulls back. My eyes have been closed, but I open them to look at him. His deep blue eyes are stormy with desire. "I wanna take my shirt off," he says. "You okay with that?"

Who wouldn't want an up close look at any of these guys? I remember my first sight of him as Wraith was working on his tattoo, and I nod. I'm very, very okay with it.

"And I want to take yours off, too."

That makes me pause. My bruises are mostly on my arms and shoulders, but what if they don't like what they see? What if my breasts are too droopy, or my stomach a little too soft?

Wraith seems to sense my hesitation and slides his hands underneath the hem of the t-shirt, not taking it off, but touching me skin to skin. He spreads one hand over my belly and slides the other up to my breast. "You're fucking beautiful, Kaylee."

"I'm not perfect," I whisper. Working in the beauty industry, I've seen more than my share of bodies, and I never ever judge, but I'm very conscious of every line, dimple and bulge on my own.

"Fuck perfect, I'll take real." Wraith's breath skates over my ear and the heat and tingles that have been pooling in my stomach make a move further down.

Oh God.

I nod again. The devilish grin on Tank's face makes it immediately worth it. There's so much naked appreciation in the way he looks at me that it's hard to stay self-conscious.

Tank leans back and crosses his arms over his torso to grab the hem of his shirt and twist it up over his head. I almost forget to breathe as I watch his muscles flex and move beneath the tanned skin and vibrant ink. It's like the unveiling of a Picasso, and when I let my gaze drift downwards to where a faint line of dark hair leads into his jeans, I see the hint of a clear patch over the hilt of the gun tattoo.

It makes me want to see the whole thing.

I put my hands on Tank's pecs. It's hard to believe this is even real. His heart beats steady under my palm, and he's so much softer than I imagined, and warm.

Behind me, Wraith pulls off his shirt, too, tossing it to the floor before taking hold of my t-shirt and slowly pulling it up until it's just below my armpits. I raise my arms and then it's done. I'm completely topless, sandwiched between two equally shirtless men. I keep telling myself I'll stop this in a minute, but…

None of me is interested in stopping.

Tank grips my butt and pulls me forwards until my legs are practically wrapped around his waist and my breasts are pressed firmly against him, the tight curls of his chest hair tickling my hard nipples. Between my legs, I can feel his erection pressing right against my core. He's huge, all over. My gasp turns his smile cocky.

While I'm grinding against Tank's length—and I am, I can't help it—Wraith tips my head back, making me lean into him with Tank's strong grip keeping me from falling.

Arched back so far that I'm looking right into Wraith's eyes as he looms over me, my breasts are pointed straight up. Then both of their mouths are on me at once, Wraith claiming my lips while Tank takes a nipple in his hot, wet mouth. I gasp into Wraith's kiss at the sensation.

Up until now, my dating history has been extremely... normal. A few high school boyfriends that didn't make it much farther than kissing, and one not particularly exciting relationship with a slightly older guy after I graduated where I had sex more to find out what I was missing than anything. He was fine. It was fine.

But never ever in my life have I been on fire like I am right now. I never thought I'd be the kind of girl that would fool around with two guys at once, but now that I am, I'm starting to see the advantages.

Their kisses are very different. Wraith is less brute force passion and more teasing, his tongue playing with mine as he strokes his fingers over the nipple of the breast Tank isn't worshiping. My heart pounds and my breath is coming in labored pants. I'm twisted between them with one hand behind Tank's neck for support, and the other clinging to Wraith's powerful shoulder as I hang on for my life.

Wraith's hand makes its way down to my leggings and under the stretchy waistband. I'm not wearing panties, so he ends up cupping my bare flesh instead. I groan into Wraith's mouth as he teases me with his fingertips and rubs a constant slow circle over my clit with the heel of his hand. I pull away from his kiss with a gasp, and straighten, coming face to face with Tank.

There's something incredibly erotic about riding Wraith's hand with him fit snugly behind me as Tank leans in and claims my mouth again. His hands are on my breasts, and it starts to get hard to focus on anything but the sensations they are wringing from my eager body.

"Spread her out," Wraith growls, and suddenly I'm flat on my back on the mattress, looking up at two very sexy, very intense bikers. They are looking at me the same way I was looking at that strawberry milkshake not that long ago, like they want to devour me whole.

"Um… This has been real fun, and um, you guys are amazing, but uh…" I scoot backwards over the mattress.

Fooling around with them has been a little wild and fun, but I'm not sure I'm ready to actually have sex with two men at the same time. Even one of them is probably more than my limited experience has prepared me for.

"Much as it fucking pains me, Trigger. And trust me, it fucking pains me." Tank gestures towards the massive steel pole pushing at the front of his jeans. "Just lean back and relax. We aren't doing to do shit you don't want to do."

Wraith runs a hand through his long, black hair, the red streak fanning out between his fingers. "Consider this our interview, sweetheart." He flicks his tongue at me in an unmistakable gesture.

Oh boy. I'm nodding before I even realize I've decided to agree. "Okay."

They both grin widely as Tank grabs the waist of my leggings and pulls them off in one easy motion. Completely naked for them, I can't deny I'm a little self-conscious. "Is it… Am I okay? I mean—"

"Shut up," Tank orders, spreading my legs and settling his big frame between them. He leans in and slides his broad tongue through my folds and flicks the tip against my clit, lighting me up inside like a Christmas tree.

With his hands on the backs of my thighs, holding me open, he explores through, over and around every inch of me. He studies my every reaction, learning what makes me tick. And his dedication pays off. Big time.

"Oh my God," I moan, fisting the blanket and arching my back.

Wraith laughs. "No Gods here, baby. Only us. "He moves to my side, capturing a nipple in his mouth and using his hand on the other side.

Between Tank's clever tongue and Wraith's skilled fingers and mouth, it doesn't take long before they have me right back on the edge. "More," I moan, over and over again as an orgasm builds inside me. It swells like a tidal wave approaching land, growing bigger and bigger by the second. "Harder!"

Tank listens, working my clit with fast, strong circles. I know he's strong, but the man must be doing tongue pushups in his spare time. Holy crap!

"I'm going to come," I gasp.

"Let it happen," Wraith whispers into my ear. "Shatter for us. You look so fucking gorgeous like this. All naked and open."

I feel like a goddess, worshiped by two very dedicated attendants. Sex has never been like this before, and their clothes aren't even off! When it hits, it's only them holding me down that keeps me from flying right off the mattress. My fingers find their way into Wraith's silky hair, and I can't stop moaning as I explode right onto Tank's tongue. For a moment, time loses all meaning.

They slowly bring me back to Earth until I'm completely boneless in their embrace. I yawn and close my eyes, fighting the pull of sleep but having days of rest to catch up on.

"Sleep, baby. We'll watch over you," Tank murmurs.

"Promise?" I ask, snuggling into the covers as they tuck me in.

Wraith smooths a hand over my forehead. "Promise."

16

KAYLEE

"Come on, princess. Let's just go walk around." Nitro grins, but his sexy green eyes look a little concerned. "Just because you can't go home doesn't mean you can't leave this fucking room. You've gotten the okay to move around so long as one of us is with you."

Cross-legged on the bed, I fiddle with the strings on the front of the hoodie he loaned me. "Are you sure it's okay? People were really mad at me when you brought me here. Maybe it's safer if I just stay in the room. I don't want you to get in trouble or anything. Actually, yeah. I think it's probably best for everyone if I just stay here."

I deal myself another round of solitaire, spreading the cards out on the blanket. With no phone, no laptop, no nothing, all I have to entertain myself with is a pack of cards and some weird old sci-fi books full of strange aliens and women with oversized breasts.

He sighs and sits down across from me. I peek up through my lashes, hoping he doesn't see me looking. Does Nitro know what I did with Wraith and Tank? He hasn't said anything, but guys talk, right? I feel a little unfaithful and I have no idea why.

"Put your fucking shoes on. We're going out." Nitro sweeps a hand through the cards

"Hey! What are you doing?"

"I'm saving you from your fucking self," he growls. "Take it from someone who's been blown up a couple times. Hiding can fuck you up almost as much as the shit that made you hide in the first place. We aren't your enemies. The club took a hit and guys like Sledge want someone to blame. You ain't it, but hurt people, hurt people, right?"

I gape at him.

"What? You think I don't read? I spent six years in the Army, princess. As much of it deployed as they'd let me. This?" He gestures to himself. "This is me after I worked through some of my shit. I'm still fucked up, but I'm a self-aware fuck up. Now put your fucking shoes on. You need to touch grass before you forget you're not a dainty little hairdresser anymore. You're a badass motherfucker who resisted torture."

My jaw drops even farther. Nitro puts a finger under my chin and pushes it up with a sexy emerald wink.

I don't feel much like a badass as he leads me out of Cannon's old room and towards the common area, but in the light of day after sleep, food, getting clean and... other stuff, it's not quite as scary. "Hey, Nitro? Do you think it would be okay if I said thank you to the woman who got me the clothes and stuff?"

"Yeah, sure." He looks around. "Snark! Is Alessa home?"

A wiry man with short cropped hair looks up from a laptop he has set up on the bar. "Last I knew."

"Thanks."

I stick to Nitro's side like glue. The glances I get aren't very friendly, but it mostly feels like people aren't sure how I fit in, and they need to assess if I'm a threat or not.

A couple women who look like the definition of 'biker chicks' wander out of a door in the back of the room. One has awesome long pink hair, and the other is a bottle blonde whose yellow tones make my fingers itch to fix. Their looks are assessing, too, but they don't seem hostile, just curious.

"Where does Alessa live?" I ask Nitro as he holds the door open for us to go outside. A blast of February air hits me and I pull my hands into the ends of Nitro's hoodie. We don't get snow here like at my grandparents' place in Colorado, but it's still pretty cold if you ask me.

"Round the side. Their house is in the compound. Don't fucking know how they are making it work with five adults and three kids in that house."

"Five adults? Do they have family living with them? Even living with my parents feels like a lot sometimes."

"Nah, it's just them." Nitro says like that answers anything. He slips off his jacket and puts it around my shoulders without even asking if I need it. Immediately I'm enveloped by his body heat and the rich scent of leather and his cologne.

On cue, Alessa, the pretty, dark haired woman from the meeting is standing in the doorway of one of the houses inside the compound. She has a toddler with a mop of shaggy blond hair on her hip. "Izzy. Take your brother, go next door and see if Liam wants help walking Jupiter."

"I wanna hold the leash!" an adorable little boy shouts, bursting out the door, followed by a young girl who must be Izzy. She looks like a miniature version of her mother. They glance our way, but head straight to the house next door.

It looks so... normal.

From the outside, I would never in a million years have thought that this kind of scene was inside the walls of the Screaming Eagles compound. That there would be families here. Mothers and kids alongside ferocious looking bikers. The door to the next house opens up and a big boxer bursts out, dragging a young boy behind it.

"Jupe!" he yells. "Heel!"

The dog slows down but doesn't stop, and it takes Izzy grabbing the leash as well to rein him in. Izzy's younger brother thinks the whole thing is hilarious and is laughing his little head off.

Alessa shakes her head and looks away from the kids as I approach with Nitro behind me. She smiles, but there are dark circles under her eyes. "Any news?"

"No, not yet," Nitro answers. "But we've got the best men on it. If anyone knows that, it's you and Em."

"Hi." I say with a little, nervous wave. "I just... I wanted to say thank you for the things. I didn't have anything when I got here, and it was really nice of you to think of me."

At least her look at me is friendly. "It's the least we can do. Trust me, I think most of us know what it's like to end up here with nothing but the clothes on our backs. If you stick around long enough, you'll probably hear some of the stories." She looks over my shoulder at Nitro. "Miriam's taking this pretty hard. She's been spending a lot of time over at Emily's"

He puts his hand on my shoulder. "We'll get Eagle-eye back. We'll get them all back."

A lean man with short black hair that has a bright green streak through it steps out of the neighboring house. I like the color. He's carrying a little girl who looks about the same age as Alessa's toddler. "Alessa? Can you watch Chloe for a bit?"

She nods. "Sure. I'll take them over to Summer's and see how she's doing."

He jogs over and puts the little girl down. She stands for a bit and then drops to her butt on the cold ground, poking chubby little fingers at the dry winter grass. "Thanks. It's a fucking mad house over there and I've got shit to do. Kaylee, right? I'm Wild Child." His eyes are green, matching his streak, and nearly as nice as Nitro's, but not quite.

"Nice to meet you," I answer automatically, holding out my hand.

He shakes it with a laugh. "So polite. Em was like that when we met her, too."

Two more men come out of Alessa's house. Bear and Viking I think, unless I've gotten names mixed up. Bear kisses both Alessa and the baby with such tenderness that it makes me smile.

And then Viking does the same. What the heck?

Viking looks at Nitro. "The lawyers are on their way. They've got no fucking reason to hold Prez and the others but we think it would be a good idea if you, Wraith and Tank move Kaylee off compound for a bit. We don't want to give even a fucking hint that we had anything to do with what went down last night. We'll call you when it's clear."

Nitro smirks mischievously. "I'm sure we'll find something to do."

17

KAYLEE

A FEW MINUTES LATER, I'M ON THE BACK OF NITRO'S bike with my arms wrapped around his waist as we glide through the streets towards Haunted Ink. Tank and Wraith are already there. Riding a motorcycle is a lot more fun when I'm not fleeing for my life or in shock from almost getting blown up. The steady vibration... well, it gives a girl thoughts. Especially after Tank and Wraith showed me just how good bad boys can be.

God, I can't believe I let them do that. Let them? Practically begged them.

I don't believe Nitro when he says I'm a badass, but my world has definitely been turned on its head. The last time at Haunted Ink was only a few days ago, and I barely remember who I was when my biggest worry was that someone might break into my car.

RIP my car and the Christmas returns I still had in my trunk. I clutch Nitro harder and lean my head against his back.

These men aren't mine. I'm not that naive, but despite being—let's face it—kidnapped by the Screaming Eagles, it actually feels like they care. Like they really do want to keep me safe, and not just because I can testify that they didn't do what the cops are accusing them of.

I might as well have been abducted by aliens and dropped into a parallel universe, because I don't know how to get back to the life I used to have from here. Or if I even want to. What's waiting for me out there? My parents, obviously. God, I want to tell them I'm safe. But Harris and the others know where I live. I can't go home, not yet.

Nitro, Wraith and Tank might only be mine for now, but right now is all I can worry about. They've rescued me twice and I trust them to keep me safe. It's better that people worry until I come back, than that I don't come back at all.

Nitro parks his bike around the back of the building alongside two other motorcycles that must belong to Wraith and Tank. He helps me off, putting us face to face a moment, just long enough for me to appreciate the deep green of his beautiful eyes, then puts me down with ease. I keep forgetting how strong these guys are. I shouldn't be greedy, but now that the ball's rolling, my imagination's already coming up with lots of ideas of what it would be like to explore his powerful torso.

All three of them are fantasy-worthy, and it's hard not to have those fantasies when his hand is resting possessively on my hip as he guides me towards the back door.

God, and here I was worried that I wasn't adventurous enough? I let out a little sound that makes Nitro pause. "Something funny?"

"Ummmmm, is Alessa with both Viking and Bear?" I blurt out, covering my spicy train of thought with something else that's been on my mind.

"And Snark and Hawk." He says it so matter of factly that I nearly stumble over my own feet on the way into the tattoo parlor.

"What?"

God, before yesterday, the idea of more than one guy at once was as foreign as banana on pizza. I was shocked at two, and Alessa has four? Jeez, I don't feel as strange for fantasizing about what it would be like for Nitro to join in now. The usual rules and restrictions don't apply with these people.

"Yeah, and Wild Child? The one with the baby girl? His old lady Emily has him, Hero and King," he says as he guides me into the room where Wraith and Tank are. The same room I was interviewed in.

"Is this a biker thing? Do all the women have a whole bunch of guys?"

"Nah, not everyone. But a lot do, or at least it's turned out that way in the Screaming Eagles," Wraith says, rolling his chair back from a desk in the tattoo area. He has a sketchbook in his lap and a drawing pencil in his hand. "I'd tell you the benefits, but you already got a taste, didn't you?"

Nitro chuckles, as does Tank who's flipping through a book with pictures of finished tattoos.

I spin around and look at Nitro. "You know?"

"About them helping you relax? Fuck yeah, and I'm jealous as shit. I was stuck doing dumbass riding drills with the prospects."

"Can I ask you guys a question?" My face is on fire but I have to know. "What do the guys get out of it?"

Tank snorts. "You joking?"

"No. I thought all guys want a bunch of girls to like, fawn all over them and do stuff to each other."

Nitro leans in close. "Some do, but fucking serious, I've only got one dick, you know? It's a lot more fun to make one woman lose her ever-loving mind over and over until she can't remember her own damn name."

"And we're talking about women who have been fucking claimed," Wraith adds. He puts his sketchpad down and stands up, walking over with a heat in his eyes that promises something more sinful than just a little fun.

"Does that make it different?"

"It makes all the difference, Trigger," Tank answers. "Nothing wrong with fucking around for fun, but claiming someone is about absolute fucking loyalty. Any woman we claimed would be ours. Ours to protect and ours to make scream."

I really like the sound of that while they're all looking at me like they want to tear my clothes off, but the irrational idea that there might be a nameless, faceless woman in the future that would have all this energy devoted to her? I want to claw her eyes out and she doesn't even exist yet.

"Did you ever want a tattoo?" asks Wraith, changing the subject, his eyes crinkled in amusement.

"I've always thought they looked cool, but watching you tattoo Tank was a lot more intense than I expected. I'm fine with a piercing gun, but something about the buzzing and stabbing…" My stomach twists just thinking about it.

"How about this?" He takes a marker from his tattoo station. "I use this to put down a template when I'm free-handing, and there's no canvas I'd rather fucking draw on than you. You're a piece of art, sweetheart."

Oh. Wow. "I guess that should be fine. What am I getting?"

He grins like I just gave him an early birthday present. "Artist's choice."

"I'll make sure she sits still," Nitro says, pulling me into one of the chairs right over his lap. He puts his arms around me, and as I wiggle to get comfortable, I notice I'm not the only one that found talking about sex a little exciting. Is packing serious heat a biker requirement or something? My first instinct is to move away, but I'm feeling naughty enough to wiggle again and I'm rewarded with a soft groan and a quick, "Fuck," breathed into my ear.

"How about our names?" asks Tank. He pulls down the zipper on the front of my hoodie and they pull it off me. He runs his fingers over my arm, stroking my sensitive forearm where the bruises are still visible. "Start with me, here. I don't want these to be all you see."

"Good idea. A nice, neutral starting spot," Wraith says, pulling up a stool and arranging my arm on a rest. Then he starts drawing.

I watch closely, amazed at how steady his hand is, and how perfectly he draws the letters in a bold heavy metal style. The marker tickles a little, but it's kind of fun, especially watching him add little vine and thorn flourishes to make it pretty.

"Me next," says Nitro. "On her side." His hand's already sliding underneath my T-shirt, pulling it up to reveal my ribcage.

"Um, guys, I'm—"

Tank grins. "Don't worry. We're professionals."

Nitro adjusts me in his lap, stretching out my arm and leaning me so Wraith has complete access. That one of his hands happens to be supporting me by holding my breast is completely accidental I'm sure, but I don't complain. I suck in a breath as Wraith's cool fingers smooth over my ribs and he starts sketching the outline of the letters. I crane my neck and watch.

The lettering is completely different. It looks like the kind of retro font you'd see on the side of an old school race car with more jagged embellishments and an outline around the letters. It's five, maybe six inches long and wraps around my right side, a little below my breast.

"I like seeing our names on you," Nitro murmurs, just for me.

I kind of like it too.

"Where do you want your name?" I ask Wraith.

He licks his lips and leans back. "So many options." Standing, he repositions me like a doll, making me straddle Nitro with my knees on either side of his thighs. "There are a lot of places I want to put my ink, but I think for this I want it somewhere people can see. I want them to see our marks on you."

My body feels loose and pliable as they help me out of my shirt. I've been going without a bra for so long that I've almost stopped paying attention to it, but being topless in Nitro's lap makes it hard to ignore. I have to close my eyes a moment and pretend this is all perfectly normal.

Wraith twists my hair up and out of the way, and then strokes all the way from the nape of my neck to the small of my back. I have to fight the urge to arch like a cat looking for more attention. My arms rest on Nitro's shoulders, leaving my breasts hanging right there for him to see.

"Are you still jealous?" I tease.

Nitro's expression is downright devilish. He reaches up and his thumbs stroke over my nipples. "I will be until I hear you scream my name."

18

NITRO

I've wanted to do this since I first saw her right here in the shop. She's so fucking pretty. Way too good for assholes like us, but I learned long ago not to question fate. I love the weight of her in my hands. When I flick my thumbs over her already hard nipples, she lets out a sudden sigh. Not of surprise, but relief it's finally happening.

That makes two of us, because I've been hard as a fucking rock since she started asking about why a man would want to share a woman. With the way she's been wiggling over my cock, I'll be more than fucking happy to show her.

"Oh," she says in a little whimper as Wraith starts sketching across her shoulders. He's only using markers, but as always, he's completely focused on his work.

I can't kiss her full lips from here, but press a kiss between her breasts and blow over the damp spot my lips left behind. She shivers and shifts in my lap.

"Sit still," Wraith grumbles as he signs his name on her body.

"I'm trying," she moans as I do it again.

I fucking hate seeing the marks that those cop assholes left on her body. How the hell did they take someone as sweet as Kaylee and treat her like that? I want to string those fuckers up and give them a solid dose of their own fucking medicine before I make it so they can't hurt anyone else, ever again.

"There." Wraith leans back to look at his work. He takes a picture with his phone and shows it to Kaylee. His name spans the whole top of her back in an arch, written in bold, black lettering that looks like a ragged version of what they used to label old fashioned maps. It looks fucking badass, like she already is on the inside, but now everyone can see it.

Kaylee's eyes go wide. "Wow. I feel—"

"Owned?" suggests Tank.

She blushes, and I can tell she really fucking likes that idea. "If I was really a biker chick, what would you do to me?"

"You want to play dirty, princess?" I ask.

The answer is a whisper, "Yes."

She's fucking putty in our hands, moaning deep in her throat as I recapture her beautiful breasts. Her nipples are pebbles between my fingers, and from the way she keeps wiggling, she loves the way I play with them.

Wraith throws the marker aside. "Put her on the couch. It's my turn for a taste," he growls.

Tank picks her up easily and spreads her out on the leather couch. Between the two of them, they strip off the rest of her clothes, leaving her gorgeously naked just for us. She looks up, her pale gray eyes wide but full of complete trust. She looks so fucking small compared to us, and it makes me want to both protect her, and do horrible fucking amazing things to her curvy body.

The surprised gasp she lets out when Wraith gets between her legs is pure sex. "Your beard tickles," she moans.

"All part of the service," he responds, then does something to make her eyes close and her head fall back.

"You really want to know what it would be like to be one of the girls at the club? One of the sluts?" I ask, my hand going to my belt.

Lost in bliss, she nods.

"First we'll get you good and fucking ready for us. Touch your breasts, I want to see you play with yourself while Wraith eats that pretty pussy."

Kaylee obeys without hesitation. Those small hands cup her tits, lifting and squeezing them the way I want to. Her eyes are locked on Wraith between her thighs, her chest heaving and her skin flushed pink. She looks so fucking good, especially with my name on her.

I undo my jeans and take my aching cock in my hand. Kaylee's eyes go wide when she sees it, but she licks her lips and keeps playing with herself like a good little girl. On the other side of her, Tank does the same. It's been a while since we've all shared, but it feels so damn right with her. More than it should, because we're supposed to be watching her, not fucking her.

"Open those sexy legs a little wider, princess. Wraith is going to make you come so hard, and then you're going to show me how grateful you are, aren't you? I missed out last time so it's only fair I'm the first one who gets to feel your mouth wrapped around me."

Her response is a strangled cry and my name on her lips as Wraith works his magic. Kaylee arches off the couch, her eyes squeezed shut as her whole body trembles. Fuck, that is so damn hot.

"You like it when we talk dirty, don't you, Trigger?" Tank chuckles, stroking his cock in long, languid motions as he watches her squirm.

Kaylee nods, panting for breath. Her nipples stand out from between her fingers like plump cherries, begging to be plucked and sucked. I reach out and tweak one and she cries out.

"Again," Tank orders. "Harder."

She gasps as I do it, but not from pain. Letting go of her tits, Kaylee threads her fingers into Wraith's hair as her hips jerk against his mouth, searching for release. Kaylee moans and shakes her head. "It's too much. I can't. I—"

"You fucking can. You're so fucking close. We can all see it. Come on Wraith's tongue and then open those pretty lips."

Kaylee cries out, her whole body going rigid. Wraith focuses his mouth on her clit and starts working a finger into her tight pussy. He holds her there, trapped and shuddering as he brings her over the edge. I edge closer, unable to take my eyes off her. This girl is so fucking beautiful when she comes.

Wraith moves out of the way and I climb onto the couch, straddling her and pointing my cock at her welcoming mouth. Her eyes are bright with lust and she's already got her tongue out, ready to taste the precum that's seeping from the tip. Fuuuuuck.

She engulfs the head of my cock with her sweet pink lips and I'm in fucking heaven. Her lashes flutter and she reaches up to grab my hips as I thrust a little deeper. The wet heat surrounding my crown has me too fucking close to coming already. I hiss, fighting the need to take her hard and fast before she's ready. She moans around me, sending the most delicious vibrations through my whole body. Tank groans and Wraith mutters a curse. Kaylee's eyes flick his way, and her cheeks hollow as she sucks on me.

"Fuck. Look at that," Wraith growls. "Show him how good you can take it, baby."

Kaylee opens wider, and I push deeper. She gags a little, but wraps her hand around my shaft to control the depth, her grip tight and fucking perfect.

"Holy shit. Good girl," Tank groans.

I grip the back of the couch and close my eyes, focusing on the slide of my cock between her fingers and into the hot depths of her mouth. My orgasm hits not as a slow build but as a flash flood. The surge comes suddenly, just as she reaches out and slides her fingertips over my balls. With a deep groan racking my whole damn body, I give her everything. Her eyes go wide, but she takes it all, swallowing fast. Her cheeks cave as I pull out, totally fucking drained.

Tank's moving to take my place when my back pocket starts to vibrate. I pull out my phone. "Hey, Chef. What's—"

"Get back. There's been a fucking incident with the prospects."

19

KAYLEE

Wraith, Tank and Nitro stalk into the warehouse like they're going to war. I hurry along between them, glad I'm not the one they're looking for. I'm still reeling from the way they switched immediately into business mode as soon as Nitro got that call.

"This is fucking bullshit," an angry male voice booms from inside the common room. "Who are you going to believe? Me or that bitch slut?"

The way he says those words feels like a slap. Calling the women who hang out at the club 'sluts' doesn't exactly sit easily with me to begin with, but while I've gotten the feeling that it's more of a crude term of endearment than an insult with these guys, there isn't any endearment in that voice.

"Go sit at the bar," Tank orders, pointing. "Stay where we can fucking see you." His anger isn't directed at me, but it's still there, simmering under the surface and making me uneasy.

On one of the couches by the TV, the pink haired woman I saw earlier is comforting a crying brunette with a torn shirt. Around her are several men. I don't really know any of them by name, but I've seen most of them around by now.

"Jewel? What the fuck is going on?" Wraith snaps.

A man with a shaved head wearing a black vest with a patch that just says 'prospect' on it crosses his arms in front of his chest and scowls. "You going to listen to her side first?"

"Shut the fuck up, Deuce."

Jewel—the woman with the pink hair—looks absolutely furious. "I was hanging out with the girls when he and his buddy came over looking for some fun while they watched a game. They're just prospects, but there wasn't much going on and Kaia didn't mind."

"Kaia?" Tank prompts.

The brunette looks up, messy black circles under her eyes from her makeup. "They wanted me to suck them off, but I said no. Mad Dog bitched about it, but I offered to give him a handie and then he was chill." She glares at Deuce. "But he grabbed my head and tried to force me. When I put up a fight, he—" She sits up straighter so we can all see the growing red mark on the side of her face.

Deuce rolls his eyes. "It was a fucking love tap. What the hell are they here for if they say no?"

"You fucking joking?" Nitro asks, spitting venom with each word. "If you've got a problem with the sluts, you take it to us or another officer. Nobody forces them to do shit. If that's the kind of club you're looking for, you walk out the fucking door right now. You're already on thin ice and you know it."

Something ugly flashes across Deuce's face before he pushes it down and nods. "Fine."

Tank's eyes narrow. Without a word, he cocks his arm and punches Deuce right in the side of his head. Deuce staggers back, cursing. It's fast and brutal. I've always thought violence wasn't the answer, but deep inside, watching them punish Deuce soothes part of the hurt I felt when Harris slapped me and nobody cared.

"Get the fuck out, both of you. You're both banned from the clubhouse until you hear otherwise."

"If you fuck this up for me, I'll rip your dick off," Mad Dog snarls at Deuce, grabbing his arm and hauling him out of the room.

Behind me at the bar, a man with a red dragon tattoo that wraps around his head and down his neck growls. "One more strike and that asshole's out."

"They should have let Kaia kick him in the balls." It drops out of me before I think to wonder if my opinion is even welcome around here.

The man bursts out laughing. "I'd love to see that, but it would fuck shit up for her and she knows it. Your bodyguards there are helping show the prospects the ropes. Getting reprimanded might piss them off, but it's part of life in the club. We have a hierarchy and the prospects are on the bottom of it."

"I'm confused. Wouldn't that mean the sluts are higher up?"

He snorts. "Women aren't members. Members have members, old ladies belong to their men, and the sluts are here because they like the lifestyle and men like having pretty girls around. So long as they're here, we make sure people don't fuck with them, but that's because it's basic human decency and real fucking men don't hurt people weaker than them."

I can tell it's not that simple. When they look at their wives, old ladies, whatever you want to call it, I can tell that these men would die for their families, but biker culture sounds like it's still very much a men's club. This is their world. Like it or leave it.

"I'm Chef, by the way. You want a drink or are you just going to sit there taking up space?"

"Um… a coke, please?"

The look Chef gives me makes me reconsider all of my life choices up to and including asking for a soda in a private motorcycle club bar.

"Do you have Pepsi? Because that's okay, too. I don't really mind either way as long as it isn't diet." I'm babbling, but it's hard to stop when he keeps looking at me like that. "I wish I did like diet soda. My friends keep telling me the taste of the sweetener will grow on me, but I'm in my twenties. It would've happened by now, right?"

Jewel walks behind the bar, takes Chef's face in her hands and kisses him. There's a lot of tongue. So much that I start feeling like I should find somewhere else to be, but eventually she breaks it off and pats him on the cheek. He grunts and rolls his eyes, but there's a hint of a smile as he begrudgingly pulls a Coke out of the fridge and slides the can my way.

Two bikers come up, they nod at me. The taller one, with short hair and a neatly trimmed beard calls to Chef. "Three beers and a virgin Blue Hawaiian."

"Sure, Preacher. How's Summer?" Jewel asks. "I heard the news. Congratulations."

"Thanks. It's fucking crazy. I can't believe in like half a year we'll almost be outnumbered."

The other guy glances over his shoulder. "Put a rush on it. We need to get back before they start playing a little game of what we've been calling 'oh no, stepbro'.

Jewel bursts out laughing. She sees me watching, utterly confused. "Their old lady Summer is pregnant. Triplets. Her third man is Crash. They used to be step-siblings."

"Maybe I should start drinking. The gossip around here is even better than at the salon." And some of the stuff I've heard at work when people forget the person washing their hair has ears? Crazy.

"Oh, this is nothing. Thunder and Lighting are twins, right? I heard—"

"Hey, baby," Tank says, interrupting before I get more juicy details. "You okay?"

I take a sip of my soda and spin around, finding them all behind me. "Yeah, I'm fine. Chef was just explaining club life to me."

"Shit, now we'll never be able to convince you to stay," Nitro says with a laugh.

My heart flops. He's teasing, I know it, but an hour ago we were… I don't know if I'm cut out for this. For being the kind of girl who can fool around with men like them without getting my heart broken at least a little bit.

"He didn't tell me everything. I have so many more questions. Like what are prospects? Do you have to call sluts, sluts? Do you guys know each other's real names? Do you change them legally? Like, if I sent Thank You cards after all this is over, do I put Tank on the envelope? What about if—"

Wraith kisses me, really hard, his hand capturing the side of my face and tilting my head so we line up. Everything good about the world seems to bubble right up from my stomach and percolate around my head, and I shut my eyes tight and lean into it. His long beard is scratchy around my lips and against my chin, but that's part of what makes it a kiss with Wraith, and I don't think I'd ever want it to be any different.

When he finally pulls away, I swallow thickly. No more questions, only tingles. "Was that to shut me up?"

"Yes," he deadpans. "I also just wanted to kiss you."

"Oh, okay." When it's kissing like that, I can live with it.

"No rush, Trigger, but do you want to hang out here or would you like to go somewhere a little more private. Maybe we can pick up where we left off," Tank whispers in my ear.

I am soooo getting my heart broken, but it'll be worth it. "Yes, please."

20

KAYLEE

I don't even have to walk there on my own. The moment I say yes, Tank sweeps me up and carries me in his arms like we're newlyweds, straight through the club towards the corridor that leads to the bikers' private quarters. A chorus of hoots and cheers follow us the whole way, which would normally embarrass the crap out of me, but around here it doesn't feel judgmental.

Bikers seem to feel like why wouldn't you go have wild crazy sex if everyone wants to do it? A badass biker chick would go do it, right? I want to be that, not a scared little girl like the cops made me feel.

But I'm still working on it. I bury my face in Tank's chest so nobody can see that my face is about the same shade as a tomato at all the cheering. The noise dies down behind us as we go deeper into the clubhouse, right up to Tank's door.

"It's open," he says, and Nitro opens it up for us.

I'm tossed on the bed so suddenly, I lose my breath, before I roll over to find all three of them looming over me. "Don't I get a tour first?"

Tank looks around. "Bed. Fridge. Table. Bathroom. Couch. TV. Weights." With each word, he points to a different spot in his room. It's a little bigger than the one I've been staying in, but not a lot.

"Strip," demands Wraith gruffly as he unbuttons his jeans. "This time we're doing you proper, and we've got all fucking night."

I start to, but then I stop. "No, you guys take your clothes off first. It's about time I get the first show."

The looks I get make me wonder if I should just capitulate now and get naked before someone has to donate more clothes when these end up shredded, but then Tank laughs.

"You want a show? We'll give you a show." He picks up a remote from the table and pushes a button.

Hard, driving music flows from speakers and the lights dim but don't turn off.

He pulls his shirt off and twirls it over his head before starting on his belt. With the crack of leather, it's off and soon his jeans hit the floor to be kicked aside. All he's wearing is boxer briefs, which are showing off a bulge that scares me in a really fun way. The way it's stretching out his underwear makes it look like he's literally packing a baseball bat.

Wraith and Nitro aren't far behind, making sure I get a good look at them stripping off their clothes and revealing sooooo much gorgeous male flesh. They are all covered in ink, but Wraith is exceptional. I'm not sure there's a place on his body aside from his face that has more than a hand sized patch of untouched skin.

Nitro turns to put his phone on the table and oh my God. That ass.

I don't know what these guys do for exercise, but being in a motorcycle club is apparently hard work. All three of them are ripped, and in different ways. Wraith is leaner, deadly looking. Nitro and Tank could be football players, Nitro the quarterback and Tank a defensive lineman.

Tank flexes his biceps for me, and my eyes must be wide as dinner plates. I'm pretty sure those upper arms are bigger around than my waist, and I've never been a size zero.

If I could take pictures right now, I could sell so many calendars none of us would have to work ever again.

I'd tell them so, but their egos are more than big enough as it is. "Not bad. I could recommend a few skin treatments, and I'm pretty good at waxing, but—"

Tank freaking tackles me on his bed. It's a good thing we're using his room because most bed frames wouldn't survive this kind of a beating.

"Guys, guys! I can undress myself," I shout, laughing as they work my clothes off. My shoes and leggings are the first to go, then the hoodie and shirt. I end up on all fours. Someone smacks my ass. "Hey! Watch it!"

"Oh, I was," says Nitro, just before leaning in and kissing the same spot and making me shiver.

A moment later, all my clothes are on the floor and of course they've all still got their underwear on. "I told you guys to go first."

Tank crawls over the bed until he's close enough to touch. "Must have forgotten. How about you do the honors?"

Chewing my bottom lip nervously, I reach for the elastic and hook my fingers in, then yank my hand back. "You're, um, a lot more than I'm used to. Not that I'm used to anything. Well, I'm not not used to it. But I'm not used to it. You know?"

"What are you trying to say?" Wraith asks as they all look at me, confused.

"You're big!" I blurt out, pointing to Tank's bulge.

He chuckles and the bulge grows even more impressive. "Yell that a little louder. Just in case there's someone in the next room."

"Shut up." Summoning my inner badass, I yank down his briefs. A huge cock bounces free, every bit as impressive as advertised. Long and hard. I finally get to see the full gun tattoo, with its smoking barrel ending right above the base of his cock. I wasn't sure if I'd been imagining his size since I was pretty distracted when we were in the parlor.

Distracted by…

Nitro, the only one I've had a real up close and personal experience with. Smirking, he shucks off his underwear and gives his cock a stroke. My mouth goes dry, remembering.

And last, but certainly not least…

Wraith's underwear is long gone, and his cock is already slick with precum, like he just can't wait to get inside me. Now that I'm sitting here with the three biggest cocks I've ever seen, it's honestly a little imposing. I wet my lips, and all three follow the movement closely. "How do I even start?"

"One step at a time." Tank pulls my hand to him, wrapping my fingers around his girth. My fingertips aren't close to touching. It's the same arm that still has his name drawn on it. "Stroke me."

I obey, the order slicing through me and drawing my nipples into tight points. Nitro puts himself in my other hand, so I'm stroking both of them at once.

Wraith moves in front. He's so heavily inked that it doesn't occur to me right away that one of the swirls actually goes down onto his cock. He winks when he sees me staring. "Yeah it hurt, still worth it. Now open up, sweetheart."

I do.

The salty flavor of Wraith bursts over my tongue. It's so hard to concentrate on three things at once, but they don't seem to mind. They're all so hard for me. So eager. I don't feel dirty, I feel like a goddess. Their goddess.

I close my eyes and let Wraith set the pace. He cups the side of my face with one hand and strokes my hair with his other, taking it nice and slow by pushing between my lips and then pulling back out so I can explore every ridge and bump with my tongue.

Tank and Nitro shift so they can play with my body without me disrupting the rhythm of my hands along their shafts. Their powerful hands stroke my breasts and thighs, smoothing down my spine and over the swell of my ass. Three pairs of hands are on me, and it feels incredible.

I tingle everywhere, wiggling and swaying more and more against their touch. It starts light and teasing, slowly growing more forceful until Tank slides his thick finger in between my splayed thighs and finds me slick and ready to take things to the next level. Nitro plays my hard nipples like a musician, every touch and twist surging pleasure straight to my core. Now it's Wraith that it's hard to concentrate on, but I do my best.

"Good girl," he murmurs, threading his strong fingers through my hair until he has a good grip on my head, then guiding me up and down his length.

I feel powerful but completely vulnerable. This is a test of trust. They could manhandle me any way they want, make me do anything. That edge of danger is exciting, but only because I really do trust them not to go too far.

Nitro pulls away, shoving my knees apart and sliding under me. He grabs my hips and pulls me down until my pussy is hovering right over his mouth. With my own mouth full, I can't really say anything, but oh my God do I moan as his tongue parts my folds and pushes inside.

Wraith groans. "Fuck, make her do that again."

He does.

They are all clearly really good at oral, and I can't even be jealous. I send up a silent thanks to whoever helped bring them to where they are. Up until I met them, my only experience with actually receiving was a few boring licks, and right now, I'm pretty sure Nitro could make me forget my own name.

Wraith pulls away, though he keeps his fingers wrapped in my hair. He lets out a held breath. "Goddamn, you're too fucking hot. I'm not ready to be done yet."

I don't get to respond before Tank is in his place. He rubs his thick crown against my lips and I open for him, wrapping my hand as far as I can around his base to keep him from going too deep as he thrusts his slick cock into my mouth. With a shuddering groan, I find myself rocking back and forth between Tank's cock and Nitro's tongue and fingers, balancing right on the edge of coming.

"Beautiful," whispers Wraith, tracing a finger over his name across my shoulders. "Let us watch you come."

I do, letting the orgasm wash over me like the shockwave of a nuclear bomb. I rear back off Tank's cock and scream as it washes away any trace of anyone who isn't these men. I feel reborn.

When I finally slump to my hands and knees, they guide over onto my back. The soft mattress is like floating on a cloud while I wait for my heart to stop racing and my breathing to return to normal. "Holy crap," I whisper.

Wraith crawls up the bed so that he's above me, his long locks spilling down over his shoulders, the red streak in disarray as it's fallen out of the leather thong he uses to keep it in place. His knees are between my legs, and his hard cock is glistening above my stomach. "I want to fuck you," he says simply.

I glance down, already imagining what it'll be like. "I meant it before. I've never been with anyone as big as you guys."

He smirks confidently. "I know what I'm fucking doing. It'll be good. Real fucking good."

It's the final surrender. I could say no right now and we might keep fooling around, but I'd always wonder what it would've been like. A badass wouldn't back down.

"Okay," I say with a nervous nod, trusting them with this one more thing.

Tank opens the nightstand drawer and pulls out a little plastic packet that he tosses to Wraith. God, they have me so hot I was more worried about getting split in two than getting pregnant.

Tank and Nitro are there, surrounding us, but it's Wraith that fills my senses as he looms over me and rests a hand next to my head. He nudges his cock against my entrance, sliding it up and down through my folds, making sure we're both good and ready.

Coal-dark eyes stare directly into my soul as he presses his narrow hips forwards and the head of him spreads me open. I let out a soft moan and wrap my arms around his neck as he pushes deeper, slowly, but with determination. I'm so full, and he just keeps coming.

His nostrils flare, and a throaty moan rumbles deep in his chest. "You're so fucking tight, so good."

I'm not going to argue. He's stretching me to my limit, but it feels like he was meant to be inside me. I tilt my hips up to accept him and he slides the last inch home, fully inside. There are no words. Wraith moves, easing almost all of that cock back out of me before thrusting to the hilt.

I gasp. "God…" I whisper.

"No, not God. Whose cock are you feeling?" Wraith growls.

"Yours."

"That's right."

Faster and faster. His thickness fills me like no one ever has, touching every sensitive spot in me at once. Now that I've adjusted, we move smoothly together. I still feel stretched around him like a glove, but I love it, rocking against him as he shatters my world.

Then Nitro's there on one side and Tank comes in on the other. Their hands slide over my skin, caressing me all over as Wraith relentlessly fills me over and over, driving me back to that precipice of pleasure, like I'm riding a barrel towards a waterfall. It's roaring in my ears as I shut my eyes and just let the sensations of three men's touch overwhelm me.

I'm not sure who hits their climax first, me or Wraith. We moan together, the sounds of his skin against mine echoing in the room, and just as he tenses up, I burst around him. His cock swells as he comes, but I'm too lost in my own bliss to fully register all of it. So many sensations and feelings, too many to hold onto all at once. We stay connected until we find our breaths again.

Wraith pulls out slowly and rolls over, with a deep groan. "Fucking hell."

I slide my fingers through Tank's short hair and Nitro's wavy locks as they move into the space Wraith just opened up. They tease my breasts with their lips and tongues. Nitro moves up to kiss me, and I wrap my arms around him. His hardness presses into my hip, and I know we're not done yet. Not that I want to be.

The nightstand drawer rattles and Nitro catches something as he rolls me onto my side and slides his knee between my legs, making room. He puts his hand over the temporary tattoo of his name and nips my earlobe. "Ready for one more?"

I'm usually a one and done kind of girl, but tonight I'm testing my limits. "Definitely," I say as I look down to watch him slide on the condom. This time I get to watch as he spoons behind me and lines himself up.

"So fucking wet for us," he hisses, then pushes all the way in one long stroke.

"Yes," I moan. "Do it again."

"As you command, princess." He grins widely and settles into a steady rhythm of long strokes that picks up right where Wraith left off.

Tank strokes himself in front of us watching as Nitro fucks me from behind. "Play with yourself, Trigger."

I watch him watching me as my hand moves between my legs. I splay my fingers around Nitro's cock as it drives inside, gathering my own wetness and spreading it over my clit. It's too swollen and sensitive to go hard, but I find a nice rhythm and lose myself in the feeling of being stuffed full. It's dirty and amazing to feel this visual connection to Tank while it's Nitro in my body.

"I'm going to come," I say in a horse whisper, surprising myself with how easy it is with them. It hits hard and fast, without the slow build I'm used to. Stealing the air from my lungs and leaving me gasping.

"Holy shit," Nitro groans, burying himself deep inside and holding his hips still as his cock pulses over and over. He falls back, slipping out and breathing heavily.

I feel wrecked, but I'm not leaving this room without knowing all of them. "Go easy on me, okay?" I say with a little laugh, eyeing Tank's monster a little nervously in spite of the warmup.

He gets on his back and guides me on top. "You're in control, got it?"

I nod, already slick with sweat and still tingling from my last orgasm. He's such a big guy, that he easily holds my hips and helps me get in position so his cock is right where I need it to be. I tease both of us, rotating my hips over the blunt head until I'm ready.

Oh my God. "You're huge," I groan as gravity does the work and I get my first real sense of him.

"You can do this. You're fucking made for me." Every second stretches me open around him. Sexy tingles rush through me as I spread for him, letting him in, one glorious inch at a time.

"So good," I moan, accepting his thickness.

He holds me with hands that could do such violence but are so gentle. More and more finds its way inside, but it works. It feels amazing, right on the edge of what I can take, just enough to drive me crazy. After Wraith, Nitro and now Tank, how can I ever go back to anyone else?

When I'm finally sitting flush on his hips, I'm shocked. "I took it all," I whisper.

"Fuck, you're perfect," he breathes. "Just fucking perfect."

I can feel his heartbeat as he pulses inside me, but he's right. It's perfect. We're perfect. I smile, letting him know I'm ready for more.

And God, he does. With his hands on my hips, I might be on top, but he's in control. He groans as he presses himself into my tightness, and my nails dig into his shoulders as he fills me with his size. I don't know how long I can take this for, but I'm going to ride it right up to the limit, because it's the most amazing thing I've ever felt.

There's no room for anything in me but Tank, and it's building up to what might be the strongest orgasm of my life. At least that's what it feels like as my muscles go taut, I arch my back and a guttural growl starts deep inside me, a kind of noise I didn't even know I could make. A tidal wave of explosive metaphors crash down on me all at once, and as I go off around him with a howl, he groans and pulls me to his hips one last time. Every pulse as he comes causes my pussy to squeeze him back, driving each other through our orgasms together until we finally come down and I slump over his chest, barely conscious.

"God fucking damn," Nitro whispers.

The wall thumps as someone pounds on it. "We're fucking trying to sleep over here!" comes muffled through the wall.

"Oh my God," I say with shock, putting my hand to my mouth. "Were we that loud?"

"Like a fucking banshee, baby," Wraith says with a laugh. "Perfect."

21

KAYLEE

THE BOYS ARE DEEP IN CONVERSATION WITH OTHER members by the bar while I'm curled up on the couch, deep in a book about a man who was sent to Mars and is on a mission from an alien queen with six breasts to retrieve her virgin daughter when something brushes by my leg. "What the—"

Big brown eyes look up at me. Four of them. Two belong to the energetic boxer I saw the other day, and two are in the gray muzzled face of a pittie. The pittie has a very slobbered on looking rope toy in its mouth and drops it right at my feet.

"Aw, that looks like a lot of fun, but I really don't want to touch it," I say in a friendly baby voice to the dogs. "No I don't. Nope nope nope." The boxer puts his head on my leg and looks at me like his world is falling apart.

"Jupiter, King, leave her alone," says a voice behind me. I turn to see the girl with the bad bleach job behind me.

I know I'm young, but up close I can tell she isn't much more than eighteen or nineteen. Three or four years might not mean much, but should she be hanging out in this place at her age?

"King isn't... King's dog, is he?"

The girl laughs. "No, and don't bring it up around him. King—the dog, I mean—belongs to Summer and her guys, but Jupiter's been so depressed without Eagle-eye around that they've been hanging out together more than usual."

"I'm Kaylee." She seems friendly enough, and it would be nice to have people to talk to besides men. Up until this mess started, I spent most of my days almost exclusively around women and I kind of miss it.

She cocks her head. "I know who you are. Everyone was talking about you for days. There was a rumor that it was your fault Eagle-eye's in the slammer, but I guess since you're sitting out here and not locked in the pit, that's probably not true."

"The pit?"

She shakes her head. "I don't really know. I've only heard them say it and it doesn't sound good." Her eyes cut to the table where Nitro, Wraith and Tank are sitting. "Are you with them now?"

That's a very good question, and I'm not really sure what the answer is, but I'm not about to tell this child anything that makes her think she can go sit on one of their laps. Or maybe she has already? I really don't like that idea. "Yeah. They're mine."

She giggles. "You don't have to worry about me. I'm new. No way am I going to chance pissing someone off by trying to poach their man. I'm Lace."

"Nice to meet you, Lace." I reach out and touch the ends of her hair. "Did you do this yourself?"

Her nose wrinkles. "Yeah. It didn't turn out the way I wanted it to, though."

"I could help you fix it, maybe."

"You think?" Her face lights up. "We've got a lot of random supplies in the locker room. Do you do your own hair? It's really pretty."

"Yeah, I did, but like, right now? I mean... I guess I can go see what you have."

Lace takes my hand and pulls me towards the back of the room, suddenly eager.

"Where you going?" Tank shouts.

"She's going to help me with my hair!" Lace shouts back.

The locker room is exactly that. It's not fancy, but it's clearly a feminine space in a fortress of testosterone. There are already a few girls hanging out towards the back where someone set up patched lounge chairs, including Kaia, the girl Deuce was bothering.

The showers have pretty curtains, and there are baskets full of things like tampons, condoms and even... disposable underwear? I didn't even know that was a thing, but I guess in a place like this it might come in handy. Under one of the sinks is a big bin that Lace goes straight to.

"Don't do it," says a curvy girl with tight red curls as she points at Kaia. "I know you think they're going to be cute, but trust me, baby bangs are never a good idea." She looks up when she notices us. "Tell her, Lace."

Lace chews her lip. "They *could* be cute?"

"If you really want to try it, order a cheap clip-in piece and style that," I suggest. "Even if it isn't a perfect match you can see if you like it before committing to growing your own hair back for forever. Baby bangs are rough."

The redhead frowns. "Who made you an expert?"

"Um, the State Board of Cosmetology? And I work in a salon."

Lace comes to my support. "See? She's cool, Indie. She's going to try to fix my hair."

"You're seriously a hairdresser?" Kaia asks. "From the way everyone was talking about you, I thought you were some big important person. Like a lawyer or something."

"Nope. And I'm not even a full stylist. I mean I could be, I have my license, but I don't have my own chair yet."

"You seriously know how to do hair?"

I feel more like the new girl at school than a badass, but I nod eagerly. "Yeah, seriously. If you want a change, I could do curtain bangs. It's way less drastic and much easier to grow out. I think it would be pretty on you, too."

"You think?"

"Yeah, but what do I know? I just do this for a living."

Kaia laughs. "Fine. Show me what you got when you're done with Lace."

Hanging out with the club girls ends up being the most fun I've had since I was in school. There's no bonding like beauty bonding. I don't care how much someone is into makeup or hair, everyone wants to look nice, and trusting someone else to help means revealing your insecurities.

I find a half empty bottle of toner in the hair bin and get Lace set up. Then while that's cooking, I wash Kaia's hair and trim the ends. The girls all gather around as I explain how to section off her hair for bangs.

We chat as I work, everyone telling stories about their worst haircuts and dye jobs. I admit to the time I was a teenager and didn't have the patience to do things right and ended up with a gross, washed out copper green color instead of the deep blue I was aiming for.

Oh, and the summer I tried to grow out an undercut I gave myself and couldn't put my hair up without it sticking out like a badly trimmed shrubbery.

"So why aren't you a full stylist yet?" asks Lace, sitting on the sink counter letting her legs swing.

"Because I work at my mom's salon and she never thinks I'm ready. All her clients have been going there for decades and nobody wants a new stylist. Even when I do get to fill in for someone, it's just a bunch of old ladies who need their roots touched up or a wash and a blowout."

"Sounds boring as fuck," Indie says.

The other girls agree.

"That's why I was interviewing at Haunted Ink in the first place. I looked for something that I was qualified for but would be totally different. More exciting. I just got more than I bargained for. I guess you all have more interesting lives."

Lace shrugs. "I ran away from home. Didn't finish high school. This place is fun, and the guys treat us pretty good, but it's not a forever gig. Sluts pretty much never actually end up an old lady. Jewel got really lucky hooking up with Chef right away."

Kaia nods. "I needed a place to hide from my ex for a while. He wouldn't dare come in here. It's usually safe, but I saw you there when that asshole prospect tried to make me blow him. Even if the guys deal with it afterwards, shit still happens sometimes."

"I never liked that guy," Indie says with a frown. "Him and Mad Dog are bad news. I bet they don't get voted in." Lace and Kaia nod.

"Why?" I wash the toner out of Lace's hair and it looks much better already. "You should use a purple shampoo to keep the yellow tint out, but the color is still pretty flat. If we had a slightly darker blonde I could make it look more natural."

"I don't know. There's just a vibe. Being a prospect for the Screaming Eagles is a big deal and they're always acting like they're better than everyone else. Who's Deuce's sponsor?"

"I think it was Cannon," Indie answers.

"The guy who moved out?"

"Yeah."

22

TANK

"I don't fucking like this," I growl, staring at the security screen.

Blade nods. "It's awfully convenient that the most recognizable asshole from Kaylee's description shows up at our fucking gate the day we're meeting with the Giordanos."

I press the intercom button. "What the fuck do you want?"

The scarred biker looks around and shoves his hands in his pockets. "You really want me talking about it out here? I've got shit you'll want to hear."

"What's the catch?"

"Asylum and then safe passage to somewhere way the fuck away from here."

"Reaper. Go get King, Nitro and Kaylee. If you can't find King, get as many fucking officers as you can."

He nods. "On it."

He's already pulling his phone out of his pocket as he runs from the watch post to the clubhouse. I wasn't sure about him at first, but unlike Mad Dog who started out strong and seems to be sliding, Reaper's growing on me.

"Let's bring him in and see what he has to say." Blade presses the button and leans towards the mic. "We can't fucking give that to you on the spot and you know it, but you can come in and say your fucking piece."

The guy doesn't look happy, but he nods. "Fine."

I click the safety off my gun and adjust the holster under my cut to make sure I can get it out fast. Blade taps several spots on his clothes, probably double checking the knives he never leaves behind.

We let him in, and I glare at the fucker until he looks away. He looks like he could belong to an MC, even if he isn't ours. Jeans, motorcycle boots, jean jacket with a leather vest over it. Blue bandanna. Almost like a costume, if you ask me. Just a little too fucking on point. He's built strong, though, and some fucker did a number on his face at some time in his past. Vicious scars cover a good half of it, continuing down his neck, like someone tried to carve his skin off and only half failed to do it.

Reaper comes out of the clubhouse with King, Hero, Wraith, Nitro and Kaylee. She takes one look and stops in her tracks. "It's him," she whispers, pale blue eyes wide and scared.

Members are starting to notice something's up and are casually moving to the opening of the garage to get a view. News is gonna travel fast.

It's tempting to kill this asshole on the spot for scaring our girl, but if things hadn't gone down the way they did, we never would've seen her again after that fucking interview.

"You've got balls showing up here. I'll give you that." King gives him a once over, turns his head and spits on the ground. "Talk."

"I'm fucking dead either way. The others are already gone," he says.

There's a tinge of desperation in his voice, but is it real? I know my mind's already really fucking biased against him. Even if he's telling the truth, he isn't getting a lot of fucking sympathy from us.

Hero, an officer and part of King's family with Emily, shares a dark look with King. "And we should give a fuck because why?"

The guy shakes his head. "Asylum first. I'm not telling you shit until you promise to get me out of this city."

"I don't trust him," Wraith says in a low, deadly voice. "What club are you with?"

"None. I was with the Unwanted before you destroyed them but I saw the writing on the wall and got the fuck out. Been an independent since."

I cross my arms in front of my chest. "That's fucking convenient. We'll just go raise the dead to verify your story."

He scowls at us. "Believe me or don't. Do we have a deal?"

King nods. "Follow us. If your info's good, we'll get you set up out of state, and if not? I won't kill you, but I'll drop you back on the street and let you find a new rock to scramble under."

And then we can track him down and make him pay for giving Kaylee fucking nightmares.

He gives it a moment's thought before he nods. "Yeah. Alright. Deal."

"You got a name?" King asks.

"Scar," he says.

Well that's really fucking unoriginal. I see Deuce and Shrapnel hanging out in the garage, watching. "You two! Put some sheets and shit in the cell. He can make his own bed, just make sure he's got what he needs."

They nod and scramble to follow my order.

Nitro pulls me aside. "I'm going to take Kaylee back to the clubhouse. She doesn't need to see this."

"Do it."

"Don't suppose I could get a beer? Running for my life has me fucking parched," Scar says, leering at Kaylee's ass as she walks away.

Oh, I'm going to kill this asshole if someone doesn't beat me to it.

Blade grabs a beer out of the workshop fridge on the way to the interrogation room in one of the outbuildings. The same one with the cell that Scar will be sleeping in tonight. It's a glorified shed that we use when we don't trust people in the clubhouse.

He sits down, puts his feet on the table and twists the cap off his bottle. "The whole fucking thing was a setup."

King cracks his knuckles. "No shit. If that's your big reveal, get ready to run."

"No, not you, asshole. I mean we were told where to be and who to shoot. The Eagles were supposed to get the blame, but it was an internal fucking matter if you catch my drift."

"The mob?" Wraith asks. "What the fuck would the Giordanos have to gain by that?"

"Well, we weren't exactly privy to their meetings, but I got the feeling not everyone was equally happy to be sucking your dicks. I got paid and I didn't ask questions." Scar shrugs and flashes a lopsided grin.

King stands. "Lock him in."

Scar's leaning back in his chair, and I kick the legs out from under it, landing him on his ass, hard. The beer goes everywhere. "What the fuck, man?"

"Whoops."

The prospects worked fast, already having the cell ready by the time we're out of the room. It's a box room, with nothing but a cot and a pot to piss in, but it will keep him out of the way until we can figure out what to do with him. Wraith pats him down, takes his phone, and shoves Scar through the door, sliding the deadbolt from the outside.

"Do you believe him?" I ask King.

The VP shakes his head. "I believe he knows something, but his story fucking stinks. Tonight's our meeting with the Giordanos. They're expecting something, and we don't have shit to show them. The leads are going nowhere. If Scar's story is true, then we're the ones with some big fucking questions tonight, and either way, I have a feeling Arturo will be very interested in interrogating Scar himself."

23

WRAITH

I pound my fist on the outside of Scar's accommodations. "Put your pencil dick away, we're coming in. Time to earn your keep."

There's no answer.

Nitro slips his hand into his jacket and palms his gun. "It's too fucking quiet. Be ready in case he's planning on jumping us," he says under his breath.

I nod and throw back the deadbolt, staying clear of the door.

The door swings open, and nothing happens. Cautiously, we look and there he is, rolled over on the cot with his back to us like he's got nothing better to fucking do.

"Rise and fucking shine, Miss America!" Tank shouts.

Not even a twitch.

That's when I notice the bright coppery scent of blood and the dark puddle growing under the cot. There's a slow dripping sound as Scar's life slips out onto the floor.

"Fuuuuuck," Nitro says.

I put my hand on his shoulder and there's no response. He rolls over easily, the whole front of his shirt soaked red. A bone deep gash straight across his throat makes the cause of death pretty fucking obvious. "Motherfucker," I groan. "He's still warm."

"Jesus fuck," says Tank, grimacing. "That's disgusting. Do you see a knife? Maybe he offed himself? It's only been a couple hours."

I have a strong stomach, but searching his lifeless, bloody body for a knife I might have missed earlier is a sensation that's going to stick with me. "Nothing."

Nitro crouches to get a better look. "Clean cut, straight across the throat. The door's still locked from the outside. I think he knew his attacker, or at least trusted him."

"Are you saying we have a fucking traitor?" Tank asks.

"What else makes sense?" Nitro stands. "Call King now. Kaylee's with them waiting for the Giordanos. I trust the officers, but they're not fucking handing her over to anyone but us. Whoever took out this asshole was trying to shut him up and we need to find out why. Fuck, what a mess."

I nod, staring down at Scar's glassy lifeless eyes. "Literally. She's our fucking responsibility. Not just because of this, but because she's her. I fucking like how she fits with us."

We haven't talked about what we want with Kaylee, and over a still dripping corpse is a shitty fucking time to bring it up, but I need to know if they're on board or not. I have no fucking intention of dropping her off and not looking back this time around.

Tank nods. "Same."

"She might want to walk away when this is over," Nitro says, staring down at the corpse. "I wouldn't fucking blame her."

"Then we're not doing our job," I say with a grim smile. "Now go grab a bag so we can get this asshole off the grounds. The stink is making me fucking sick."

Ten minutes later, standing in the alley behind the Roost, I pull the bag back from Scar's head. King swears. He'd already been updated, but the body hasn't gotten any prettier looking or smelling since we found it.

Arturo holds his hand in front of his nose with a disgusted look on his face. "This is your update? A dead man and a wild story that implicates us in our own attack? *Cazzo!* You're making it very hard to trust you, King."

"Give me a fucking break. You think I would slice a man's throat just to stall for time? Come inside and watch the video for yourself."

"If you're willing to murder three of my men, then what's one more?"

Back in the meeting room above the bar, we show Arturo and his men the interrogation room footage, where Scar strings us along with hints about there being a rift in the Giordanos that someone is trying to widen. They watch in stony silence, and I spend the whole fucking time trying to figure out who our traitor is and what their end game might be.

Viking scratches at his beard and leans back. "You said yourself that not everyone in the Family is happy about us working together. Can you really say with one hundred fucking percent certainty that this guy was wrong?"

"One of the dead was my fucking nephew, King!" Arturo snaps. He slams his palm into the table so hard the beer bottles jump. "Do you think we have been sitting on our hands for the past week? We've been looking into why our men stopped at that gas station when they did, and there was no good reason. While you tell me to clean my own house, perhaps you want to explain how your informant ended up dead in less than twenty-four hours."

King looks ready to rip someone's head off. "If we wanted to start a war, we would have just done so. What would we gain by all this playing around?"

"If nobody wants a war, then who the fuck benefits?" Tank asks, sounding like he's talking to himself more than anyone else. When we all look his way, he seems surprised. "What?"

"Bring the girl in," King orders. "I think we need to ask more questions."

I go to the room next door where she's waiting with Nitro. "They want to talk to Kaylee."

"Do I have to?" She looks so fucking small and nervous. I hate putting her through this.

"Yeah, baby, but when this is over, we're going somewhere nice. No blood, no torture, just the four of us and white fucking sand."

"Promise?"

"We fucking promise," Nitro swears.

Kaylee takes a deep breath and nods. In the meeting, we sit her down between us with Tank at our backs again, wanting to show both her and everyone else that she's really fucking important.

"Miss Thompson," Arturo starts. "You said there were three men involved in your time with the police. What do you remember about them? I want to hear everything, even if it's something you think you've already told us."

She nods. "Anderson and Harris picked me up at my house. Harris said he was a detective, but I think

Anderson is just a regular police officer. It was actually kinda weird though. They took me to the station downtown, but I didn't talk to anyone else, or sign in or anything. They just kept me in a room by myself and then took me straight to the apartment where you found me."

"When did the third man show up?" King asks.

"Lancer? The next day I think. He said he was with organized crime I think? We didn't exactly sit around and chat about our lives."

I laugh. "Pretty sure he's out of the picture. We didn't stop to check his pulse but he looked ready for the final check-out last we saw him."

King pushes off the table to pace. "I think someone's fucking playing us both and we're letting them do it. The question is, how far does the rot go?"

Arturo doesn't look surprised. Pissed, but not surprised. "We haven't seen significant force from the police in six years. Perhaps they've had time to lick their wounds."

"Or we're on the completely wrong fucking track." I look at Kaylee. "Right now, she's the only one we know who can identify both the people at the shooting, and the cops involved. And they know it. I hate to fucking say it, but we can't take her back to the compound and sit around until this blows up in our faces."

King holds his hand out to Arturo. "What we've said here doesn't leave this room. As far as the Eagles and the Giordanos know, we are still on the verge of war."

It goes unsaid, that if we don't figure shit out, it's the fucking truth.

Arturo hesitates.

Viking speaks up. "Alessa will arrange something with her father to get Kaylee out of the way. The Eagles trust us, and you trust Luca," Viking says. "Is that common ground enough for cooperation? At least until we have more information. We can start shooting at each other then, if necessary." He shrugs like it doesn't matter to him.

After a moment's thought, Arturo nods. "Very well. Luca is Family that I trust. But I don't like this."

"Yeah, none of us do. Then we just need to feed the rumor mill a little." Viking stands up and after a confirming glance at King, throws open the door and screams down the hallway, "If you won't trust us, why the fuck are you even here? Get the fuck out of our territory!" It's loud enough that it's bound to carry to at least a few ears.

With a pained sigh, Arturo clasps King's hand before leaving. "Keep me posted. We're hanging onto a thin thread right now."

King nods. "Same."

Well, at least we're not at fucking war.

Yet.

24

KAYLEE

When Wraith said he had the perfect place to hide me until they arranged a more secure location, I have to admit I didn't expect a bookshop.

"You're lucky I trust Wraith, Tank and Nitro," Faith tells me with just enough acid in her voice to let me know that I'd better tread carefully.

I'm having a hard time reconciling the fact that Eagle-eye's daughter, and a woman who is hooked up with three bikers of her own, is also a cute, nerdy looking bookshop owner. An hour ago I was sitting in a meeting about murder and war, and now I'm sitting in a deep, comfy chair and sipping coffee in a quiet little reading nook. Every time I think I'm starting to figure out the Screaming Eagles, they throw me a curveball.

Or in this case, a curve cookie.

"Do you want another one?" Natalie, Faith's business partner, asks, holding out a little plate full of chocolate chip cookies. I take one gratefully. "It's not that we don't trust you. It's just that with both Eagle-eye and Alpha in jail, things are a little tense."

"I get it." I'd be snippy too, if I thought it might be her fault that my dad and one of my guys were behind bars.

My guys?

It's been such a short time since I met them, so thinking about them like that seems so ridiculous, but it's been so intense. The way they make me feel is unlike anything else I've ever experienced. It's pretty clear they don't mind sharing, and if it wasn't for all the other stuff, I have to admit that the upsides are pretty amazing.

But the 'other stuff' is guns, explosions and death, so… There's a lot to think about.

Faith crosses her arms over her chest and glares at me. I try to look as inoffensive as possible, as abstract as that sounds.

She shakes her head. "You know what? I'm sorry. I know you didn't intend any of this, and I know what it's like to get pulled into biker business when you're just trying to live your life. I'm just nervous and edgy and frustrated and... God, I really miss Alpha and Dad." She puts her weight on the sales counter with both hands, and nearly shakes with frustration. I can't imagine being in her place, with two loved ones behind bars, wrongfully.

"The lawyers say it could happen any time," says Natalie, her tone soothing. "They're just stalling for time, losing papers, not answering phones, stuff like that."

"I know!" Faith seems more frustrated with herself than anything at this point. She draws a sharp breath, then lets it out slowly. "Kaylee, is there anything else we can get you?"

I look around at the shelves. "A book that doesn't involve aliens?"

Natalie's laugh is rich and bright. "Are you sure, because I've got some really good alien romance. Living with three guys is pretty much like staring in a romance novel anyway, so I don't have to fantasize much, but even Animal, Badass and Quickshot can't make their junk spin on command. Or have the little wiggly bits at the end that make you come instantly." She cuts an amused glance to Faith "For some reason, almost all of our books are ménage, but if you want one on one stuff we probably have it."

"Um… ménage sounds good…"

Faith grins. "We have lots of biker romance, too, but maybe you've had enough of that? It's not very realistic, but it's a heck of a lot of fun to read."

"Honestly, I think I'm too nervous to enjoy a book right now, but thanks. Believe it or not, my life was pretty boring right up a few days ago. Can you believe I was wishing for something, *anything* exciting to happen to me? Now I'm on the run from the police, dodging a killer and hoping that I haven't somehow started a war between the Mafia and the Screaming Eagles without even trying."

"Unbelievable," Faith replies dryly. "Let me know when a guy ruling a mall from Santa's throne tries to kill you."

What the heck is her story? Or Natalie's for that matter. Were they as wild as mine, because they don't seem super impressed.

"Can I ask you guys something? Do your guys ever get jealous?"

"What do you mean?" asks Natalie.

"I mean, they have to share you. How do you make sure everyone's happy? Do you schedule time slots? Do you have separate bedrooms, or just share one big bedroom? I've never met guys who'd happily share with one another, never mind three sharing at once. Not that I need to know personally, of course."

Natalie chuckles. "Do you want to?"

I grab another cookie. "No. I mean, I don't think so. They've been so good to me, but eventually this part has to end, right? How do I introduce them to my parents? 'Hi, Mom and Dad, these are the three MC club members that I've fallen in love with.' They would flip." I laugh briefly at the image, but then frown, because I'd happily deal with all of that awkwardness if it meant we all make it out alive and I can hug them again and let them know that I'm safe.

"I think," Faith says as she runs her fingers along the top of the books on the shelf beside us, "that if you end up with bikers, you'll find that there is no one answer. They live every moment from one to the next. What's important to them is the club, and the safety of their families. If they choose you for their old lady, they're yours for life. Just like you're theirs. So if you're going to make that choice, make sure that you're sure. Because they will always be there."

That sounds both amazing and terrifying at the same time.

"Listen." I start to pull myself out of the chair, no matter how comfortable it is. "Maybe it would be better if I just found my own spot to hide. That way nobody would—"

"Sit your ass down, before I knock it right back down into that chair," says Faith in absolutely no uncertain terms. She goes behind the counter and pulls out a handgun, placing it very visibly in front of her. "Now eat your cookies and read a fucking book."

"I just wanted more coffee! I wasn't going anywhere!"

"Damn straight you weren't. Look, I like you, Kaylee. If you're still around, you're welcome to come by with your men for Easter, but right now, you could be the difference between my little girl growing up with all her fathers and grandfather… or not." On cue, a cry comes from a baby monitor I hadn't even noticed on the counter. "Keep an eye on her, Nat. I have to go get Lotte."

Natalie smiles. With blue eyes and long blonde hair, she seems so sweet.

"So how did you end up with your guys?" I ask.

"Oh, they bought me."

Cookie crumbs stick in my throat and I fold over in a coughing fit. "Excuse me? Bought you?"

"Yeah, I was pretty expensive, too." She leans in conspiratorially. "All these books? It doesn't compare to the real thing. Have they done you at the same time yet? Like not in a row, but together?"

If my hands could get as hot as my cheeks, it would boil my coffee. "We haven't—they didn't—it's not like—"

She raises an eyebrow at me.

"No," I squeak.

A dreamy look spreads across her face. "You have so much to look forward to."

25

KAYLEE

I can't see anything, but I hear the car door shut with a loud click behind me. Or maybe it just sounds loud because of the blindfold. "Where are we?"

"Can't tell you that, but we got you," says Tank, his big hand totally engulfing my fingers.

"When can I take this off?"

"Soon. Alessa and Luca arranged for a spot for us. The fewer people who know where it is the better, and that includes you. Only a very short list of members are allowed to know where we are. It's safer for everyone that way." says Wraith. "Once we're inside, it will just be the four of us."

Maybe it's the kinky images Natalie's questions put in my head, but there's something about how he says it that fills me with ideas. The more of the Screaming Eagles old ladies I meet, the more I realize there are a lot of ways to be a badass biker babe. There could be room for someone like me. If they want me around, that is.

"Just us, huh? What are we supposed to do while we wait?"

"Do you have a suggestion?" Tank whispers, making me shiver.

A hand on my back guides me forwards. "Step. That's it," says Nitro, guiding me through a door. I can easily picture the sexy little smirk on his lips. "Imagine the possibilities."

"Together," repeats in my brain, courtesy of Natalie.

"Come on." I let out a little laugh. "We're hiding out. We shouldn't—"

One of them blows a little puff of air over my ear. Nitro or Wraith, I think. It's hard to decide where everyone is when I can't see them. I jerk my head aside, but a strong hand—Tank's?—captures my jaw and holds it still so someone can briefly kiss my lips. Okay, that's nice.

Definitely Tank. I'd know his forcefulness and the hint of sweet from the granola bars he carries everywhere.

"Guys…"

"Ssh," says Wraith. "The situation is fucked but we're safe here, so let's take advantage of it. I don't want to waste the opportunity."

He kisses me. I know it's him, partly because of the way his beard tickles, but I think I'd know even without it. All three of them have kissed me enough that it's a fun game to guess who is who.

With my sight gone, I'm acutely aware of everything. When I concentrate, I can hear the subtle sound of the guys breathing, and the rustle of cloth and leather as they move around me. Just before Nitro places his lips on mine, I recognize his unique leather and musk scent. God, I think I could pick them out in a lineup by their scents alone. He pulls down the zipper of my hoodie, slipping it off my shoulders.

"Cold!" I hiss as chilly fingers slip under my tank top from behind. It's warm in here, but their rough and calloused fingers haven't caught up with that yet. I think it's Wraith. Yeah, definitely, because I can feel his beard brush over my neck as he kisses my collarbone.

From in front, one of the others pulls up the hem of my shirt until I raise my arms to let him remove it. There's a deep hum of appreciation. Tank probably?

As soon as the shirt's gone, the stretchy bralette Lace gave me follows, removed while my arms are still up. Different hands slide around my sides to cup my newly freed breasts, his touch skilled and gentle. He toys with them, working me up with dexterous fingers that know exactly what to do. Our time together has been intense but not that long, but the guys are so good at learning what gets me going. I moan, letting them know they're on the right track.

The button on my jeans is popped open and my pants go down, taking my panties with them. "You're in a rush," I tease, and I have to admit that as their hands explore my naked body, squeezing and caressing me, I am too. They steady me so I don't fall as Tank sweeps me off my feet and the rest of my clothes drop away. When he puts me down, my toes sink into thick, soft carpeting.

Someone pinches my butt, making me squeak and take a surprised step forwards. "Watch it!" I yelp.

"Oh, I was," comes Nitro's husky reply. "I can't take my fucking eyes off it when you're around."

A hot and wet mouth settles around my nipple. I gasp, my hands coming up automatically. I find his hair and bury my hands in the long strands so I can guide him. It's Wraith, obviously. He's the only one with hair this gorgeous. I love how it feels running through my fingers.

Someone else kisses and nibbles my belly and waist, in no pattern that I can pick out, so every new touch is a little surprise. And hands, everywhere. Hips, thighs, sides, breasts, across my throat, through my hair. When I can't see who's who, it's like there are a thousand men in here with me, not just three.

I feel so exposed. Am I the only one naked? There's a strange intensity in not being able to see anything. It's a little scary too, but I trust the guys. Nothing's going to hurt me. If I panic and try to tear the blindfold off, I don't even think they'll stop me anymore, but it's hot too, and they aren't the only ones that want to put the outside world on hold for a minute and play a little.

"Come," orders Tank, and the guys release me so I can move forwards, though they hold my arms on either side so I don't fall if I trip. "Where are you taking me?"

Hands cup my breasts to stop me. Here, I guess. I'm still on the soft carpet, so it wasn't far.

"On your knees, sweetheart," Wraith hisses into my ear. A hand on my shoulder urges me down.

Licking my lips, I obey. Then I'm pushed forward and my hands guided until I'm touching bare skin. I explore him and figure out pretty quickly that I'm kneeling between someone's bare legs. Someone who's sitting down. Running my hands up his thighs, I find a proud cock straining upwards, and wrap my fingers around it. It's thick, but they all are.

Big, strong fingers thread themselves through my hair and pull me forwards. Whoever it is, he's sitting down so I lean my weight on him and open my mouth.

Tank.

They're all big, but he's in a class all of his own. I swirl my tongue around the head and he proves it's him when he groans. "Oh, fuck, Kaylee, that's good. Suck me, Trigger." He's already dripping precum, and I savor the salty flavor of him coating my tongue.

A hand settles on my ass, while another presses on the insides of my thighs, urging my knees further apart. I moan as a slippery finger slides easily into my pussy. Am I really that wet already? I arch my back, rocking against the hand and taking him deeper. It feels nice, a sexy warmup for what I'm sure is coming next.

Then it's gone, and I moan around Tank's cock and wiggle my butt. I'm rewarded by one, and then a second finger, sliding back into me. The way they're moving—is it both Nitro and Wraith with a finger each? I can't tell, and it frustrates me, but I don't want to know for sure, either. God, it feels good. Maybe there's something to this sensory deprivation thing. I never know what's coming next. And it's distracting. I get a little tap on my head, reminding me to get back to work. Happily.

Something wet and slippery drips onto my butt. I draw a little breath through my nose at the sudden coolness, but it's quickly soothed by warm fingers rubbing it into my skin, going closer and closer to… really?

While two fingers are sliding in and out of my dripping pussy, a third scoops up the slickness and spreads it around my back entrance instead. With a little bit of pressure, the tip pushes in. Not far, just a little. Just exploring, testing me. Probably waiting to see if I push it away or beg for more.

"Give me a second," I say in a shaky voice. "I've never done this before."

"Say the word and it stops." It's Nitro.

I nod, moving my hips carefully to explore the sensation on my own terms. It doesn't hurt, not with all that lube, but I feel incredibly full, with fingers both front and back, never mind the big cock hovering right in front of my face. With a little nod, I signal I'm willing to keep going. The two fingers in my pussy stretch me open as the one in my ass teases me with new sensations. I lean forward and suck Tank's cock back into my mouth, reveling in the feel of so much happening at the same time.

Is this what Natalie meant by all together? Oh God.

I know it's theoretically possible, but really? A way to be with all of them at the same time?

My thighs tremble, their sinful touches giving me goosebumps. Every time I think I've learned the rhythm, things get so overwhelming that I have to pull off Tank to get my breathing back under control.

And then suddenly, I'm empty.

"Guys? What—"

I shriek in surprise before I laugh as they pick me up. I'm carried a short way before they lower me again. Something thick and hard nudges against my pussy. Like a ragdoll, I'm impaled slowly onto a massive cock that I know has to be Tank. Inch by amazing, delicious inch stretches me open, making me glad all the lube made it down front too. He's a lot.

"Ooooooh," I gasp. My pulse races, thundering when I'm finally settled in his lap, all that dick inside me. God, it feels good.

I brace my palms against his muscular chest, then move my hips, just a little bit up and a little bit down. Big hands grip my ass, and then the next time

I rise, he helps me right up, and when I come back down, he groans too as I find just a little more of him to take.

A hand presses between my shoulder blades, directing me forwards. Now what? I lean forwards, resting my head into the hollow between Tank's neck and shoulder. More slick liquid is poured over my ass before the finger returns, reminding me what it's like to be filled both front and back, but this time, there's a real cock in my pussy. A shiver raises goosebumps all over my body. It's a stretch, but it feels amazing.

"You like that, baby?" Wraith says in a low growl. Is it his finger? Nitro's? I don't know. "Are you ready for more?"

A second finger joins the first in my ass, and I find myself moving back and forth, fucking both Tank and the fingers together. Stretched, in a dirty, erotic, sinful way that old Kaylee would've thought was just the realm of twisted fantasy and naughty romance novels, but now is becoming decadent reality.

I moan into Tank's neck, clinging to him and letting the sensations fill me, overwhelm me. And then pause as the fingers are taken away. "Don't have to stop," I moan.

"Oh, we're not," says Nitro, and then there's a new pressure there, along with new squirts of lube.

I groan, deep in my throat, as a cock presses against my ass. "Slow. Go slow," I get out between pants. Tank keeps still so I only have to worry about one cock at once. Like his monster somehow isn't enough.

"We're not gonna hurt you, sweetheart."

It starts with little thrusts, slow and careful, just easing a little more inside with each one, and constantly adding more lube every time I so much as wince. Amazingly, while I'm feeling fuller and fuller, and more and more stretched around them, it doesn't hurt. A little ache, a stretch well beyond what I'm used to, but it's nothing compared to how it excites me. I'm being sandwiched between two of my three favorite men as they claim me in a way I wouldn't have thought possible.

When he finally bottoms out, I'm at my limit, but I've done it. I've taken two of them. Two huge cocks, at once. Holy freaking cow. "Just… wait a little. Let me adjust—get used to it."

"Of course." He shifts just a little as he wraps his fingers in my hair and tugs just a little.

Tank slides his hands from my hips, and up my sides until he can cup my breasts from the front. His thumbs stroke my rock hard nipples. My whole body tenses. I swear I can feel both of their pulses through their cocks, one in front, one in back. I swallow hard, building some courage.

And then I try to move.

I ease forward, and now that I'm getting used to the fullness, the feeling of both of them sliding out feels strange. Like something's missing. I don't go far, before I push my ass back, taking them right back to their roots. God, there it is, that fullness again.

"Jesus fuck," Wraith whispers, giving away that it's him fucking me alongside Tank. His hands go tight around my waist, and I can feel the tension in his grip as he fights to keep from letting loose. It's got to be as excruciating for him as it is for me. He hisses hoarsely, his voice dark and smoldering with passion, "Fuck, Kaylee, stop me now, or I'm not going to be fucking able to."

"I didn't ask you to," I push back at him, and that's all he needs. Wraith's grip tightens, and he starts to fuck.

My breath is pushed right out of me in a guttural moan. I don't even have words to describe how crazy it feels. So freaking sexy.

And then Tank starts to move beneath me, his hands moving back to my thighs and gripping them as he thrusts upwards. I dig my fingernails into Tank's shoulders and cry out. Even behind the blindfold, my eyes squeeze shut, and bright shapes dance over the insides of my eyelids.

Wraith's strokes are steady, fast, just refusing to stop, while Tank's technique is slower, more languid, a little less predictable. Sometimes one's pulling out while the other thrusts in, but other times, they both drive in at once, and that's when I have to hold on just a little extra, digging my nails into Tank's chest. I ache, but it's so good. I feel so stretched, but so connected to them, like we're all one big oversexed organism that can't stop.

They're taking me, using me for their own needs, as their steadily thrusting cocks drive me closer and closer to that magical moment where I already know I'm going to completely fall apart.

They're so big, and I don't just mean their thick cocks, but all of them. I'm a very average sized woman, but with them I feel so tiny. "Wh—what do we look like?"

Nitro lets out a harsh laugh. "It's fucking obscene how sexy you look taking them. I'm going to have to get my dick in your mouth before I come all over the sheets like a fucking kid just from watching."

"So do it."

"Shit, there's the badass, I knew she was hiding in there somewhere." Nitro's fingers slide into my hair and make a fist so they can control me, and then the hot, smooth tip of his cock is pressed against my lips.

My cheeks cave as I suck Nitro in, making my lips as tight around him as I can. It's hard to control the speed or depth while I'm getting rocked from behind, and I drive just a little too far. He bumps against the back of my throat, making my stomach clench. All three of them groan at once.

"So fucking good, Trigger," Tank moans.

I'm actually doing it. Pleasing all of them at once, and it's not just for their pleasure. I'm one big nerve ending, tingling all over, from my head to my toes. It's rough and primal in the best way. I don't care if Nitro pushes a little too hard sometimes, or if I cry out when both Tank and Wraith drive in at once. I bet my nails are drawing blood from Tank's chest. This wildness, this... it's what I've been looking for. Wanting. Needing, even if I didn't know it. That chance to break away from everything that's boring old me, and to just be wild.

They're giving it to me, and it's only because I know I'm safe in their hands that I can really let go. The four of us together is almost like a religious experience.

"Fuck, I'm close," groans Nitro. My scalp tingles as his fingers twist and his thrusts get faster and faster.

Wraith's hands tighten on my hips, and Tank's hips are pistoning off the bed as he drives up into me. A hand—probably Tank?—slips between us and brushes my clit. I lunge forward with a groan, taking Nitro deeper than before.

He bites out a curse, and then thick cum spills over my tongue and down my throat. I swallow as fast as

I can. You'd think it'd been months since the last time, even though I know for a fact that's not true. But he's just the start of the chain reaction, and his pleasure lights the match to set me off like fireworks.

I explode around my guys, my whole body going tight as a bow. I've never come this hard in my whole life. Head spinning and toes curling, stars float in the darkness in front of my eyes. I scream as I come, the sound loud in my ears and scratching my throat.

"Fuck," groans Tank and Wraith at the same time, and they swell impossibly big as they come with me. Stretched tight around both of them, it's like I can feel every vein, every contour of their amazing cocks as they finish together. For a long moment, time stands still, and then we collapse together, me against Tank's chest and Wraith against my back, all of us breathing like we just finished a marathon.

"Oh my God," I whisper, my pulse thundering in my head.

Wraith pulls out slowly and carefully before Tank gently rolls me off him. Being empty so suddenly is like walking outside and getting hit by a strong winter wind that goes straight through your clothes.

I shiver and someone big and naked wraps around me from behind, enveloping me in a hug that keeps my naked body cozy and warm.

"Close your eyes," Tank says, giving me a moment to do so before he pulls off the blindfold.

I didn't realize how dark it was under there until the light hits my eyelids. I ease my eyes open slowly, adjusting to the change.

The first things I see are Nitro's deep green eyes. "Fuck, baby, that was hot. You okay?"

I snuggle into Tank. "Yeah. But wow, that was intense. If the bad guys show up, you'll have to carry me."

Wraith emerges from a bathroom after shutting off the sink. "Good, that means we're doing our job."

Tank and Nitro chuckle, like there's a joke there I'm missing.

I can't bring myself to ask. As I relax, I look around to see where we are. The windows are tall and narrow, and covered by blinds. A lot of small details make it feel fancy. We're recovering on a massive four post bed. Fancy paintings hang on the walls, and there's a crystal light fixture above us. I guess if we're going to hide out somewhere, it's a bonus that it's nice.

"Come on, princess. There's a hot tub if you want to soak and relax."

Oh yeah, this is the kind of protective custody I could get used to.

26

KING

Eagle-eye returns like fucking royalty, and I for one am fucking thrilled to turn over the crown.

As the van with our men pulls into the courtyard in front of the clubhouse, every member of the club is out to welcome them home. Cheers echo off the walls as the door opens and the fucking man himself steps out, looking around with that piercing gray eye.

Thank fuck the lawyers finally came through. Bail made the club war chest bleed, but it was fucking worth it to get him, Alpha and Beast back where they belong. There's a very good chance that one of the faces in this crowd is a fucking traitor. It's time to take control of the situation again.

"Dad!" Faith yells, handing Charlotte over to Blade and running towards her father.

She's going to have to work on her sprint, because Jupiter launches himself out of the clubhouse like he hasn't seen the old man for fucking years. Eagle-eye laughs, bending to scratch Jupe's stomach with both hands as the dog rolls around barking like a maniac. But when Faith and Miriam get to him, he stands and wraps his arms around them, pulling them close and whispering to the crying women.

Faith nods, breaking away. Eagle-eye kisses Miriam fucking senseless, earning another round of cheering. Not a single fucker in the yard would say shit about a man just out of prison showing his fucking family he cares.

"It's good to have him back," Emily says, her arm tight around my waist. "I've never seen Mom like this. She was a wreck. I don't think she ever loved my father like she does Eagle-eye. Not that I blame her, but I had a real hard time seeing her with Eagle-eye in the beginning."

"Yeah, they're good for each other. She settles him."

Then Alpha steps out, and it's Faith's turn to get kissed senseless. Behind her, Ripper and Blade stand proud, welcoming their brother back. Strike Team Motherfucking Alpha is whole again.

Fuck, I try to imagine what it'd be like to be separated for that long from Em and the others, trapped behind bars in some shithole prison. Even the thought makes me furious. Never mind what it would do to the kids. Faith and the boys' little girl is still a fucking baby. She won't remember Alpha being missing for a week, but ours are old enough to demand answers and still too fucking young to understand.

Beast's only a prospect and doesn't have a woman, but he gets a round of cheers from the boys anyway. His head's bandaged, and his face still looks raw even if it's healing, but at least he's fucking standing. Razor, his sponsor, claps him on the back, and he looks a little embarrassed.

Eagle-eye's keen gaze finds me. He disengages from Miriam, who wipes her arm across her eyes, but stands aside. She's been here long enough to know when club business comes first. We're all gonna steer clear of the common room tonight though. Sound fucking carries from his rooms on the second floor and I don't need to hear that shit.

"King," he says, extending his hand.

I take it, clasping forearms and pulling him into a fucking bear hug. "Good to have you back, Prez."

"Good to be here. I'd love to shoot the shit and fucking relax but we need to have a sit down. Now."

I nod.

"Get the officers together. My office. There's shit coming down the pipeline."

Fucking perfect. That's exactly what we need.

Fifteen minutes later, we're all piled into his office above the common room. I've caught him up on our end of things, including the Scar getting his throat slit, the second meeting with the Giordanos, and Wraith, Tank and Nitro being in hiding with Kaylee.

"They're fucking her, aren't they?" he asks.

I laugh. Damn, I missed this bastard. "You want me to say no?"

"That's a yes." He shakes his head. "Doesn't even surprise me anymore. I could tell they were already thinking with their dicks when I talked to her that first night. So long as they do their fucking jobs, we have bigger problems."

"No shit. So what's your news?"

He looks up, his face hard. "Hawthorne's out."

"The fuck?"

"What do you mean, he's out?" Viking growls. Even in February, he's only wearing a vest with nothing under. I swear his parents were fucking polar bears. He tugs the braids in his beard, his icy blues focused and alert. "Why haven't we heard anything?"

"Officially? He's a high interest target and they want to keep it out of the press. He's been playing good fucking prisoner long enough that with the right amount of money, the system that put him away is the same one that's sucking his dick first chance it gets. If anyone's thinking, 'Huh, could this possibly have anything to do with all the shit going on?' then congratulations. You can see the obvious." Eagle-eye crosses his arms over his chest and glares around the room. "If he isn't already on the streets, he will be soon. The only reason I even know is because that fucker isn't the only one with contacts behind the prison walls. A silver lining to being in that hellhole was having a few strings to pull."

"Too bad you weren't cell mates, huh?" jokes Wild Child. He grins at the thought. He's switched out the purple streak in his hair for green this week.

"They would've fucking had me on murder," growls Eagle-eye. "If I could make sure that fucker never even crossed Miriam or Emily's minds again, I'd take the opportunity in a fucking heartbeat."

Fuck yeah. Hawthorne might technically be my father-in-law, but if I was in a cell with him, I'd do the same fucking thing.

That fucker never gave a shit about the women in his care. He tried to have Emily killed—his own fucking daughter—never mind the fact that he thought knocking her around was good fucking parenting. He's the kind of man that inspires you to be better than him, and that's the best fucking thing I can say about him.

"So let me see if I follow." Ripper scratches his chin with his good hand. His wrist stump on the other arm doesn't have anything attached right now. "A bunch of unknown fuckers gun down some mob goons. The cops kidnapped that girl to set us up and use it as an excuse to get you out of the way. The Giordanos might be behind it, but that's only based on the word of one of the gun fuckers, and someone in the club shut him up good so we can't even fucking press the truth out of him. Oh, and Hawthorne's up our asses again. I know he's a manipulative shit with money and connections, but that seems like a lot of fucking work. It's not like we don't have other enemies."

"Fair." Eagle-eye nods. "But there's one more piece of the puzzle that points in his direction."

"And that is?"

"The detective Kaylee told you about? Harris? He used to be on Hawthorne's staff. He got punched straight back to beat cop when his boss went away, but he was on that fucking task force that Hawthorne tried to use to take us out six years ago."

"Thor's balls," says Viking with a laugh. "Only you would go into the fucking slammer and come out with more dirt than when you went in."

Eagle-eye grunts. "Never fucking underestimate the power of gossip when people don't have shit else to trade in, boys. There's a lot of fucking balls in motion right now, and I'll be honest. I don't know how they all fit together, but our number one priority right now is to stop the bleed. We need to find the fucking traitor."

"Yeah, I think—"

Someone hammers on the door like they're trying to break it down. "Trouble!" Sounds like Bear. I'm surprised the door's fucking holding, to be honest. I let him in.

He looks ready to claw someone's face. "Luca just called Alessa. They have Kaylee stashed at her old apartment, and news just came through that the police are mobilizing. I don't know how they fucking found out this fast, but we need to get them moved."

"Motherfucker! When I find out who the fuck it is, Jupiter and King are going to be shitting his fingers for a week."

Wild Child snickers. "I didn't know you liked finger food."

I smack the back of his head. "Let's go. They're gonna need support."

The guys pause, looking between me and Eagle-eye, but Prez nods. "You heard what he said. Every single fucking member needs to be accounted for. Anyone who gives you shit? Assume they can't be trusted. I'd rather take the traitor with us than leave him here with our fucking women and kids."

We pound down the stairs and start rounding up the boys. Everyone from blooded members old as Snake to the freshest kids. We need all the manpower we can get. I grab the nearest prospect, Mad Dog. "We need you guys on bikes, pronto. Stick with your group. It's time to show us you what you've got."

He snaps a nod and runs for his bike.

Shrapnel's already straddling his ride, ready to go. Deuce is still getting his shit together. Beast gets a pass for his injury and he was in fucking jail with Eagle-eye when Scar was killed. "Where the fuck is Reaper?"

"Coming!" He comes running out of the garage, rolling his bike with him.

"Where are we going?" asks Mad Dog as he settles into the saddle. "What the fuck's going on?"

"Just keep up with the formation. Shit's gonna get hot and we don't need a repeat of the last fuck up." I wait impatiently for Deuce and Mad Dog.

"Do I have time to fuel up? Was gonna fill later today." Shrapnel sounds embarrassed for being caught unprepared.

Deuce rolls up and looks over Shrapnel's shoulder. "You're good."

Something about his answer itches my brain. "What do you mean?"

His eyes go wide for a split second before he schools his reaction. "Huh? He's got half a tank. City's not that fucking big."

"You think they're in the city? Why?" I wave a hand, capturing Wild Child and Hero's attention, as they're right here, getting ready to ride with me.

"It just makes sense. You don't think that I—" Suddenly, he kicks his bike into action. I get a grip on his jacket, but it slips as he revs and sets a course straight for the open gate.

"Stop that motherfucker!" Members throw themselves out of the way to keep from being run down. I draw, but there's a lot of fucking people in front of the clubhouse and if I miss—fuck!

Except Bear's right there, and he's fast when he needs to be. Just as Deuce is flying by, instead of jumping aside, he extends an arm thick as my fucking thigh. Deuce doesn't have a chance. With a grunt loud enough that I hear it from here, Deuce drops off the back of his bike and onto the pavement. Then Bear's on top of him, pinning him down.

"Throw him in the pit. I don't care if he's sleeping in Scar's blood. Wild Child? I fucking hate to leave you behind, but I need someone I know I can trust. Take Sledge and Thunder and lock down the rest of the prospects. We don't have time to play detective. Find out who Deuce's sponsor is and start asking questions. If anyone causes shit? Gun'em down."

"Understood," Wild Child says with a nod, all business. When the shit hits the fan, even he can be serious.

The last one out of the clubhouse is Eagle-eye, on the phone. "I don't care what you're in the fucking middle of. You need to get the hell out. Now!" He jams the phone into his pocket and gets onto his classic machine.

"Screaming Eagles," he roars in his gravelly bass. "Roll the fuck out!"

27

KAYLEE

I flop my arm over the side of the sofa and rest my chin on my shoulder. "I miss my phone. Don't get me wrong, this is heaven compared to last time I was in protective custody, but I'm bored." Nitro raises his hand, but before he says anything, I cut him off. "Not yet. At this rate I'll never be able to walk out of here when we're finally able to leave."

"Mission successful," Wraith says with a quiet laugh. The other two chuckle.

Tank wraps a big, protective arm around me and pulls me close. "Truth or dare," he says suddenly.

"Seriously? I haven't played that in ages." I shift a little to get more comfortable. "Who starts? No, wait.

I know you guys. No sex dares for at least... three rounds."

Wraith laughs. "Fine. I'm game."

"Only three rounds before the fun stuff? Okay. Let's do it." Nitro grabs a couple of fancy import beers from the fridge and a sparkling water for me. He passes them out and drops into a chair, putting his feet up on the fancy glass coffee table. I think the base is actually gold plated. It just seems impractical in all sorts of ways. And Alessa lived with Izzy here when she was a baby? Maybe they put new furniture in after she moved out.

"I'll start," Wraith says with a smirk. "Kaylee, truth or dare?"

"Um... truth."

"Which one of us is the best looking and why is it me?" he asks as he leans back in the chair and winks.

"No! I'm not going to answer questions that compare you guys. That shouldn't be allowed." I stick my tongue out at him. "Ask real stuff. We should actually get to know each other, right?"

Tank holds up a hand. "I'm with her on this one. No causing bad blood, and it's no fun if she's just getting set up the whole time."

"Fine." Wraith leans in. "Why did you kiss me when we dropped you off the first night?"

My cheeks flare. He remembers that? "You were the one I rode with, okay? And I just thought… You guys were the sexiest men I'd ever seen and I thought I'd never get another chance. So I took it."

"Shit, I should've moved faster and gotten you behind me," Tank says with a laugh.

"My turn. And I'm going to take every other turn, because you guys already know each other. It'd be three on one."

Nitro squeezes into the couch next to me, on the opposite side from Tank. It's a little bigger than a loveseat, which means it's getting cozy. "I thought you liked three on one. It didn't seem to bother you last night."

"Moving on! Nitro, truth or dare?"

He considers it. "Truth."

"What's the stupidest thing you guys have ever done together?"

"Oh fuck." Wraith looks at the ceiling while he scratches his beard thoughtfully.

After what feels like an awful long time without getting an answer, I get impatient. "What? Avoiding the question?"

Nitro shakes his head. "Nah, but I've known these assholes for a while and… there's a lot to fucking choose from."

"The fence," Wraith suggests.

"Shit, I forgot about that. You're right." Nitro laughs. "About three years ago—three? Think so—we were on a ride out in the sticks. Someone was running a chop shop in a barn or some shit? Doesn't matter. Anyway, we pulled over to piss in the middle of fucking nowhere. Dudes being dudes, we aim for the nearest target which happened to be a wire fence…"

"Oh no." I put my hands to my mouth, pretty sure I know what's coming.

"Fucking yes. The damn thing was electric. We put the screaming in Screaming Eagles that night."

Tank winces and squeezes his thighs together like he can still feel it. "Fuck, that hurt."

I try to be sympathetic, I really do, but… the image of the three of them, God—I should feel bad.

"Glad you take so much enjoyment in our pain," comments Wraith dryly.

"Well, it doesn't seem to have done any lasting damage," I manage to get out in spite of laughing my head off.

"Truth or dare, Kaylee," says Tank, giving my thigh a firm squeeze. "Before you fucking pass out."

I pause long enough to draw a deep breath to center myself. A snort escapes me and I almost lose it again, but then I hold up a hand. "Okay. I'm good. I'm good. Truth."

"What's the wildest thing you've ever done?" Tank grins in anticipation.

I blink at him. "Are you kidding?"

"Nope. I want details."

"Well, I hate to disappoint you, but all the wildest things I've done have happened since I met you. Saved by bikers from an exploding gas station, kidnapped by cops, had sex with three guys at once… I mean, nothing in my life has even come close to that. I'm a cosmetologist who lives in my parents' house. Excitement used to be finding an onion ring in my fries."

Tank scowls. "Shit, let me think of a different question."

"No! You asked and I answered. Tank, truth or dare?"

He cocks his head and thinks about it. "Truth. I like this getting to know each other shit."

"Okay, how did you end up in the Screaming Eagles? Actually. Do you guys mind if I ask you all? I know it's not exactly how the game works."

Tank chuckles. "Nah, it's fine"

"I grew up in the life," says Wraith, surprising me a little by going first. "Dad was a Night Roller and Mom was his old lady. He kept our home away from the clubhouse, but I saw a lot of shit."

"So you started out in another club?"

He shakes his head. "Nah, I didn't join anywhere until the Eagles. Dad struggled with a lot of shit.

Alcohol, drugs, a mean fucking temper. He wasn't the worst, but he wasn't fucking father of the year either. He's not around anymore, and that wasn't a legacy I was interested in continuing. My mother was an amazing fucking painter. She wanted me to go to art school, but all the traditional shit isn't for me. I got into tattooing and never looked back."

"But you're in a club now. What changed?"

"I was a broke ass kid living in South Side, so it was hard to not notice the club. They seemed to be doing good for the neighborhood, but I wasn't interested in signing up. Eagles kept coming to my tattoo studio to get their ink. They noticed I rode so we had common ground and got friendly. I found out Eagle-eye had noticed my work and was keeping an eye on the studio. That's how I got to know these two jokers." He gestures. "The Screaming Eagles reminded me of the best of what I had growing up, without nearly as much of the shit I ran away from. Sure, we've got our fingers in some dirty pies, but none of the worst shit, and probably not as much as people think now that the legit businesses are up and running. I respected the bar Eagle-eye set, so when he asked if I was interested, I said hell yeah."

"That's… that's more reasonable than I expected. To be honest, I was just assuming it was a rough childhood and the only way out was a life of crime or something."

"Oh, that's me," says Tank, raising a hand. "I grew up shit poor and I was always big, even when I was small." He laughs. "School didn't sit well with me. Kids are cruel when you're different, and when I had four to six inches on most of them, I was a pretty big fucking target. I could handle 'em one on one, but when they worked together, I couldn't do shit about it. My folks were working two jobs each. They couldn't pick up and move because their kid was having a hard time at school. I'm not fucking proud of it, but I got cornered one day in high-school and just fucking lost it. I put two guys in the hospital. I dropped out before they could kick my ass to the curb."

I wrap my arms around him, at least as far as they get, and squeeze him as hard as I can. Tank is one of the sweetest people I've ever met, but I can just imagine him with his back against the wall and forced to do what he had to.

He puts his arm around me again and pulls me closer. "Anyway, all I've really got to bring to the table is my size, so that's what I used. Started fighting in an underground ring, the rougher the better. You remember the guy who was working the bar the night we first talked? That was Badass. He fought in the same circuit, though he'd been there a while. That's probably why Eagle-eye started keeping his eye on it. One day after a fight, he asked if I wanted to do anything with my life. Offered me a chance to belong somewhere. Best thing that's ever happened to me."

I look at Nitro.

"Wish I had a sob story too so I could have you wrapped around me like that, but nah. You know my history. I'm just another ex-soldier who couldn't hack it when I came home." He puts his hand on my arm and slowly strokes the bare skin with his fingertips. It's not directly sexy, but it definitely reminds me of what it's like to have skin on skin contact with him and the others.

"Yeah, but you didn't tell me how you actually joined. Eagle-eye doesn't hang around recruiting veterans too, does he?"

"Nah, not that I know of. We tend to find him. I had a good time in the Army, mostly blowing shit up, but eventually I knew I needed to either get out or get used to the idea that I was there for good. I wanted a change so I went home and civilian life nearly bored me right back in. The only thing I really enjoyed was riding and fucking up. I was headed down a really shitty path when I met Eagle-eye and a couple of the old timers at a bar. It was like…" Nitro makes everything sound like a joke, but I can tell there's a lot more behind the words. "He saw me drowning and tossed me a lifeline."

Nitro leans in to give my ear a little nibble. His voice is seductive. "So now you've gotten three truths for the price of one. It's our turn. Dare ya to take a dare."

"I don't think it's how this works."

"You broke the rules first," he says, his voice darkening just a little, adding a hint of smolder. "My throat's sore from talking. Maybe there's something else we can do. Something more physical."

There's a tingle in my stomach that's threatening to become something more. So maybe I'll play along. "Okay, I'll do a dare."

"Been waiting for that," says Nitro, rubbing his hands together, and suddenly I wonder how much trouble I'm in.

28

KAYLEE

"I dare you to give me a lap dance," says Nitro in a sexy voice with a twinkle in his eye. "I wanna see exactly how hard you can make me."

I blink. That escalated quickly. "Lap dance? I've never—I mean, I have no idea how." That sounds so lame, but it's the truth. The only thing I know about lap dances is from TV and movies. And not even the really spicy kind.

"First you need music." Wraith does something on his phone and brings up a song with a steady, thumping beat on the TV, using it as a speaker. Of course the apartment has a fancy sound system too. There must be a bass speaker under the couch, since the whole thing starts vibrating in time with the music. "Just do your best," he says, already adjusting himself in his jeans. "It's about having fun, not paying rent. You're gonna be fucking sexy, no matter what you do."

I haven't danced since they made us learn to square dance in middle school gym. They have no idea how freaking unsexy I can look. "I'm going to look dumb."

"You're gonna look fucking fantastic," says Tank, with so much sincerity that I almost believe him. "You already do. Anything else you do'll only make it better."

"There's no touching in a lap dance, right? Hands at your sides." I'm pretty sure I remember that from the movies.

"You'll be begging me to use them soon enough," Nitro says with a cocky smirk, shoving Tank over to make more room around him on the couch.

He's probably right, but I won't give him the satisfaction of agreeing. "You wish. Sit back and keep your hands to yourself." And then I start to move to the music.

Square dancing is out, I'm not that lame. I spin away, putting my back to him. Weaving my butt in time with the music, I pull my hair up to the top of my head and get my shoulders into it. That's sexy right?

"My lap's over here, princess," he reminds me, patting his thighs.

"I'm coming, I'm coming."

"Not yet, but we'll get there," promises Tank.

Guess I walked right into that one. I close my eyes and just start moving to the music as I back towards him. Nitro has his legs together to give me room to move, but it's still a lot to straddle. "Okay, I'm going to do my best, okay?"

"I'm loving the effort, baby." He puts his hands behind his head and leans back.

I put a little more sway in my hips and shuffle back until I feel his chest behind me. Then I let myself go lower, drawing a little surprised breath when I feel he's already getting hard, the length of him easily noticeable even through his jeans.

"Is this enough for the dare? Does it get any harder than that? Because you're pretty hard." I press harder against him, and take distinct pleasure in hearing him groan. Then I start a steady, figure eight with my hips, grinding over his cock. "It's hard to miss it, it's right there."

He puts his hands on my hips and it takes me a second to remember we're still playing a game. "No hands!"

Nitro leans close to whisper in my ear, "You should've been more specific, baby."

"What? Oh!"

Hands at his sides, Nitro shows off his strength by lifting his hips while still sitting, meeting my grinding with a steady push of his own. I moan in spite of myself.

This isn't awkward teenage dry humping in the back of a car, it's hot, dirty and amazing. His jeans are rough against the softness of my pajama bottoms. I try to keep my whimpers quiet, but I'm not fooling anyone. He's not the only one who's getting all built up from this. Maybe I'll allow some touching after all.

"Fuck, you win," he says, grabbing my hips and pushing me to my feet.

"What? Didn't you like it?" I look back over my shoulder. He's about to bust right out of his jeans. My hips are still swaying a little to the music, so I exaggerate that for him. "Was I doing too good of a job?"

"Fuck, your ass is built for sin, just like the rest of you. Someone else." He adjusts himself, but it still looks uncomfortable.

"Is it my turn now?"

"I think the game might be over, sweetheart," says Wraith, his hand stroking the outside of his jeans.

"You don't even know what my dare is." I wanted to be a little wilder, right? Well, I'll show them wild. "I dare all of you to stroke yourselves for me. Show me what you've got. If I have to get you guys hard, it's only fair I get to see the result."

Apparently it's a perfectly acceptable dare, because suddenly I'm surrounded by three half naked men. The music plays as one by one, they wrap their fists around their eager cocks and watch me hungrily. I'm not sure this game is going to last much longer, and I'm not even sure they will be the first to break.

"Strip," orders Wraith hoarsely. "Keep dancing and strip for us. Show us how fucking beautiful you are."

"I'm not that—"

"You fucking are, Kaylee. I dare you to look me in the eye and tell me we don't know beauty when we see it. Strip." Wraith's words slide through me like a knife through hot butter, leaving me absolutely dripping.

I start moving again, taking little steps and swaying around the middle of the room. Everywhere I turn, there's a rock hard cock pointing my way. Then I peel up my top.

"Fuck yeah," growls Nitro as I throw the shirt away, dancing in just my pajama pants.

Normally, I would feel silly, but they look at me like I'm the only thing in the world that matters. It makes me feel wanted. Sexy. I cup my breasts as I dance past them. "Like this?"

"Everything," snarls Tank. He's stroking himself slowly, almost not at all, like he's right on the edge. I want to see him lose it, so I turn my ass towards him, then bend over at the waist and pull my pajama pants down. I'm still wiggling my hips to the music, shifting my butt back and forth while I reveal my panties. "Motherfucker." When I look over my shoulder, he's not even touching himself.

"Hey, I said I wanted a show, too." I try to sound stern, but it feels a little weak when I know any one of them could throw me over the couch and I'd go happily.

"You're fucking killing me," he growls, but resumes touching himself. His cock glistens with his slickness, a thick drop sliding down from the tip.

I sway to the music, my hands covering my breasts. The guys follow me with their eyes like I'm the only woman left on the planet. Like they're hypnotized. It's an intoxicating feeling.

Nervously biting my lip, I move my hands until my breasts are revealed. I'm so wet by now that I bet there's a damp spot forming on my panties. I start to pull them down, eager to get to whatever's next, when Wraith growls from his chair. "Over here. I want the honors."

If it means getting his hands on me, I'm more than ready. I dance over to him, and as soon as I'm within reach, he grabs me by the ass and pulls me close so suddenly I tumble right into him.

He presses a wet kiss to my belly, then hooks his fingers in the skimpy fabric and pulls. My fingers dig into his shoulders as my panties are dragged over my hips and thighs. He drops them to pool around my feet. "Step out, sweetheart." His hand is already stroking the inside of my thigh, getting awfully close to where I'm most sensitive.

The game might be over, but I'm pretty sure I'm about to win.

"Fuck, I need in you," growls Wraith. He rises from the chair, and throws me over his shoulder like I'm made of feathers. I squirm and laugh as he carries me right past Tank and Nitro and into the bedroom. They're not slow in following.

He puts me down on the mattress, and they stand at the end of the bed, removing the last of their clothing. Every single one of them is so hard it looks painful. Tall, strong, broad and generously endowed, they're every girl's wettest dream come true. And I can have all of them at once.

Me. Little, boring me.

Except maybe I'm not so boring anymore.

Wraith is the first to climb onto the bed. He pushes my legs open so he can get between them, lowering himself so his mouth is only a couple of inches away from my pussy. "One more dare for you, sweetheart," he says in a lust-darkened voice that sends tingles racing up my spine. "Beg me to eat you out. Plead for my tongue on your clit. Let me hear exactly how bad you fucking want it."

Oh God.

Tank gets on one side of me and Nitro on the other. They trail their fingers over my sensitive skin, exploring my sides, my belly, definitely my breasts. As Tank swirls a big finger around my nipple, I let out a soft mewl and flex my hips at Wraith, trying to entice him without having to say it.

"Say it, Trigger," Tank prompts.

"Please?"

All three of them laugh. "What the fuck was that?" asks Wraith. "That didn't sound like fucking begging to me. Let me fucking hear it."

I wet my lips, looking between all three of them. They're all looking right back, smirking and waiting for me. I get it. Nothing's going to happen before I do. "You boys are cruel."

Nitro shakes his head. "You've fucking teased us, told us to get our cocks out, and then stripped. What's a few words more? Final dare."

"And then?"

"And then we make you come until you can't walk."

I swallow thickly, knowing they're not kidding. "Please, lick me."

"You can do better than that. Louder. What exactly?" Wraith teases me with a quick kiss on my pussy, right on the lips. My hips lurch in response to his sudden touch. "Let's hear it."

"Please, will you lick my pussy until I come?" I say, louder and hopefully convincing enough.

He responds by drawing his broad tongue right in between my folds, flicking it over my clit as he comes up. All the built-up tension in me releases in a guttural moan. God, that felt nice. Then he hooks his hands around my thighs and pulls me closer, so he can do it all over again.

Sparks race across my skin, little bolts of arc lightning that light the way to my nipples, like there's a direct line between them and my pussy. And when Tank and Nitro lean in and sucks my nipples into their hot mouths, the circuit is complete.

I bury one hand in Nitro's wavy locks and the other grasps Tank's short cut, pulling them both against me. If I'm going to have to beg for their attention, then I'm going to make sure I make the most of it when I have it.

"You gonna come for us?" asks Tank in a husky voice. "You gonna show us how fucking beautiful you are when you go over the edge. I haven't seen it enough times yet." Then he goes back to teasing my nipple with his tongue.

I don't even have the breath to answer. I'm right there. So close. "Ffffuck…" I hiss.

"She's swearing, Nitro. You're doing a good job," says Tank with a little laugh, before he sucks my nipple right into his mouth and gives it a little bite. I gasp, my fingers digging in harder.

He doesn't answer, too busy driving me absolutely wild. His tongue is magic.

I try to move away a little, to reduce the intensity, but his grip is too strong. I'm going to come all over Wraith's face, whether I'm ready to or not. "Please," I moan.

"Please what?" asks Nitro teasingly. "Please stop? Do you want Wraith to slow down? Or do you want him to make you fucking come?"

I'm not even sure. I both want release, and the buildup to last forever. But too long, and I'd just die, I think. Either way, I don't have the breath to answer him, because Wraith makes the decision for me.

He guns it, and pleasure explodes from my pussy in a wave that washes over me. I explode beneath him. I press against the bed in a tight arch, quivering like I've got a fever until I collapse back onto the sheets, breathing like I just finished a marathon for the first time in my life.

Tank and Nitro are there before I have time to recover. Tank slides inside from behind, his big hands wrapped around my waist. His thickness fills me just perfectly, just big enough to ache the way I'm learning to love. I moan deep in my throat, which Nitro takes as an opportunity, and suddenly he's at my front, lifting my leg and—

A phone rings.

"Just fucking ignore it," growls Tank as he absolutely destroys me in the best way.

No one argues. I wrap my arms around Nitro's neck and—

Another phone rings.

"Jesus Christ," groans Nitro.

"I'll check," Wraith says with a heavy sigh, sliding off the bed. "Fuck, it's Eagle-eye. He must be out." Everyone freezes as he answers. "We what? Fuck. Yes, sir. We're on it."

29

TANK

My cock's fucking screaming at me. I haven't gotten my clothes on so fast since I was sixteen and got caught with my boss's daughter. She didn't hold a candle to Kaylee, though.

"What's happening?" I pull my shirt over my head while Kaylee's digging clothes out of her duffel bag, and yanking them on as quickly as she can. It's like hiding art. I'm gonna insist she goes naked anytime she's home.

Fuck, home?

Jesus, there won't be a home to make with her if we can't keep her safe.

Wraith looks pissed. "Our location leaked. Cops are on their way. We're fucking compromised. There's no time to pack, just hurry the fuck up. We need to get on the bikes and vanish."

"Working on it!" Nitro pulls a shirt over his head, throws on his jacket.

"I'm good." She's got on jeans that hug her hips just fucking perfectly—Alessa knows how to pick clothes, that's for fucking sure—and a t-shirt and jacket.

Wraith waves for us to follow, spinning his keys around a finger. "Let's get the fuck on the road. The sooner we get the hell outta here, the more distance we'll put between us and the cops."

He's just about to open the door when I happen to look out the window. "Fuck! Hang back! There's a fucking army out there."

"Shit." Nitro glances out too, then over at Kaylee. She looks between us with wide eyes, her expression terrified. This was supposed to be fucking safe.

"How the fuck did they find us?" Wraith bolts the door.

"Maybe they're about to do a drug bust next door?" I suggest with a grim smile, drawing my gun. They're not gonna get us cheap, I can fucking promise them that.

"This is fucked," Wraith growls. "The club's on the way but they can't fucking teleport."

"But Eagle-eye's back?"

Wraith nods. "Apparently."

"Can we go out the back?" Nitro asks.

Wraith shakes his head. "It's too open. There's no cover that way. This is a shitty fucking hideout."

"You can't let them take me," Kaylee says, her voice barely above a whimper. "Not again. Please."

I take her in my arms and pull her close. She's shivering like she's naked in winter. "We're not gonna let them have you, baby. Over our dead fucking bodies."

"I don't want that either." She shudders. "If it means staying alive, then give me to them. They won't want to kill me, right?"

"Not right away, at least." I hope. Unless they've decided to just eliminate the complications. "We're not dead yet, okay? The cavalry's on its way."

Nitro is carefully looking out the front. "Neighbors are getting curious. Unless we do something stupid, they can't just take us out execution style with this many witnesses. Fuck, that's Harris."

Motherfucker.

"Surrender now! Release the hostage and this won't have to turn ugly," Harris yells through a megaphone.

"Hostage?" Kaylee gasps. "Does he mean me? I'm not a hostage. I'll go yell it, if I have to."

"No fucking chance," I snap. "It's a trap. He's just covering his ass by saying what makes the witnesses sympathetic when they take us out. He might shoot you, he might not, but don't trust a world out of his fucking mouth."

She shakes her head. "I know. He's—he's horrible." Fuck, the way her voice cracks cuts deep.

One day, I'm gonna break all his fucking ribs and pull them out, one by one, while he's still awake to feel it, just for what he did to her. But the most important thing now is that we get her outta here, and alive.

"You have exactly five minutes," Harris's grating voice echoes through the megaphone, "and then we're coming in. We do not negotiate with terrorists!"

"Terrorists? I'm gonna make sure I save a bullet for that motherfucker's face." Wraith has his piece out, too.

Nitro pulls out his phone. "Calling Alessa," he explains.

A moment later she picks up. Her voice is so loud, it carries. "Are you guys safe?"

"Not even fucking close. Tell me your place has a secret exit, escape tunnel, bomb shelter, a backpack of hand grenades, something. We'll take fucking anything at this point."

"Fuck," she hisses. "No, I never needed it. I just lived there, out of sight. Crap, I don't know how the cops found it, but no. I'm sorry."

"Guess it was too much to hope for. Alright. We'll figure something out."

"Good luck."

"We need to distract them until help gets here," I say. "Any thoughts?"

"He says he won't negotiate, but if he doesn't, and we have a hostage, then he's gonna look at least as bad as he would if he just started gunning." Wraith's expression is dark, but determined. "Here's to me not getting my head shot off."

"Wraith!" Nitro, Kaylee and I say it all at once as he cracks open the door, ignoring us.

"Harris!" he yells. "We'll give her up, but you need to give us a little more time."

"Why the fuck would I do that?" There's triumph in his voice that carries easily even through the muddling of the megaphone. He's got us pinned like bugs and he fucking knows it. Goddamn it. I hate feeling trapped.

"You don't think we'd fucking make so you could just walk in here and take her, do you? Unless you want the whole fucking building to go, you'll give us time," Wraith yells back.

We all know that Harris doesn't give a shit if we all blow up, but the neighbors sure as fuck do, and with more and more of a crowd gathering, he's got to keep some kind of public face to this.

I hope.

"Fine! Five more minutes! After that, we're coming for you."

Wraith shuts the door and looks back over his shoulder. "Five more minutes. That enough for anything?"

"Not without a distraction," Nitro looks thoughtful. "But, maybe…"

"Get going on it," snaps Wraith. "Whatever the fuck it is, we'll draw things out as much as we can."

Nitro nods, then disappears into the kitchen and starts rummaging. Knowing him, whatever he's planning is going to make a big fucking boom.

The rumble of engines gets my attention. Fuck, could it be…

People scream outside and scatter as a whole fucking armada of motorcycles appears down the road. They're here. They're fucking here. "It's the Eagles!"

Not that the cops are gonna make it easy on us. When Nitro pokes his head out of the kitchen,

Wraith yells, "Keep doing whatever you're doing. No guarantees yet. I'll yell if you're good."

"Got it."

At least the cavalry's forcing the cops to regroup. If we're lucky, we can make a fire line that gets us a path out. For Kaylee, if nothing else. "Fuck, I hate having to watch from in here while they're having all the fun."

Wraith chuckles. "I'm just as happy without a fucking bullet through my head. Just keep an eye open for an opportunity. We have to get Kaylee the hell outta here."

"We have to get all of us out of here," she says, clinging to my side. "I'm not running without you."

"You can and you fucking will," I say, putting all the command I've fucking got into my voice. "We can take care of ourselves a lot better if we know you're safe."

"I'm not a child!"

"No, you're not, Trigger, but if you get hurt, I'm never gonna fucking forgive myself. If we can get all of us out, awesome. But if the opportunity comes, you go, and we'll follow." She doesn't look convinced, but she doesn't argue. "I mean it. Don't do anything stupid. We can take care of ourselves, alright?"

Gunshots ring out between the buildings. "Sounds like negotiations broke down," sneers Wraith.

Fuck, there's a full on battle out there, and people are gonna fucking die. It's bound to fucking happen. I just hope it won't be any of ours. It looks like the cops weren't anticipating this much resistance, though. They've set up a line that puts us on the Eagle side of things. Only problem's that there's a lot of fucking wide open space. We'd be fish in a fucking barrel. I bet Harris wants Kaylee back, but the second best thing is to get rid of her. She knows way too fucking much at this point.

A couple of stray bullets come in through one of the windows, shattering it. I pull her into my chest and take the brunt of the glass on my jacket. She screams and covers her head.

Wraith's phone rings.

"Yeah? Yeah… got it. We'll be ready." He jams the phone in his pocket. "They've captured some of the riot shields. They're gonna try to use them to get us outta here. Nitro! Get over here! Be ready."

"Can those things take a bullet?" Have to admit I'm a little fucking skeptical. They always looked flimsy to me.

"They'll take more than my head." Wraith shrugs. "I'm not seeing a lot of options."

"Fucking great." I give Kaylee a squeeze. "You ready, baby? You're going out first."

"Wait, we aren't all going?"

"Eagle-eye won't be able to spare many people while keeping the cops pinned down." As if to emphasize my point, the gunfire outside swells. "It's gonna be one at a time. We get you out, and then we'll be right behind you. Promise."

Fuck, the way she looks up at me breaks my heart, but there's no other way to do this.

Lightning, Badass and Hero come running across the no man's land between us and the closest cover out there, keeping down and jumping over a low stone wall that lines the walk up to the apartment. They've got the riot shields up between them and the cops, and it doesn't take long before they're taking hits. Hero's almost knocked over by a burst, but he keeps it up, and the three of them keep close together so they make a kind of mobile shield wall. Wraith throws open the door and jumps out of the way as they barrel into the living room.

Wraith grins. "Sorry to be shitty hosts, but we don't have much food in the house. First rounds on us later?"

Badass's grin is battle ugly. "Sounds like a fucking plan. Who's coming first?"

I give Kaylee a little shove, since she seems unwilling to let go of me. "Go on, baby. We'll be right behind you. They'll take care of you."

"Tank…" She looks between me and Wraith before throwing a long look at the kitchen. "You guys better come right away. I need you."

"You're never fucking getting rid of us, sweetheart." Wraith pulls her close real quick and puts a big kiss on top of her head. "Never."

I agree. "Never."

Nitro sticks his head out. "We got this, princess. Go! We'll find you."

She looks tiny between her rescue squad. "Make us proud, boys," I growl. "She'd better fucking be in one piece when it's our turn."

"We got her," says Hero, and then they're out the door. Watching them cover Kaylee as they dash across the battle field has to be about the scariest thing I've watched in my fucking life.

I only just get to see them get behind cover when something smashes through the remaining window and hits the couch, smoking.

"Down!" Wraith yells, then pushes me back, away from it. We fall together into the narrow hall, just as the cloud is replaced by a fwoosh of bright-hot flame. The fuckers threw a firebomb.

"Fuck!"

30

KAYLEE

A MASSIVE BLACK CLOUD COMES BARRELING OUT OF the narrow windows of Alessa's old apartment, followed by long tongues of flame. "Noooo!" I scream, realizing everything's gone as wrong as it possibly could. "Let me go!" If Badass and Hero weren't holding me back, I'd be running right back through the gunfire to get to the three men who own my heart.

My men.

The heart that's about to explode in my chest, and I don't know if it's because it's working so hard, or because it just got hopelessly, irreparably shattered. I scream, over and over, using the hands holding me back as something to fight against, something to take my furious grief and frustration out on.

They told me—they freaking told me—less than a minute ago that they were going to be right behind me. With me. Following me. Here to keep me safe.

They lied. They freaking lied.

I keep fighting, but I'm also desperately watching the apartment for any kind of sign of life, of movement. Them making a mad dash for it. Anything would be better than them burning up in front of me.

"Go get them!" I shriek to Badass, Hero and anyone else who can pick up a riot shield to go get Tank, Wraith and Nitro. "Hurry, before they burn!"

"Fuck," growls Badass. "We're going, but you have to fucking stay here, you get it? If you're charging in on your own you'll only hurt yourself, and if you get hurt, they're gonna fucking kill us. Stay!"

I stop fighting. If they're going in, I'll wait here. I don't want to, but I will. I even take a step back to give them space, keeping behind the wall we're using for cover. God, the whole scene is chaos. Bikers, cops, guns going off like the fireworks finale on the fourth of July. I'm safe here, at least for now, but I don't care.

Hero, Lightning and Badass grab the riot shields and move to where another step will put them in the line of fire. "Wraith!" Hero calls out. "Tank! Fucking say something! We're coming over!"

Please, please, please, say something.

"Go!" commands Badass, and they start moving. Immediately, bullets ricochet off their shields. Oh God, please don't let them get hurt either. This is all my fault, but I don't know what I can do about it.

There's a boom, much too deep to be normal gunfire that makes my heart skip a beat. Badass's shield is hit so hard he's spun around and knocked to the ground. He rolls right back up, and they retreat into cover. No, no. They can't give up.

In my head, I know perfectly well that if they can't even make it over there, there's no way they can bring anyone back safely, but… Tank, Wraith and Nitro are in there. There's so much I want to tell them, to do with them—I just want them back. No matter how.

My chest is one tight ball of terror. I touch my face, finding it wet and not even being aware that I'm crying. I refuse to give up. I can't give up. I refuse to—

The whole front of the apartment shudders and tries to lift off the ground as a shockwave blows out the door and window frames with a boom that shakes the whole neighborhood. Thick black smoke billows out of the remains of the facade in such thick swells that nothing is visible anymore. For a moment, all the gunfire stops as both sides stop to see what just happened.

I stand there, suddenly numb. Expressionless. I'm trapped again, just like before at the gas station. I can't go back, and there's nothing for me to move towards. Not with the men I love most likely dying inside the apartment where we were just… I can still feel the echo of them inside me!

I fall to my knees, staring without really seeing.

The smoke dissipates slowly, but deep inside the building, there's this terrible creak, an awful crunch as something starts to happen. And whatever it is, it's not good.

The whole front of the building slides down like snow off a melting roof, bringing with it tons of dust, stone, glass and metal. The force launches a whole bunch of it into the air like a wave crashing. I hate myself for moving further away from what's probably become the dusty grave of Nitro, Wraith and Tank, but my instincts send me scrambling away from all the bits of house that are falling from the sky.

I get so far back that I end up mixed into the crowd that's watching. Neighbors who are probably freaking out about their own home alongside rubberneckers who just want to watch the destruction. With a shriek that burns my throat and lungs, I scream my grief into the cold and uncaring universe. And then I do it again.

An older man comes up to me. He reminds me a bit of the bikers, with a trimmed gray beard, and soft eyes that are full of concern set in a face that looks like life has left its toll. He puts his arm around me, trying to comfort me from the deepest pain I've felt in my life, and while I know he can never actually succeed, I bury my face into his leather jacket anyway. My body is racked with sobs while he rubs my back.

"It's alright, it's alright," he says. "Come on. You can't stay here. If the cops get their hands on you, who knows what they'll do."

"Wh... What?" My brain isn't working at one hundred percent. I don't recognize this guy, but I don't know most of the Screaming Eagles. "Who are you?"

"I'm Emily's father. I came to help. You've met her, right? You're safe with me."

"She's King's old lady, right? And Hero?" There was a third, right? I can't remember. "What are you doing here?"

"I'll explain everything once you're safe. You can't stay here."

I nod, too distraught to question anything. "Um, yeah. Okay."

He leads me away from the fighting that's starting to kick back up now that the smoke has cleared. We round a corner or two, leaving it all behind. Aside from distant shouting and a few shots, everything fades.

But as we leave the immediate danger, my brain starts working again. "Where are we going? Is Emily here? Is she waiting for her men to come back?" The hole in my chest gapes wide in the shape of Wraith, Nitro and Tank, stealing my breath.

"Oh, no. My daughter isn't anywhere near here."

There's something in his tone of voice that makes me look up. "So where—"

"And here you go," he says to someone else. "You catch more flies with honey than vinegar."

"Indeed. I'll have to remember that, Mr. Hawthorne."

31

NITRO

All I can fucking see is dust.

"Tank! Shit, fuck!" A length of rebar got me in the shoulder and it fucking hurts, but I can move it okay, so I don't think it's serious. Fuck, that was a closer call than I like. "Wraith!"

A deep, hacking cough sounds in the dust cloud to my right. "Here." It sounds like a whole section of broken building shifts as Tank gets himself loose, but I'm guessing he's alright, since he doesn't say anything else.

"Wraith!"

"Stop shouting," comes his bitchy voice from my left. "My leg's trapped, but I think I'm okay. Just fucking stuck."

"Coming." Either the shooting paused when I blew out the back of Alessa's apartment, or I just can't hear shit anymore. We need to get the fuck outta here before all the dust settles and they catch us out in the open.

A massive shadow emerges from the cloud, revealing Tank. His jacket's got some vicious shreds in it, and there's blood oozing down from an ugly scrape on his neck, but he's moving. I bet I don't look any fucking better.

"Jesus fucking Christ on a goddamn motorcycle," Wraith groans. "What the hell did you do? I wanted a distraction, not demolition."

"Por que no los dos? If you think mixing cleaning supplies and gunpowder the right way in the middle of a fucking siege, and still making sure it's definitely enough to open up the back wall of a fucking house without blowing us apart is easy, then you can make the next fucking bomb, deal? They got Kaylee out, right? I was a little busy."

Wraith laughs hoarsely. "Yeah, Hero and Badass got her clear. Fucking help me out, here."

We find him under a collapsed section of wall. There's blood coming from a cut on his forehead and the tattoo on his forearm is gonna need a touchup once the gash there has healed, but he looks mostly angry at being trapped instead of hurt.

Tank grabs one part, and I grab the other. "Ready?" he growls.

"Go for it. Lift with your legs, not your back, fellas."

Tank and I both give him the finger, then get back in position. We groan as we lift. Fuck, this is heavy. Every muscle I've fucking got is straining. Even Tank, who usually takes shit like this with one arm is giving it his all, those huge fucking biceps of his swelling as he pulls. The wall segment shifts, and Wraith pulls himself upward.

"Hurry, can't fucking hold it for long," Tank hisses through gritted teeth, and I can only nod in agreement.

Wraith doesn't waste any time, getting himself clear as soon as there's any give. He gets to his feet, dusts himself off then nods. "Let's go find Kaylee."

Using what's left of the dust cloud for cover, we rush behind the neighboring unit. I don't know what choice I had, but the thought that the cops might not have bothered clearing out the residents before opening fire makes me sick. And they'll blame all this on us, even though they were the ones that went in with fucking firebombs in a residential neighborhood. Kids live here, assholes.

We keep low along the back wall, using the chaos for as much cover as possible until we can get around to tell everyone we're still breathing. No one wins a fucking shootout like this, so the sooner we can just get the fuck back to the clubhouse, the better.

King's the first one to spot us. Relief flashes across his face. "Boys! Fuck, am I glad to see you alive and walking!"

"Where's Kaylee?" is our first question, and we all fucking ask it at once.

"I was hoping you fucking knew. Hero and Badass got her out, but she vanished when the fucking walls came down and everyone scattered. Do you have any way of contacting her? A number maybe?"

I shake my head. "Hasn't exactly been time to shop for phones. We should've fucking sorted a burner for her, but she's been with at least one of us since we snatched her from the cops." I scan the street, looking for any sign. By now the fight is breaking up, there are still potshots being fired from both sides, but Harris is nowhere to be seen.

"Would she run away?" Tank frowns, considering options, and it's obvious he's not liking all of the answers.

"She wouldn't leave us," Wraith says with utter confidence.

He's right. She wouldn't, not after all this. I refuse to fucking accept that and my gut's telling me that's the fucking truth. "No, but she might try to get clear of the danger."

King nods. "I don't fucking like it. Where's your bikes?"

"Parking garage around the block." Wraith points down the street, then glances over at the smoking ruins of Alessa's apartment. "Didn't wanna advertise that we were there. Not that it did us a lot of good."

"Hey, it means they didn't just blow sky high. Good. We're pulling out. If we've got her, she comes with us. If not, we're not accomplishing anything here."

King barks a few commands to the closest guys, and they start spreading the word.

Badass makes his way over. "Find her yet?"

"No, she was with you last we saw." Wraith says grimly. "What the fuck happened?"

"The whole fucking place blew up, that's what happened. I asked around and a lady saw a girl that matches Kaylee get led away by an older man. He seemed to be helping her. We tried looking for them, but no luck." As Badass finishes, Eagle-eye arrives with Hero, looking all of us over with his one-eyed glare.

Tank scratches his head. "Who the fuck would she go with? Where was this? Take us there!"

Hero leads the way. "We don't known for sure, because witnesses are fucking useless, but over this way."

"Kaylee!" Tank yells, and then Wraith and I join in. We're not gonna take the fucking chance that she's not having cocoa in someone's apartment while they're waiting for the fire department.

We turn down a couple of alleys and side streets, looking for any sign, but it's not until I spot something on the ground that the sinking feeling deep in my gut drops all way to my fucking feet.

I pick it up. It's one of Kaylee's gloves. "She was here. Someone fucking grabbed her." Fuck, it could be significant, or it could mean nothing at all. My gut tells me it means something, though.

Badass waves at us, holding his phone. "Eagle-eye says we need to go. There's more cops coming. We gotta get outta here. Stay and be killed."

Leaving is the last thing I want to do, but there's no way to help her if we're dead or behind bars. Fuck. "Fine. Coming."

On the ride back, I can't shake the feeling that we've fucking abandoned Kaylee. What the fuck happened? And who was the man she was seen with? There's a big fucking ball of spiky worry in my gut, and it's not gonna go away until I've got Kaylee back in my arms.

And I'm willing to do some pretty fucked up shit to make that happen.

32

KAYLEE

THE ROPES CHEW INTO MY WRISTS, AND EVERYTHING'S black. This time, being blindfolded isn't nearly as much fun. In fact, it's terrifying.

I'm in a car, a limo. I saw that much before they put the blindfold on and shoved me in here. Anderson and Harris are sitting on either side of me, with our backs to the driver. I have no idea which one's which though. They haven't said anything since I was shoved in here, and that just makes them even more eerie.

"You've caused us a lot of trouble, Ms. Thompson," says Hawthorne from the seat across from us. As soon as we met up with the others, he dropped the fatherly persona like a snake shedding its skin. "But it'll all be worth it in the end. The Screaming Eagles and the Giordanos can wipe each other out, and whatever's left, we'll mop up easily. It's too bad, really. The Mafia used to be reasonable to work with, but those damn hooligans ruined everything."

I need to think of a plan, but I feel numb. Nitro, Tank and Wraith are probably dead, and there's a good chance I'll join them if I don't cooperate. The only thing keeping me going is knowing that the guys would want the club to survive, and there are so many people I met in the Screaming Eagles that I don't want to see hurt.

If I can keep him talking, maybe I'll learn something I can use.

"How did you know about Emily?"

"What do you mean?" He sounds amused, like he's pulled one over on me. I guess he did.

"Pretending to be her dad."

"Oh, baby girl. I wasn't pretending. I am Emily's father. And Miriam's ex-husband. Eagle-eye and I, we have a history. We go way back. The only chance I took was hoping nobody would have bothered telling someone like you enough details to make you doubt me." He chuckles.

God, I hope he never calls me baby girl again. The chills that rush down my back freeze my spine from the inside. He's actually Emily's dad? I just bet he and Eagle-eye have history. "Someone like me?"

"Please. Harris has told me all about you. You're a nothing. A pawn with a cunt. You were given the chance to do the right thing and instead you decided to become a slut for those animals."

"I'd rather be one of their sluts than lie for you bastards any day," I spit.

Ok, maybe that was a bit much.

But he doesn't seem bothered. He's in charge, so I guess he doesn't care how mouthy I get. "You're all sluts. Whores who throw yourselves on your backs, spread your legs and wait for a filthy biker to fall in. You, Emily, Miriam, and any other woman in that shithole. This city won't be clean until we've gotten rid of every single one of them. Of you."

The pure venom in his tone as he finishes is chilling. This guy isn't stable, and I already know his little henchmen that are crowding me in here aren't either. The moment he decides he doesn't need me anymore, I'm going to be turned into a statistic. Whether that's murder victim, mysterious disappearance or something else still remains to be seen.

"Where are we going?"

"Am I supposed to tell you my dastardly plan? Please. We're getting out of this disgusting city. That's all you're getting." He laughs darkly.

"Do you even believe you're doing the right thing? People are dying, and it's not the men you call animals that are responsible."

"If me being the villain is what it takes to clear the world of the crime that infests this city then so be it. If there's anything I learned from my time in prison, it's that my means are not… good. Just necessary. Look at you. I've kidnapped you, put you in the hands of zealots like Harris and Anderson, and I'm instigating a gang war in the city I once was the mayor of. A city I love. But sometimes, tough love is required, and that means breaking a few eggs."

Anderson chuckles, making my stomach flip at the mention of eggs.

"I don't expect anyone to remember me as a great humanitarian, a wonderful philanthropist or even some kind of twisted Robin Hood, but if something better can grow out of the rubble I leave behind then that will be my legacy. And you're but a little, but useful, piece of that puzzle."

"I'm never going to help you."

"You already are. Everything is playing into my hands. The explosion will be easy enough to pin on the Eagles. So many people have the wrong impression, seeing them as some sort of heroes fighting the power and protecting the sewer of South Side, but they'll be swayed, and once the Eagles are gone, we can bulldoze the whole district and rezone it. Build it up right."

Built on the deaths of the men I love. My feelings are so obvious now, and I never got the chance to say it to them. I wiggle my wrists against the rope, but it's not giving at all. My hands are getting a little tingly, they're so tight.

The surface under the car changes as we slow and turn. Now it's the crunch of gravel. Wherever we're going, I think we're almost there. God, I could be anywhere, and no one saw me get stolen away. The boys found me once, but I don't know that it's possible for them to do it again.

The car stops, a door opens, and the car rocks a little as Hawthorne gets out. Then the blindfold is removed. I shy back when I open my eyes to see Harris right in front of my face, grinning viciously.

"Boo," he says calmly. "We're here. Get out." Then he climbs out, leaving me to struggle out of the limo with my hands tied.

It's awkward and humiliating, which I'm sure is the point, but I manage. I look around while Anderson climbs out behind me. Nobody is ever going to find me.

The place is a mansion in the woods on the edge of a lake. There are terraces, balconies, and everything shines in white stucco and glass. I bet it's beautiful here in the summer, but right now a freezing wind is blowing in over the water, making me shiver almost as much as being back with Harris and Anderson.

Hawthorne sets a course up a sloped stone tile path that leads to a big double door with gold handles. There are armed guards on either side of the door and more by the big doors that lead into the garage under the house.

Harris shoves me in the center of my back. "Move it, bitch. You owe me."

Hawthorne extends his arms and lets the chill of the lake wash over him. "Perfect, just perfect. Let's get inside where it's warm. I think we'll be able to make you see reason after a while, despite your protests. Besides, it's not like your heroes are around to save you this time." His statement is all flat, like it's just an afterthought. The three best men in the world, dead, and he doesn't even care.

But I do.

I'm trying so hard not to cry. So, so hard.

I want my heroes back.

33

WRAITH

When we pull up in front of the clubhouse, Snark's already waiting for us. Eagle-eye had Badass call ahead with the little info he had. From the shit eating grin on Snark's face, he's already got something for us.

"Talk to us," I say as I shut my bike off and dismount.

"What the man said," King agrees. "Time's of the essence."

"That's for fucking sure." Snark's expression sobers immediately, as if he just remembered that there's something bigger going on than bragging about his digital skills. "Hawthorne."

"What about him?" growls Eagle-eye, pushing his way forwards. I wasn't in the club when that whole mess went down, but I know that's not good. That it's fucking bad.

Snark swings his laptop around while gesturing at it like we're gonna understand anything of the dense lines of text and numbers on the screen. "It took me a while, but I found a neighborhood camera group that was as secure as PAP." He looks at us like we should find that funny. "Whatever. That would land at DEF CON. The image was blurry, and he's grown a beard while he's been away, but if that isn't Hawthorne, I'm gonna eat my fucking patch."

"God fucking damn it!" Tank explodes. I can't fucking remember the last time I saw him this angry. "Everything we did, and now she's right the fuck back where we started. And probably back in the hands of Harris and the egg guy—exactly what we fucking promised would never happen!"

"Wait, I got one more thing," Snark says. "It's about Deuce."

King and Eagle-eye filled us in on Hawthorne and his connection to the crooked cops on the way back, and Deuce's betrayal. That little fucker. I never really liked him, but I don't like a lot of people and that doesn't make them traitors.

"What about him?"

"He isn't Deuce."

Eagle-eye's nostrils flare. "What do you mean?"

"I tracked down Cannon, who was listed as his sponsor. Except the guy Cannon knows as Deuce is in fucking Australia. He's the son of a buddy of his. He put his name forward, but didn't have a fucking clue that someone'd actually showed up."

"So who the fuck do we have locked up?" King asks.

"Maybe it's time to ask." I crack my knuckles. "I'm real eager for a… conversation."

Nitro licks his lips, nothing pleasant in his crooked grin. "Same."

We set course for the pit, and I'm gonna be very disappointed if Deuce sings too quickly, since my fists are itching. He looks up when we open the door, his eyes widening.

"Deuce," Eagle-eye says conversationally. "There's been some miscommunication."

His eyes go wide. "Yeah, I mean, I didn't—"

Perfect. Grabbing his jacket with both fists, I yank him off the bench and throw him into the fucking wall. He grunts as the back of his head connects. "You didn't what, *Deuce*? Are you with the cops? Or just an asshole who's willing to take their money?"

He swings at me, but if he thinks a shit like him is gonna get the upper hand on me, he's even fucking stupider than I thought. Tank blocks with one arm, then drives a fist into his gut. He doubles over and starts coughing.

"I didn't—"

Nitro gets up in his face. "Fuck you! No wonder you were fucking everywhere you shouldn't. No wonder you fucked up our escape and got Eagle-eye arrested. How did you learn about Alessa's apartment? That one I wanna know."

"Fuck," he groans. "I heard the mob guy talking to his daughter, okay? Didn't take a genius."

King lands a punch that sends a tooth flying. "If you want to even have the chance of surviving your stay, you're going to tell us where Hawthorne has the girl."

"I don't know shit about that!"

My next hit drops him to the floor, where he groans and tries to push himself back up. I put my boot on his back and keep him there. "Are you sure? Really fucking sure? I'd hate to get an answer I don't like."

"They'll fucking kill me," Deuce gets out through a tongue that's probably swelling by now.

Eagle-eye, who's been content to stand back and watch us beat the shit out of this shitstain, crouches down and grabs him by the hair, forcing him to look up. "We'll fucking kill you, so pick your poison. Do I make myself clear? Look around. Do you think anyone gives a shit what happens to a weasel like you? Who's coming to rescue you? Cooperate and maybe we'll think about not cutting out your tongue and letting you choke on the blood."

"I only saw Hawthorne once," he forces out, like he has to convince himself to make the words.

I smile. "Now we're fucking getting somewhere. Keep going."

"I swear to God! All I know is he's got a fancy place somewhere, but they never took me there. What I don't know can't be tortured out of me, so do your fucking worst."

I can almost appreciate his attitude, but nah.

Snark comes into the cell, takes one look and fake gags. "Who dropped a Deuce in here? The Giordanos are on their way. They're really interested in getting a chance to talk to this shit."

The traitor pales. "Wait, you're not gonna give me to the mob, are you?"

I don't feel a shred of pity for his limp form on the floor. "You know, it's kinda fucking impressive. You've managed to set yourself up as a target for not just us, but the Mafia too. Few people are that fucking dumb."

There's the sound of flesh hitting flesh, and what sounds like vomit before Eagle-eye and the rest come out of the cell. Emily and Miriam are waiting in the courtyard. We share what little information about Hawthorne we got out of Deuce.

"Blue Lake," says Emily.

Miriam nods. "It makes sense. He got it in the divorce. I always hated that place because he loved it so much."

"Do we go?" Tank eyes me, standing tensely. I understand. It's better to do something than nothing. But what if it's the wrong something?

Nitro nods. "We can't sit around waiting. That fucker's been setting us up against the Giordanos, hoping we'd all just take each other out. Much as I hate to say it, Kaylee's just caught in the crossfire."

"Fuck, you don't think…" I trail off, not even wanting to fucking say it. But if she's not important to them anymore, has he killed her?

"I don't think so." Nitro looks hopeful, and I worry that he's letting that guide his thoughts, but if there's anyone on the team who's good at reasoning, it's him. "They thought they could use her once to set us up, but if he took her, he has to know she's important to us. That should buy her some time."

Eagle-eye grunts. "Miriam, get us directions for the house. Wraith, Tank and Nitro, we're going to check it out. I trust you guys to make the right call. We need to regroup here and get the club ready for what might come next, but if there's a chance at Hawthorne, I'm going to fucking be there. King, you'll be in charge here."

"What?" King looks at him like he's crazy. "No. You got your old lady and daughter here. You stay. I'll bring the boys and assist."

"No fucking way. This isn't just politics. This is personal. Besides, your old lady is Miriam's girl. She's like a daughter to me."

King snorts. "Should I start calling you daddy?"

"Oh, Jesus fucking Christ, that'd be too fucking weird. I said like a daughter. One is enough." He shakes his head.

Miriam goes white as a ghost. Emily reaches over and grabs her mother's hand.

Eagle-eye catches it right away. "What's wrong?"

Miriam shakes her head. "It's nothing, I just—"

"Fucking tell me, woman."

Emily rolls her eyes. "Mom's pregnant."

34

KAYLEE

The door slams behind me, and it feels like that's the last time I'm going to see daylight, because I'm never going to cooperate. I owe my men and the Screaming Eagles that much. And I don't think Harris will take no for an answer. It's a pretty bleak truth to acknowledge.

But for the moment, I'm alive, and as long as I'm alive, I'll do my best to keep it that way. I just have to play docile and wait for an opportunity.

Just.

At least they've taken off the ropes. I'm still rubbing my wrists as I look around. The inside of the mansion is at least as luxurious as Alessa's apartment was. I have to pinch my lips tight a moment as a flash of Tank, Wraith, Nitro and me laughing and playing truth or dare passes through my brain.

It's only been hours. It feels like years.

The first room they bring me through is a large sitting room, a full two stories tall with a cathedral ceiling and huge windows overlooking the lake. Thick wool rugs cover the floors, dampening my footsteps. The couches look designer, the coffee table looks designer, the massive open fireplace looks designer, and oil paintings in thick, ornate frames hang on all the walls.

A split staircase follows the walls and meets at the top in the back of the room, and that's where they bring me, before walking me down a hall with more fancy paintings on the walls, and into a smaller sitting room. Maybe more like a permanently covered terrace. Is that an observatory? I've never been in a house this fancy before.

It's shaped like a quarter circle, with domed windows that go all the way from the floor to the middle of the ceiling, giving an amazing view of the lake and the dreary winter woods next to it. A pier extends from the house, where a speedboat and a couple of jet skis are moored. A perfect vacation spot for the one percent. Or a prison for me.

Maybe I could break the window and jump, but I'm three floors up. Even if I broke through, I'd break my legs, at best. At worst, it'd be a short and embarrassing end to my captivity.

In the middle of the room is an ornate table and some chairs. "Have a seat," says Harris and points. The binder I recognize all too well lies on the table.

"I'm never going to testify," I repeat with all the conviction I can muster. Anything else feels like I'm betraying the guys' memory.

Harris cracks his knuckles. "Who gives a fuck?"

"Then why are you—"

"Because you know too fucking much. Isn't that obvious? You know what we look like, you know what the killers look like, and we don't even know anymore how much you've overheard. We can't risk keeping you around." He grins, a grimace of pure evil. "Only reason you're still alive is that the Eagles want you, and we can use that. The war's still brewing, and the more unhinged we get them, the easier it's gonna be to force it. The Screaming Eagles will be eradicated, and I'm looking forward to you watching it all before I fucking beat you to death, you little bitch."

Anderson smiles. "Are you hungry?"

Oh God.

I can't let them hurt me. Play meek, play docile. Be the girl they want. When I get out of here—when, not if—I can find a spot to curl up into a tiny ball and cry for a long, long time. Probably some therapy. But until then, I need to stay on the ball and keep focused. An opportunity could show itself at any moment, and if I don't grip it with both hands and make the most of it... well, I'm not going to let myself think that way.

"So why the binder?"

Harris glances at the table as if he's forgotten it's even there. "Just placating Hawthorne. I think he's still got some ideas about running a trial, but you and I, we both know that's not gonna happen."

"So I'm just going to sit here and... what?"

"Frankly, Ms. Thompson. I don't give a shit. Sit here and cry if it helps you pass the time. I'll be back." Then they leave me alone in the room, shutting the double doors behind them. The click of the lock tells me I'm locked in. Trapped, again.

With nothing else to do, I flip through the book. My heart lurches when I find Wraith, then Nitro and Tank. I put my fingers on their pictures, and this time I can't keep my tears back. They drip onto the pages, staining them, and I don't care if I ruin Harris's stupid binder.

I slam the book shut and get up to pace the room. I'm supposed to be a biker chick badass, right? That's what my men keep telling me. What would a biker chick badass do?

Maybe there's something in here I can use. The chairs? They look old, like antiques. I try each of them, and three of them are steady as rocks, but the fourth one… is the leg loose? I try to wrench it, but it refuses to budge. I lean it forward so it's balanced on a diagonal between the floor and the edge of the table. Then I lean as much weight on the bad leg as possible.

It doesn't do anything. At least not right away, but then, as I start to bounce, there's a soft creak.

Maybe?

I try harder, grabbing the edge of the table to pull myself down for every bounce, trying to put as much force on the chair as possible, and it creaks louder.

It snaps, the chair crashing to the floor with me on top of it. I slam into the floor, jarring my teeth together and knocking my head against the table's edge, but the leg has broken off. I try to ignore the throbbing in my head and the ache that tells me I've scraped up my shin as I pick up the makeshift club. It's pretty solid. I give it a little test swing. Maybe I can't overpower Harris or Anderson, but it's heavy enough to give me a chance.

The only chance I have right now.

35

TANK

When we reach the courtyard, the Giordanos are already here. Arturo, Luca and Nicholas stand in front of their black SUV, Arturo with his arms crossed over his chest and glowering. A second SUV just like his pulls in behind waved in by Viking at the gate.

"Is it true?" Arturo asks. "You've found the man responsible for the death of my men?"

"Yes, but he was Hawthorne's tool," replies Eagle-eye. "We're working on tracking down Hawthorne's location now. If you'd like to join the hunt, I'd love to see the look on that asshole's face when he sees us working together."

"Hawthorne? *Cazzo*. Tempting, but I can't risk it." He nods his head sideways. "Nicholas, go with them. I want a full report."

"Of course."

Our group is small, but it's solid. Me, Nitro, Tank and Eagle-eye, with Nicholas following behind in one of the mob cars. I raise my hand into the air. Eagle-eye, Nitro and Tank pull up next to me, revving their engines. "Everyone good to go?" When all of them give me a signal, I nod. "Then let's roll out. It's time to get Kaylee back."

We follow the GPS until it's dark and a wrought iron fence blocks our way, at least fifteen feet tall with spikes on top. On the other side a driveway disappears into the trees. The bars have way too tight spacing to slip through, and they'd be a fucking bitch to climb. And the front gate's even taller, the top of the massive doors formed into an arch.

You'd almost think Hawthorne wasn't interested in visitors.

"What do we do?" I ask. "I bet this shit goes all the way around the property."

Nitro opens the saddlebag on his bike and pulls out a piece of gray play dough. At least that's what it looks like. "I brought keys."

Wraith and I laugh. "Nice." Eagle-eye nods like he expected it all along, and the old fox probably did.

Nicholas eyes the lump suspiciously. "C-4?"

"Never leave home without it." Nitro molds and bends it, shaping it to fit around where the two halves of the gate meet. I have to admit I'm a little skeptical watching him do it. I know C-4 isn't supposed to blow up easy, but that's enough of it to make just about anyone's day a really fucking bad one. I just have to trust Nitro to know what he's doing. Luckily, he does.

He jams a detonator into it and activates a little switch. A dim red light pulses in the darkness.

"Back," he hisses, and we retreat well away from the gate. He pulls his phone out of his pocket and brings up an app with a red button. He taps it, confirms, and then the detonator goes off. The C-4 explodes with a flash of light and a loud boom, throwing the gates right off their hinges. Holy shit.

"Ding dong," Nicholas sings dryly. I snort, I didn't know Mafia types were allowed to joke.

"Let's move" says Wraith and then we rev our bikes and charge down the driveway, Nicholas leaving the car behind to ride bitch behind Wraith. Neither of them are thrilled with it, but too fucking bad. I like this plan. Subtlety was never my strong suit.

As we come around the last bend, the mansion appears in front of us. I gotta say, it's pretty fucking swank. Not exactly the cottage I expected. Doesn't fucking matter, as long as we get Kaylee outta here.

Almost immediately, guards pop out from doors and start shooting from windows. More people here than I figured too. Maybe it was good we brought the Mafia boy after all, if he knows what the fuck he's doing.

The driveway's lined with marble statues, like something out of a historical movie about the ancient Greeks or Romans or some shit like that. Tacky as fuck, but they make for decent cover. We abandon the bikes to get behind them, spreading out.

Wraith fires, and someone screams from inside. Already a promising start. The Mafia guy picks one off too, and then we're moving forward.

I get as far as almost to the garage when I have to throw myself down and take cover behind a corner of the terrace. Some fucker opened the garage door and is taking potshots using the wall for cover. I fire, duck, he pops up to fire back, and Nitro takes him right in the face. His scream cuts off halfway as he falls back, dead as a fucking doornail.

When I'm sure no one else is shooting from in there, I roll and make my way inside. "Going in!" I yell.

"We'll keep'em busy!" Eagle-eye yells back, his hand cannon booming like fucking thunder.

In a place like this, I'm assuming there's at least one door connecting to the garage, and the dumbass guarding it gave us an opening. I rush to the back and find it. The door's locked, but now we're getting to my specialty—breaking shit.

I slam my shoulder into the door, and it tears right off its hinges. This place looks like a palace but it's built like a McMansion. Did Hawthorne think nobody would find him? He'd better not have fucking hurt Kaylee, that's all I'm fucking saying.

Just as I come around a corner, a guard is coming the other way. Before he can even make a sound, I grip him by the neck of his shirt and slam his face into the wall. He drops like a fucking bean bag. Nice. I hadn't expected this to be so fucking easy.

Now where did they put her?

The place is like a fucking maze. I push through a couple doors and emerge into a big kitchen, the kind the owners never see because it's for the staff. There's a frying pan on the stove with a single egg sizzling in it. Acting purely on instinct, I dodge and another frying pan barely misses my face, hitting my shoulder instead. My arm goes numb and my gun hits the floor.

Fuck.

It's fucking Anderson with a frying pan in one hand and a big ass chef's knife in the other. "And here I fucking hoped we killed you," I growl as I get in position to fight him while looking around for something I can use for a weapon.

"I'm afraid the kitchen's off limits," he says as he approaches. His lines need work, but he's moving like he knows what he's doing. If he gets that knife in me, I'm fucked.

I back up slowly, baiting him to follow me. "Is this really what you wanna do? Go out defending an old shit like Hawthorne? He's just gonna use you and then throw you aside. Once he's on top, why's he gonna need you, huh?" I have no idea, to be honest, but I'm hoping for some henchman insecurity here.

He only chuckles, not taking the bait, as he keeps chasing me around the big kitchen. Guess not.

I grab a couple plates off the counter and throw them at him as he comes at me, but he bats them aside with the frying pan, smashing them into thousands of pieces. Even if he doesn't get me right away, all the noise is bound to attract more guards.

Fuck, I don't have time for this shit.

He throws the pan, and as I block it, I trip over something and fall backwards. The floor hits me like a fucking truck and my skull bounces off the marble tile. He's on me with the kitchen knife in a flash. Fuck, he's fast, and stronger than he looks.

Still, I get my hand around his wrist, keeping us at a stalemate as he puts his weight on it, trying to force it down into my throat. If I let go, he'll fucking kill me, and if he lets up, I'll do the same.

I'm stronger. Slowly, inch by inch, I force his arm up and back. He's gritting his teeth, his forehead's sweating, but even with all his weight on it, I'm pushing him away. "Motherfucker," he hisses, and then I twist his arm. A nasty popping noise comes from his joint and the fucker screams. He manages to hold onto the knife somehow as he steps back, but it's sticking at an unnatural angle and that's gotta hurt like a bitch.

I jump to my feet, and finding myself next to the stove, I grab the hot pan with the burning egg in it and swing towards him. He lifts his good arm to block, but takes the flat of the pan right to the face, accompanied with another scream and a satisfying sizzle. He's one of the fuckers who tried to break Kaylee and I don't give a fuck if he wasn't the one who hit her. He's just as fucking guilty.

As he's rolling on the ground and clutching his burnt face, I pick up the chef's knife from the floor and drive it deep into the back of his neck at the base of his skull, like I'm opening a lobster. He twitches once, and goes still.

"Which came first, motherfucker?"

I find my gun, and then get the fuck out. The shootout is still going, so maybe I'm lucky enough that no one noticed this, but I'm not gonna bet on it.

Pushing the next door open, I take it, emerging into a big, fancy ass sitting room. There's two guys at the windows shooting out. Apparently no one passed on the message that I got inside, and I'm about to take advantage of that when I hear a scream upstairs.

"Help! In here!"

If that's not Kaylee, I'm gonna eat my fucking bike. I take the stairs two at a time, until I get to a hallway. The screaming's down there. My feet can't fucking carry me fast enough. If we've found her already, this has to be about the smoothest rescue mission the Eagles have managed to date.

The door's locked, but I kick it open. Most of the room inside is glass with a fancy table and a broken chair in the middle, but I don't see anyone. What the fuck?

I step inside and something hard slams into my skull before everything goes black.

36

KAYLEE

"Tank?"

He's alive! Oh my God, he's alive!

If I didn't just kill him. I drop to my knees next to him and feel for a pulse. It's strong, but crap, I must've given him one heck of a concussion if he's down like that. Maybe if I find some water, or—

"Get the fuck away from him," snaps Harris as he grabs my wrist and yanks me out of the room, right over Tank's prone body. Harris pauses a moment like he considers taking the time to kill Tank, but then rushes down the hall, dragging me with him.

"Let go!" I snap and try to resist, but he's way too strong for me.

Unless I follow, I'm going to go right on my face. He takes me in the opposite direction from where I was led in, to the end of the hallway, where there's a small, personal elevator waiting. He drags me in, just as Hawthorne comes out of one of the other rooms.

"Wait! We're getting the fuck out of here!" He looks stressed as he jogs towards us. That's good, right? I try to pull away, hoping Harris is distracted, but he yanks me right back. Not yet, at least.

If Tank's alive, maybe the others are too, and that means I have a lot more to live for than just trying to bring down these guys. Please let Tank come to before one of the guards finds him. Or Anderson.

Harris hits the basement button before Hawthorne gets to us, but Hawthorne slips in just in time. "Trying to leave without me?" he snaps.

"The objective is bigger than either of us. I'm just getting it going ASAP," Harris says.

They glower at each other as the elevator descends. Is there trouble in paradise? Is that something I can use?

The elevator jolts to a sudden stop. "Now what?" growls Hawthorne. "I pay good money to have this house kept in perfect condition."

Harris slams the panel, while Hawthorne messes with the door. Harris has a gun on a holster. Can I…

I reach forward carefully, trying to pull the gun out without him noticing. When I succeed, I'm so surprised I'm not sure what I'm supposed to do next. Like, a gun? Me? And the elevator is so cramped, I don't know if I can make this work, but it's only a matter of time before Harris notices.

I jam the barrel into Hawthorne's side and try to channel my best badass biker chick voice. "Don't fucking move, or I'm gonna blow a hole in your side. There's a reason they call me Trigger."

Hawthorne freezes and Harris turns.

"Don't fucking move," I growl. "Or I'm gonna murder your boss."

Harris looks down at the situation, then laughs and reaches. Oh God, no, I didn't want him to call my bluff. I've never… shutting my eyes tight, I pull the trigger.

Except, nothing happens. The trigger doesn't even move. I get enough time to try again, before Harris slams me against the side of the elevator and pulls it from my fingers. "Next time, you little bitch, try disengaging the safety." He slams me again for good measure, and the elevator starts again. "Well, would you look at that? Just took the right kind of nudge, didn't it?" He laughs, and it's the ugliest sound I've heard in my life.

Hawthorne, on the other hand, isn't laughing. "Jesus, Harris. Pay attention. She could've killed me."

"You're fine," Harris says back. Something's changed in their dynamic. It's like Hawthorne's supervillain veneer has peeled off, and Harris is taking charge. "We'll grab the boat and get the fuck out of here. They're not going to be able to follow."

Hawthorne nods. He's sweating, wiping his brow and breathing heavily. Part of it is his age, definitely, but he looks terrified.

Good.

Gunshots grow louder. Someone screams, and I hope it's no one I know. I just got Tank back, I'm not ready to lose him again, or the hope that Wraith and Nitro are alive, too. I don't know what miracle saved them, but I refuse to waste this second chance.

The elevator reaches bottom and Hawthorne tears it open. A cold gust of wind rushes in. It opens straight into a mudroom that leads out the back near the boat dock. Harris digs his fingers into my upper arm and hauls me with him out the door.

"Stop right fucking there!" snaps a voice I know so well.

Wraith stands along the side of the house, pointing his gun at the three of us. Next to him is Nitro, Eagle-eye and a younger guy I remember was with the Giordanos. Nicholas? What the heck is he doing here?

Harris whirls me in front of him and puts his gun at my head in a blink. "Don't take a fucking step closer," he sneers as he drags me backwards down the slippery wooden planks. "If you don't want me to blow her fucking brains out over the water."

Argh! I want to fight him, but with the gun at my head, I don't dare. I bet *he* doesn't have the safety on. Like a coward, Hawthorne makes sure to keep us between him and my rescuers, leading the way towards the boat.

"Let her go," says Nitro. "There's nowhere you can go that we can't find you. Let her go now, and we'll at least give you a head start."

Harris growls. "I don't fucking believe you. No, I'm going, and I'm taking her with me. If you're good and keep away, I won't throw her overboard in the middle of the fucking lake."

I shudder at the thought. It's February. The water's going to be freezing, and the lake is big. Would I be able to swim to land? With my clothes on, before the cold got to me? I'm not that good of a swimmer.

The elevator dings, and Tank comes out, his gun up and a massive lump on the side of his forehead. Thank God. Our eyes meet, and I mouth, "Sorry."

He smirks at me, and then Harris drags me backwards, his arm locked around my throat and the barrel of his pistol digging into my temple.

"How important is she?" asks Nicholas, his gun pointed right in my direction.

That's not the kind of question that gives a girl warm fuzzies.

So I'm relieved when Wraith shakes his head. "If you make a single move that causes Kaylee to be hurt, you won't make it back to report to Arturo. Just so that's fucking clear."

But if they don't, then Harris will get away with me, and then what? I go limp, making myself as heavy as possible, hoping that he won't shoot me. If he does, he'll lose the only leverage that he has. So what can I do except resist? I try to kick Harris's leg.

"Kaylee," snaps Nitro.

"Stop it, you little bitch," Harris growls and lifts me right off my feet. His grip is cutting off my air, and I grab his arm, digging my nails in to try to make him let go. I hear him hiss, but he doesn't let up. "You're coming with me, whether you want to or not, so stop your fucking wiggling." All I can do is fight for precious oxygen as he drags me.

The boat rocks as he pulls me aboard. The water on either side of us is black, only broken up by a hint of white froth as the cold wind cuts over the lake. The guys follow, keeping their distance and their guns trained on Harris and Hawthorne, but I know none of them are going to shoot. And of course I don't want them to, but will that save me? I really don't know. The farther away from them that he takes me, the more in danger I am.

"Untie the boat," Harris orders Hawthorne, and he hops to it. "And you! If you shoot him, your little bitch is going down too."

Hawthorne loosens the rope and jumps aboard, giving the dock a push with his foot. Harris turns the key, and the motor starts up. The boat's rocking intensifies as we float away. And still, Harris has his iron grip around my throat. I'm starting to get dizzy.

"There's a guest dock on the far side of the lake," says Hawthorne as he pulls a phone out of his pocket. "Get us there, and I'll have someone pick us up."

The boat roars as Harris presses the throttle, and only Harris holding me keeps me from falling when it lurches forwards.

When we're finally out of shooting range, I'm released so suddenly that I topple right into the back of the boat. I hit the plastic seats with a grunt, then spend a few moments getting my breath back. My throat aches, almost as much as my heart does.

And behind us, the dock falls farther and farther away, along with Nicholas, Eagle-eye and the three best men on the planet.

37

NITRO

"Fuck!" Tank screams, aiming his gun after the boat, but we all know we're not shooting. Not if we might hit Kaylee.

Wraith snarls. "If they get away, we're never seeing Kaylee again."

My gaze falls to the two jet skis bobbing in the water next to the dock. "How different can they be from riding a motorcycle anyway?" I point.

Tank's eyes light up. "We're about to fucking find out." He's the first one there, dropping onto the closest one. It dips low under his weight. It starts up with a rumble that sounds awfully tinny when you're used to a proper engine between your legs, but as long as it fucking gets us there, I don't give a fuck.

"Guess we share?" Wraith asks as he jumps onto the other one. I drop onto it behind him and unhook the mooring rope.

"Nicholas and I will drive around," says Eagle-eye. "If I've got it figured out right, there's only one place on the other side. We'll meet you there."

Tank shoots off first, the roar growing more respectable as he twists the throttle, but we're not far behind. Wraith leans forwards and guns this thing for all it's worth. It wobbles hard on the waves, but so far so good.

Still, fast as we're going, Harris and Hawthorne have a good head start and the benefit of someone who knows the fucking lake. If either of those fucks hurt Kaylee, I swear they're not going to survive the night. They're already dead men walking.

The jet ski bounces in the water, making me slam my teeth together. Who the fuck does this for fun?

The boat starts as a vague shadow in the darkness, but as the moon rises and my eyes adjust, it becomes easier to make out. Have they noticed us yet? It doesn't seem like it, because they're keeping a straight line for some lights on the other side of the lake. I'm guessing that's where they've got a way out.

Eagle-eye's not afraid of riding fast, but the lake's big. Hopefully, he's able to meet us on the other side in time.

Something whizzes past my ear, followed immediately by the crack of a gunshot. Fuck, if we don't get on there quick, we're going to be target practice until they nail us.

"Hold on," Wraith yells, then starts weaving as we approach. More gunshots, but I don't hear the bullets, so maybe the evasive maneuvers are working.

"Shit!" Tank yells and veers a moment before he's back on course.

Or maybe they're just shooting at him instead. He's still hunched over the handlebars and gunning his jet ski for the boat, though, so we're all still breathing.

The icy spray hits my face and hands, making it hard to hold the gun in frozen fingers. My boots are fucking soaked and my jeans aren't much better. If any of us fall in, we're fucked. It makes me grip Wraith's jacket a little harder.

Just a little farther.

The lights on the other side are getting closer, and we're right on their tail. The shooting's died down, so either they're running low on ammo, or saving it for when we climb aboard. Hard to tell, but I'll take it.

"Gonna pull alongside," yells Wraith. "Ready?"

"Fuck yeah!" Okay, jet skis are bullshit, but this is fun.

Hawthorne's up at the front of the boat, manning the wheel, while Harris has taken cover behind the front passenger seat, clutching Kaylee in one arm and aiming a gun right for us with the other.

Fuck.

"Going!"

I let go of Wraith and jump, hoping the force of the jet ski engine gives it enough stability for me to push off of.

I strike the side of the boat, half on, half off, my boots dragging in the water under me, threatening to rip me right off and dump me in the wake. Kaylee screams, a gun fires. A sharp line of pain starts at my shoulder and drags all the way down over my shoulder blade. I don't think it's serious, but that could just be the adrenaline talking.

I pull hard and roll forwards, getting my legs inside the boat. I strike the deck hard and dive down between the back bench and the fishing seat that's mounted there.

"You'll never get away from us," I yell. "Hurt Kaylee, and you fuckers are dead."

It's a stalemate. They know we're not gonna let them live at this point, and we're not gonna shoot until we know Kaylee's safe.

Something thunks against the back of the boat, right behind me, followed by the snap of shattering plastic and an engine grinding to a stop. I look behind and see bright yellow and orange jet ski parts shooting into the air, thrown up by the propeller. Wraith is still out on the left, matching speeds with us.

Fuck, what the hell are you doing, Tank? He didn't actually drop into the water, did he? My chest tightens at the thought. Me and Tank have been battle partners for way too long for me to lose him to something that fucking dumb. I wave my arm at Wraith, trying to signal for him to look behind the boat, but a bullet almost takes my fucking hand off, so I've got other things to worry about first. Hopefully, he saw it.

"They broke the propeller!" Hawthorne's playing with the throttle, but while there's a loud whine in the back that speeds and slows the engine, whatever connects that torque to the propeller isn't doing anything anymore. At least Tank managed to fuck up the engine, but goddamn it, I'm going to fucking kill him if he drowns.

"Jump off the boat now, and I won't fucking shoot you," yells Harris. "Your buddy there can pick you up."

I don't trust that fucker any farther than I can throw this boat. There's one row of seats before the open deck. I throw myself forwards, rolling from behind the fishing chairs and finding cover behind them. A shot goes off, just a hair too late, punching a hole in the back of the boat.

"Getting nervous, Harris?" I yell. That motherfucker is only giving me more and more reasons to fucking kill him.

"Come get me, you little shit," he yells back. "I dare you to come gunning for me. I fucking dare you."

"Jesus Christ, Harris. Just shoot him. We need to get this fucking boat running again."

Wraith is back on the left side, but up around the bow, where he's hidden from the pilot's chairs, using the massive front of the boat for cover. He's shut off the jet ski, and he's pulling himself up. So if I can keep distracting Harris and Hawthorne, maybe he can get the jump on them.

"You've got Kaylee, but Hawthorne's in the open. Let her go, or I'll murder him instead."

Harris laughs. "I don't give a fuck. He was more useful in jail, funneling me money and not whining."

"You traitorous little shit! I was the one that promoted you in the first place! All these years of taking care of you, and you're ready to throw me overboard?"

"Oh, shut the fuck up, old man."

Wraith's up on the bow now, the jet ski floating down the side of the boat.

"Shit, one's behind us," yells Hawthorne, and he fires.

"Fuck," Wraith yells as he drops onto the boat, a red stain spreading on his thigh. Goddamn it. I can't wait any longer.

Using their distraction, I charge Hawthorne before he gets off another shot. He barely manages to turn before I'm on him and slam him against the dashboard or whatever the fuck you call it on a boat. He grunts and collapses. Wraith's safe, but now I'm exposed. Shit.

Harris points his gun right at me. "Bye, motherfu—"

The throaty snarl that cuts him off is all too fucking familiar and even before Tank has launched himself over the railing and crashed into Harris, I'm grinning. That crazy motherfucker. Did he cling to the outside of the boat this whole fucking time?

They go down in a pile, bringing Kaylee with them. She whimpers when she hits the deck hard. Harris is still holding his gun, which goes off once when his hand hits right by her head, and she screams like a fucking banshee. Fuck, my ears are ringing, so hers have to be in fucking pain.

It gives me great pleasure to stomp my boot down on top of his hand, which yields a very satisfying crunch and a pained roar from Harris. Once his hand's broken, it's easy enough to kick his iron away, and then he doesn't have a chance against Tank. He probably didn't anyway, because Tank's flipped the fuck out, slamming Harris into the deck over and over while flinging those massive fists at him. The sounds coming out of Tank are barely human.

I yank Kaylee out of the way, just so she doesn't get drawn into it. She clings to me, burying her face in my chest like I'm a fucking life buoy.

"Fuck, a hand?" Wraith bites out through a tight wince. He's crawled across the bow to within reach. Kaylee helps as we lower him down and into one of the chairs.

Tank finally gets up, revealing a Harris that's little more than pulp. His face is a mess, I don't think he's got a fucking tooth left, and his shirt is soaked in fucking blood. When he groans, I'm surprised he's still alive.

"Fuck that felt good." Tank's breathing hard, but he's calming, now that some of that's outta his system.

"Kaylee, you okay?" Wraith's clutching his thigh as he looks up at her.

"Oh my God, I should be asking you that!" She throws herself around his neck, squeezing him hard. "God, I thought all of you were dead, and then when I knocked out Tank, I—"

"Back up!" Wraith pulls her away so he can look at her. "You did fucking what?"

"It was a love tap," growls Tank as he scoops her up in a bear hug and squeezes her so hard she squeaks. "I'm just fucking glad you're alive."

We're all interrupted by the sound of the jet ski starting up, and Hawthorne shooting away from us, his suit jacket flapping in the wind behind him. I aim and take a shot, but either it's blowing too hard or the motion of the boat throws me off.

"Let him go," growls Wraith. "We got Kaylee back."

"Yeah. We need to get this boat moving again and get you the hell back to Doc."

A couple of flips of the on off switch, and a shove on the throttle, and something snaps behind the propeller, shooting up into the air. Whatever it was, working it loose seems to have solved the problem. The engine's a little extra grindy, but we're moving forwards. I set a course for the lights ahead of us, hoping we'll find Eagle-eye there.

"Nice," growls Tank, then he takes the wheel. "Always wanted to try being a skipper."

"I think I prefer the road, to be honest," says Wraith. Not sure if it's the wound in his leg or the rocking of the boat that's got him looking a little green. Either way, we should get him back to land.

Harris shifts in the bottom of the boat. Wouldn't you believe it, I think the fucker's trying to crawl over to his gun. This time I'm closer, grabbing the bastard that threatened the life of the woman we love—and don't think I've fucking forgotten how he knocked her around and treated her. I lift him up so his ugly mug is right in front of mine. He tries to spit, but his lips are too split and with most of his teeth missing, it just dribbles over his chin. I could almost feel bad for him.

But I don't. "Fuck you."

Then I throw him overboard.

Kaylee gasps, but I don't give a fuck. He was dead already. I just made sure of it. His head bobs above the water for a moment, and then he's gone.

38

EAGLE-EYE

The first sign of life from the water is a jet ski, coming in at high speed. Is it one of the boys? There's no fucking way all three of them and Kaylee are on that thing. I wave Nicholas back, and take a step behind one of the dock buildings to watch.

The guy on the jet ski cuts the engine and glides into the boat ramp. The moment it strikes the asphalt, he's off it and coming up. Hawthorne.

Motherfucker.

I wait for him to get to the top, then step out. "Long time, no see."

"Eagle-eye." His voice is fucking ice. Is he armed? Doesn't look like it, but that doesn't mean I'm not watching.

"Last I saw you, your boat was bigger and had more people on it. You better have a good fucking story as to what happened."

He laughs dryly. "Or what? You'll shoot me? I think we already know what's going to happen here."

"You might be right. You've caused a lot of fucking trouble, Hawthorne. Beat your daughter. Beat your wife. Hurt a lot of fucking people. If it'd been up to me, you'd never have made it as far as fucking jail, and now you're here, stirring up all the old shit all over again. Trying to start a fucking war in your own city. Getting sweet kids like Kaylee in trouble well over her fucking head. Maybe you should've stayed on the fucking boat." I loosen the gun in my belt.

He throws his hands out. "I did what I had to do. This city is turning into a fucking shithole, with your little play group at the center of it. Was it so fucking hard to grow up someday? To just act like fucking adults instead of... whatever the fuck you do? Of course I have to get rid of you. It was my fucking duty, Eagle-eye. And somehow you've managed to turn it all against me. I've got nothing left, and it's all your damn fault."

"I think I speak for just about everybody in the whole damn city except you, in saying that you brought this shit on yourself."

He shrugs. "So now what? You going to end it?"

I nod, feeling grim, but righteous. "I am. You've hurt too many people I care about, and if I let you go, you'll just keep on doing it."

"Jesus Christ. How do you even fucking sleep at night?"

"Easy," I say as I draw. "With your wife."

One shot is all it takes, and he collapses like a sack of potatoes. Do I feel satisfaction? Nah, because this doesn't undo anything that he did. But it's a fucking conclusion, and I'll accept that.

And that's when I hear the sound of a boat coming in.

39

KAYLEE

All my concerns about Nicholas were wiped away when I learned he drove to Hawthorne's place. We'll have to go back for some of the bikes, but my men were definitely not in any shape to ride. Well, Tank wanted to, but I cried until he agreed to ride with us, and I have zero regrets.

It's three in the morning, but the courtyard is packed with bikers when we pull into the club with Eagle-eye leading on his bike. I feel gross. Dirty. Both because I stink like lake water and terror, and because I've racked up a whole new pile of memories that I need to scrub away.

The reception is muted until we open the SUV door and Wraith, Tank and Nitro come out, with me in tow. Then I feel bad for all the kids who probably wake up when the members cheer at seeing everyone alive.

"I'll take him inside," says Nitro, helping Wraith up the stairs. A thick-bodied biker with short white hair and beard follows them in, followed by a woman who I think is Emily. Is he a doctor or something?

The crowd swarms Tank and Eagle-eye, as everyone wants to congratulate them on a job well done. I actually feel a little left out. And a little insecure. Now that Hawthorne is gone, Harris and Anderson are gone, and the Giordanos and Screaming Eagles are going to be mending fences, where does that leave me?

Do I go home? God, I can finally call Mom and Dad! But what do I tell them? I glance at Tank, then I look at the gate.

I could leave all this craziness behind, but where would that leave me? What would I do? Go back to washing hair and working for Mom? I can't unlearn everything I've experienced. I love Tank, Wraith and Nitro. I don't want to leave. But now everything is over. Mission successful, but how do they feel about it?

About me?

Tank's arm slips around my waist. "Let's go inside, baby."

I lean into his touch. God, it feels so good, and I don't want to leave that behind. But I'm nervous anyway. If they still want me here, it's because we're flipping a new page, because all the 'real' reasons for why I'm here are gone. For some reason, I'm worried about the answer. "You guys don't need to protect me anymore. I mean, they're all dead now. So—"

"Baby, if you think we're done protecting you, you haven't been paying fucking attention." The way he says it sends a wave of hope flowing through me. "Do you want out? I get it. It's dangerous here. Not exactly homey. Would you rather go home?"

I shake my head. "No, but how do I explain to my parents that I'm together with not just one biker, but three of them? I mean, if they want me."

"They do, and very carefully," he says as he runs his clever fingers up and down my arm. "And ideally without a shotgun nearby."

I can't help laughing. "Luckily, that's not an issue in my parents' house. Can we go see how Wraith is doing?"

"Sure." Tank refuses to take his hands off me, keeping the physical contact all the way back to Wraith's quarters. It feels nice.

The biker with the short white hair and beard is coming out as we get there. "He's fine," he says. "It's a deep graze, but it's just a graze. There's no bullet in there, and the bleeding stopped. I bet it hurt like a fucking bitch, but I've put a bandage on it and he should be back to his normal asshole self if he takes it easy for a week or two." He flashes a little grin at that.

Tank laughs. "Thanks, Doc. We'll make sure he stays in place and doesn't do anything dumb."

"I find that hard to believe, but that's your problem, not mine." And then he's off.

"Wraith!" I go in ahead of Tank. Nitro has thrown himself onto one of the chairs, and Wraith is on his bed, with his pants off and a big bandage around his injured thigh. "How are you feeling?"

Wraith huffs. "Takes more than that to put me out of action. Doc just likes to make a big deal out of it."

"He said a week or two. I'm not letting you do anything too strenuous until then."

He grins. "You gonna make me?"

"If I have to!"

"Guess you'll have to ride on top, then."

The guys laugh as I blush. You wouldn't think after everything we've done they could still do that to me.

"No, at least not until I've showered. I'm dirty and gross, and I'm just trying to forget everything that happened tonight." I swallow as it flashes back—right up to watching Harris go under. Maybe I am getting tougher, because I have no sympathy for him, not after everything he did, but that doesn't make the memory any less creepy and unsettling.

And then Tank's back around me, holding me close. "She's had a rough night. Go easy on her."

Nitro nods. "Yeah. Listen, your shower isn't big enough for three. I'll stay here and keep Wraith from stabbing his eyes out from boredom, and you get her cleaned up. We can all get caught up in the morning."

The way he says caught up hints at more than just a little talking, and I like it.

Tank nods. "My pleasure. Need anything before I go?" He looks at Wraith.

"Wait!" I hold my hands up. "I know this is a lot, but I really thought you guys were dead for a while, and I hated knowing that you died before I got to talk to you about how I feel."

They eye me curiously. Guess the stage is mine.

"When I saw that explosion and the building collapse. It nearly killed me."

"Trigger—"

"I know now that things will go back to normal, you'll want to get back to your lives. I'm just some girl, and you have plenty of girls around here, so..."

It's Nitro's turn to interrupt me. "Princess—"

"No, let me—"

"Stop," Wraith orders.

I stop, blinking at him, not sure if I'm being rejected or what.

Nitro chuckles. "Do you remember when we explained what being claimed meant? About how that meant absolute fucking loyalty? We've fucking claimed you, sweetheart. All you have to do is say yes."

"Oh."

Tank pulls me right back into his embrace.

"No. I stink and—"

"I don't fucking care. Nitro speaks truth. Truth for all three of us. When I told we weren't done protecting you, I wasn't fucking kidding. We're not gonna let you go, unless you tell us to fuck off. If you really don't want us claiming you, then we're not gonna force you. We don't want a woman who doesn't want us. But until I hear otherwise, I'm gonna keep holding you, watching for you, drag you off to the fucking shower and scrub every last remnant of those assholes that fucked around with you until you skin's fucking red and glowing, and I'm gonna pull you into my bed and fucking hold you the whole damn night." He squeezes me for emphasis. "Was that fucking clear enough?"

I nod against his broad chest. "Yeah. I—God, and here I thought I talked a lot. But I—"

Tank stops me with a finger on my lips. "No. No answers right now. No decisions. You're worn out and you've been through a lot. Come, we get you clean and a good night's rest. And that's all you have to think about right now."

"Okay."

Tank's true to his promise, and when I'm curled up in his arms, squeaky clean, scrubbed down by him personally, I don't think I've ever felt so warm and safe. The only thing better would be if all three guys were here, but then I'm not entirely sure I'd be sleeping.

And we need a bigger bed.

"Tank?"

"Hmm?" he mumbles sleepily.

"Thank you."

He pulls me in closer, and then I can't keep myself awake any longer.

40

KAYLEE

Well, the guys haven't claimed me. Not for real anyway. On the other hand, I'm now working at Haunted Ink, and in the position I originally applied for.

Plus missionary, doggy, cowgirl and any number of other positions that might strike our fancy.

The last customer leaves after I take their payment, and then I flip the sign on the door to "Closed." The days here aren't any shorter or easier than they were at Mom's salon, but my boss is certainly easier on the eyes, and when all three of them are here, it's amazing that I get any work done at all. It requires willpower—willpower, I tell you.

It's been two weeks since we got back. Mom and Dad aren't thrilled about me working in South Side, or that I seem to be keeping the company of not just one, or two, but in fact three big Screaming Eagles, but they were also so ecstatic to see me home safe and alive, that we're glossing over that for now. I slept at home for a couple of nights to make them happy, but then I missed the guys too much, so now I'm back to crashing in their rooms until we figure out something more permanent.

And yeah, when I say permanent, I mean it. I know there's no way I can go back to my old life. Not anymore. Working in Mom's salon after I've pretty much become a private stylist to all the sluts and some of the old ladies? Touch up some plain color highlights when I've now got all the hues in the rainbow to work with? It's like growing up on… on… ugh, unsalted eggs, and then finding out that there's steak and curries and candy and everything else out there. It's… possible to go back, but who'd want to. I'm sure Mom will understand eventually.

But it's not just the work and variety, of course. There's also the three gorgeous guys in the next room over, who—if I know them right—are having a beer after the last customer left and are waiting for me to come in so we can do something wild. And once you get used to that wildness, there's no going back. Everything else is underwhelming at best.

"Kaylee!" Wraith calls me from the other room. "Got a minute?"

"Just closing up. Be right there."

Once I'm sure the door's locked and everything is in order for opening tomorrow, I head into the back. I still have fond memories from when they showed me how they might tattoo me, and some other things too. Suddenly I'm hopeful that maybe we're going for a repeat.

When I come in, the tattoo chair is set up as if Wraith's expecting another customer. "Touching up one of the guys?"

"Sort of, but not really."

"Okaaay?" There's something in the air, but I'm not sure what. Just a vibe.

"We've been thinking," starts Wraith.

"Uh oh," I say and smile, trying to lighten the mood a little. "Am I in trouble?"

"Depends on how you define trouble," says Tank. He moves behind me and closes the door to the front room, in effect closing me in with them. Now, normally, that's not a problem in any way whatsoever. It usually means an amazing time for all of us. But something's weird, so now I'm not sure.

"It's been a few weeks since we got back now," says Nitro. "Wraith's fully back on his feet, Hawthorne, Harris and the rest are fading. And we're all feeling things."

"Feeling things?" I look from one to another, trying to figure out exactly what they're getting at. "What kinds of things?"

Wraith shrugs. "Things we can't ignore any longer. So we've decided that we won't."

"Won't ignore what? Tell me what's going on!" I can only take so much build-up here. I feel like they're ganging up on me a little. I just wish I knew what they're up to.

Wraith stops, then nods. "Okay, first up—your job's safe. You can work here for however long you want."

"What? Why wouldn't I be able to?"

"But... we're not gonna wait any longer."

"Would you guys just fucking say what you mean, already, before I have a fucking heart attack?"

Well, that shut them up. They blink at me like I just dropped out of the sky.

"What? I can't swear sometimes too? Is it just a biker thing?"

Tank laughs. "You know what? Fair. Fucking fair, Trigger. We've talked and we've decided. We wanna claim you. Make you ours. Fuck, we've wanted to almost since we fucking met you, but we wanted to give you a little time to settle after everything that happened. But we're not patient men, Kaylee. So tell us. Will you be ours?"

I swallow hard. "Yours?" My voice feels so small.

"Ours." Wraith moves so he's standing next to Tank. "All of ours."

"We want you as our old lady," says Nitro as he joins them. "We fucking love you, Kaylee. You have to know that."

I have no idea if my eyes are as big as they feel right now, but my chest just went so tight that the only thing I manage to squeak out is, "Love?"

"You've seen how some of the other old ladies are with their guys. Fuck, we want that too." Tank swallows, like he's feeling the intensity too. "We want that with you. Until we grow old and fucking die. So yeah, we fucking love you."

"Don't say die." I finally found my voice. "Too many people died already."

Wraith takes a step closer. "So maybe you think this is fucked up, or maybe this is what you want, but you need to let us know, sweetheart. Do you wanna spend the rest of your life with us? Be our old lady? In good and bad, sickness, health, I don't fucking know. I don't know the whole list, but I do know I fucking love you. And now you've heard it from all of us. So the question is this. What do you fucking want?"

Oh God. My heart's thundering, my pulse is so loud in my ears that I don't think I can hear anything anymore. I clench my fists so tight it hurts. "What do I want? I want you. Wraith, Tank, Nitro, all three of you. Yes. Yes! I want all of you. Who else would it be? Always you." And it's true. I feel it with every fiber of my being. No one is ever going to make me feel like my guys do. Never. "You're mine. Always." I wet my lips and smiled nervously. "Isn't this the part where you guys kiss me?"

"You bet your sexy fucking ass it is," growls Tank, and then he's the first one there, lifting me right up in his arms, propping me up with his hands under my butt as he kisses me like he'll die if he doesn't. I only get a moment to draw breath when he pulls away, as I'm passed right over to Nitro, who kisses me so fiercely I'm surprised I'm not on fire by the time he passes me to Wraith. And there's that melty kiss that he's so good at, the one I fell for that first night when they dropped me off. And it's only gotten better since then.

But then he carries me to the tattoo chair to put me down in it. I look up at the three of them, towering over me. I smile mischievously. "Are we playing with markers again?"

Wraith shakes his head. "No markers this time. Baby, if you're going to be ours, properly claimed as ours, we want the whole fucking world to know it. So the question is, will you let us?"

Oh.

Oh!

"For real?" I swallow thickly. A tattoo? Three tattoos. "Do I have to?"

"No. No one's gonna fucking force you to do anything you don't want ever again. We wouldn't put you through that." It's Wraith who says it, but all three of them nod, looking determined. I'm realizing that when they mean protect me, they mean it, from demons out there, but also any demons I have on the inside. But it's also obvious that it would mean a lot to them.

And to me.

So I nod. "Okay. Yeah. Do it. Just… keep me distracted."

Tank grins.

"No, not like that. Jeez. Just… be here with me."

Wraith nods. "Always, sweetheart. Always."

41

KAYLEE

Sun, warmth, salty air over my skin, soft white sand under me and the shade of a convenient palm tree? Wraith definitely delivered on his promise.

Tank comes my way, carrying a bottle of Coke and a beer, wearing nothing but a pair of dark blue swimming shorts. He looks freaking amazing, his broad chest and shoulders nicely tanned. It's not fair—we both slathered on sunblock, but it's like his gorgeous body is generating the soft brown shade on its own, while I'm getting nothing. Nothing!

I'll enjoy the view, though.

Behind him come Wraith and Nitro, their beers already open and carrying a huge cooler between them. It's strange to see them so out of their biker element, but at the same time, no one would ever mistake them for anything else. Just on vacation, is all.

Tank hands me my Coke, then drops onto the blanket next to me. It's me, them, the beach, the ocean, and nothing else in sight. There's an advantage to having ridden down to Mexico on motorcycles, even if my butt was so ready to not be anywhere near a bike seat by the time we got here. It means that we can go wherever we want, like beaches well away from the tourist traps. This one is so remote that there isn't another soul nearby.

"I knew that bikini would look good on you," Wraith says as he drops down next to me to inspect the tattoos. They're well healed by now, but he babies them anyway, wanting to make sure nothing happens to damage them, or me. "Shows off our tags nicely."

It's skimpier than anything I would've ever picked up in my old, boring life, but it's hard not to build a little self-confidence when you've got three hotter-than-sin guys who've seemingly decided to dedicate their lives to complimenting you. And he's right. I want to show off who I belong to. Tank, with his gothic letters down the inside of my arm. Nitro, in that jagged retro font around my side and under my boob. And of course, Wraith across my upper back, in bold, black lettering.

Claimed and marked.

They got tattoos afterwards too, all in the same place. Just above their hearts, they all have one that reads Kaylee, surrounded by roses. I thought it seemed like such a generic flower, but Wraith said it suited me. They're hardy, resilient and they have sharp points if you don't watch yourself.

Maybe he's right, but I just love all of our marks. And now that they managed to baby me through getting their names on me, I'm already starting to wonder if I could handle some more.

"Fuck, this isn't half bad," says Nitro, as he lies down next to me, leaning his weight back on his elbows.

"And not a fucking soul in sight," says Tank, shading his hands as he looks around. "I mean, fuck, we could be running around naked, and no one would know."

That's of course when all of them look my way. I shrug. "I'm good, guys, but knock yourselves out. I won't mind. Just don't come crying to me if your dicks get sunburned."

"Will you kiss them better if we do?" asks Wraith a quirk to his lips.

"If you're really, really nice to me, maybe I'll at least rub some sunblock on them before you go running around."

"I'm game," says Nitro, and off his shorts go, revealing a cock that's already hardening up.

Even knowing that we're out in the middle of nowhere, I cover my mouth in shock as I look around. Just like that. He holds the sunblock out for me to take, then leans back with his hands behind his head. "Get to it."

"I should squirt this into your mouth," I snap at him playfully, as I squirt a good glob into my hand instead.

"You know," says Tank, as he pulls off his shorts too. "That does give me some ideas."

"You guys are incorrigible," I say, but it's not a real complaint. I'm a little too excited to make sure they guys are protected all over.

I start giving them all handies, switching between the three of them and making sure they're all good and covered. I even think Wraith's about to blow from the way he's moaning, but then I stop and get up. "I don't know about you guys, but I want to swim."

"What? You're leaving us like this?" Tank points down at his undeniably impressive dick.

"For now. But maybe if you guys can think of some ways to convince me, we'll see how it goes afterwards." Then I make a run for the water.

The sand hides the sound of their footsteps, but a quick glance over my shoulder shows me all three of them coming full speed, and bare-ass naked and gunning for me. Oh no.

They tackle me into the water, and milliseconds later, my bikini is gone. It's a good thing we're alone, but with my three tattooed stallions around me, I don't think I care too much anymore. If it ever was anything more, it all devolves into a sexy wrestling match almost immediately.

We play our way out into deeper water, and then I'm kissing Nitro deeply, while the waves wash over us. God, it feels nice. His cock relaxed for the chase, but now it's back in full force, poking my stomach. Then Wraith is behind me, brushing my hair out of the way so he can kiss my neck and shoulder. It's like I've gone to Paradise. They take turns passing me around between them while we all get soaked. My hands find cocks to stroke, and their hands are all over me, teasing all my secret and not so secret spots until I'm ready to come right between the three of them.

Tank lifts me, putting his hands under my thighs and ass while I cling to him like a little monkey, my legs around his waist and my arms wrapped around his neck. I kiss him hard as he lowers me onto his length. He slots into me like we were made for each other, and then I get the long, delicious slide down until all of him is in me.

"I've never done it standing up before," I breathe hoarsely. "It's nice." It's an understatement and a half. He fills me so completely this way, and there's a lot of him to be filled by.

He lifts me, sliding me up his cock until I'm almost all the way off, then lets gravity do its thing as he drops me right back down. I moan out loud as I'm suddenly full of him again. "Oh God," I whimper.

It's like I don't weigh anything as he lifts and lowers me, over and over. All I can do is hang on for dear life and kiss him at the top of every stroke.

"Stop hogging her," growls Wraith. He presses against me from behind, and judging by the hardness nestling in between my ass cheeks, he's more than ready to go. "Bring her in so we can all get at her."

Oh, yes please. I love any time I get with any of them, but when it's all of them at once? There's nothing like it.

Tank walks right back onto land without ever letting me down, keeping me impaled on that monster of his the whole way. The motion of his walk bounces me around just enough to have me biting my lip and pressing my face against his powerful chest. If he doesn't watch it, I'm going to come just from him taking a little walk.

When we get to the blanket, he drops to his knees on it, the shock of it sending a sudden pleasure wave through me. "God, I might just want to stay on you forever."

"It'll make the ride home interesting, that's for fucking sure," Tank says with a laugh. God, even the motion of him laughing makes me moan.

I whimper in protest when Wraith and Nitro lift me off him so they can reposition, even if I know that it's going to make everything even better. I just don't have any patience right now. All I want is cock.

Luckily, there's three of them here, ready to oblige.

Nitro drops to the blanket on his back, and starts lubing up his cock. Yeah, we came prepared—beer, soda, sunblock, change of clothes... and lube. He's being generous, slathering it on, while looking at me with a smoldering look of pure lust. I could get lost and drown in the passion of those black pools.

"Face the water," he orders as I move to straddle him. I do, then ease back so I'm resting my back on his chest. At this angle, my head hangs over his shoulder and as Tank pushes my legs back and out, I'm completely open to them.

Nitro angles himself so that his thickness is pushing at my ass, then starts working himself in, a little at a time so I can adjust. It's always a challenge when we start, even if it doesn't take long before it feels amazing. And after all that fooling around in the water, I'm so horny that even if it aches a little, I don't care. I just want to get fucked. It's amazing how much the body can take once the hormones get flowing and the only thing in my mind is how I can pleasure—and be pleasured—by all my guys together.

While I work more and more of Nitro inside my ass, Tank uses the slickness of my own juices to make his fingers slippery and draw languid circles around my clit with them. Wraith leans over me and takes my nipple and the surrounding flesh into his mouth, sliding his tongue over the tight bud and the sensitive bumps around it. I dig my fingers into his long hair to keep him in place and try to remember to breathe.

Butterflies are having some sort of conference in my belly, stirred up by the clever fingers and tongues of my men. Tingles shoot through me as my ass settles fully against Nitro's hips, so that I've taken all of him. And when Wraith moves around to present his jutting cock to my lips, I open up and let him in.

In this position, with my head upside down, I want to try something I've been practicing for weeks, but haven't dared do for real yet. Kaia gave me some tips and something to practice with, and I know it's going to blow his mind if I can do it. I won't say I'm not distracted by Nitro and Tank already deep inside me, but when Wraith begins with small thrusts between my lips, I reach up so I can get a good grip on his ass, and then I start pulling him closer.

He bumps against the back of my throat, just a moment before I expect, making me gag on him. "Jesus," moans Nitro under me. He felt that. Wraith pulls back a little, but I urge him forwards again, and this time I'm ready for him. The spongy tip of him touches the entrance to my throat, and I swallow hard.

"Fuck, Kaylee, you don't have to—"

I swallow again, pull harder and then suddenly, he slips in. Just a little, but he's there. In my throat. I did it! I push him out and draw a ragged breath around him.

"Holy shit, that's—fuck."

I pull him right back in, and this time it goes easier. I'm figuring out when to swallow, when to pull, and he gets pretty deep before I push him back. It's a little sloppy. Saliva's running in a trickle down the side of my cheek, and I gag sometimes, but I keep trying, and every time, it goes a little easier and I can hold him a little longer.

"Jesus Christ," whispers Tank, his fingers still teasing me.

Nitro wraps his hand around my throat, his calloused fingers rough against my skin. Not tight, but when I take Wraith again, Nitro swears. "Fuck, I can feel it."

"Such a good little dirty girl," says Tank, and I can hear the grin in his voice as he starts easing back into me.

I gasp as Wraith lets up a moment and I'm filled by two huge men at once. Slowly, but surely, Tank slides deeper and deeper until he's all the way in me, stretching me together with Nitro in ways that are sinful, dirty and absolutely delightful. A raspy moan escapes me as they begin to move.

Wraith starts to play with my breasts as I draw a deep breath, then pull him back into my mouth. I want to truly take all of them at once. To feel every inch of all of my men inside me. Controlling my breath is a challenge and a half, but after a couple of tries, I do it. My nose bumps into Wraith, and I've got all three of them. Never in the history of the world has a woman felt so full and accomplished as I do right now. I'm sure of it.

It lasts a moment and then Tank does something around my clit that forces a gasp, and I have to push Wraith out again. And then things get a little wilder, a little less controlled as all the guys are moving in me at once. And as I get more and more worked up, and my breathing more ragged, poor Wraith has to take care of more and more business himself, because I'm only one woman in the end, and I do like breathing. Not that he seems to mind, and any time I can, I get my tongue and lips back on him.

Tank and Nitro slide in and out on a mission to drive me over the edge, and it's not going to be long. So much sensation, so many hands, cocks, ways to be touched and teased and driven right up the wall.

But Wraith's the first one who groans and pushes himself back into my mouth. I hold him off for a moment so I can draw a breath, then pull him in. I swallow, once, twice and then he's in. He swells immediately and moans deep in his chest. I just keep swallowing, milking the cum right out of him until I have to breathe again. I give him a push, and he withdraws, his cock still twitching. The last few drops spatter onto my tongue and lips, and then he settles back, breathing heavy.

Nitro and Tank don't give me any time to recover. If anything, the show seems to have turned them on further, because they speed up, both of them fucking me harder and harder. I grip Tank's powerful arms, using them for support as he drives that amazing cock of his in and out of me in long, powerful strokes. A soft keen starts in my throat as Nitro fills me, over and over, finding sexy spots I didn't even know I had. Wraith sneaks a finger onto my clit while he sucks on a nipple. It's like there's a volcano about to erupt inside me, and the churning magma is just getting hotter and hotter.

"Fuck!" Nitro growls, and he thickens in my ass as his cock starts pulsing. His hands are on my waist, keeping me moving as he drives himself in from below, over and over, coating my insides. And that's it for me, as all the feelings coalesce and my inner volcano finally bubbles over and I come like a freight train between him and Tank. I scream, my fingers and toes curling as I go tight between the guys. I moan, and then Tank drives himself home one last time, pinning me down as he comes in me.

We quiver and moan together, and if there's a better way of feeling like we all truly belong to each other, then I don't know what that is. It's not until we're all loosening up, catching our breath, that we finally separate, Tank rolling off, followed by me.

Wraith's juice is still wet on my lips and salty on my tongue, my pussy and ass are coated by Tank and Nitro. I'm well and truly claimed by the men who chose me. By the men I chose. They taught me what true wildness is, and how to live your life on your own terms, rather than what's expected of you. Even when that means falling in love with three brutal men with a tenuous relationship with the law, and leaving behind a safe and sheltered life.

Many would say that I've made a terrible mistake, but I'm living my life to the fullest. I've been through trauma and survived, and while I know my men will never be straight up good guys, they'll always be my good guys. And just as I accept them for who and what they are, when I was in the greatest danger of my life, they were the ones who came through to save me. And I know they'll keep showing up for me like that, for the rest of my life.

I press myself against Wraith's side, then reach out with a hand and a foot so that I'm touching all three of them at once, just feeling their presence. I'm going to wear their marks proudly, knowing that no matter what happens from now on, I am forever safe —or as safe as anyone can ever be in this crazy world.

And that is a life worth living.

ABOUT THE AUTHOR

International bestselling author Stephanie Brother writes high heat love stories with a hint of the forbidden. Since 2015, she's been bringing to life handsome, flawed heroes who know how to treat their women. If you enjoy stories involving multiple lovers, including twins, triplets, stepbrothers and their friends, you're in the right place. When it comes to books and men, Stephanie truly believes it's the more, the merrier.

She spends most of her day typing, drinking coffee, and interacting with readers.

Her books have been translated into German, French, and Spanish, and she has hit the Amazon bestseller list in seven countries.

Printed in Great Britain
by Amazon